Bolan reached the summit first

Below, the sparkling river beckoned to him. Across the water, between the Tigris and Euphrates, lay the alluvial plain that had once been called Mesopotamia. The place was alive with history, Bolan knew.

It was the region in which Hammurabi's Code, the world's first set of written laws, had laid the groundwork for all future systems of justice. The area had exemplified the best that mankind had to offer. And the worst. The ancient kingdom had also introduced oppression, terror and ruthless militancy to the world.

The cradle of civilization, some had called it. Bolan wondered wryly if it might not end up being the *grave* of civilization.

The Executioner wiped sand from his eyes as he stared at the camp a quarter mile away. His weary vision finally focused on a line of tents, with U.S. M2 Bradley Fighting Vehicles and M-109 howitzers parked to the side.

"No chance to take them on now," Katz said.

Bolan shook his head. "Not with one assault rifle and pistols."

Manning fell forward next to them, exhausted. "So much for heading back to Kuwait," he whispered.

Bolan turned to the other men. "We'll head toward the water. After we're rested, we'll travel north."

"You mean . . . ?" Calvin James began, letting his voice drift off.

The Executioner nodded wearily, then looked at each of his warriors. "We're going to Baghdad."

Accolades for America's greatest hero Mack Bolan

"Very, very action-oriented.... Highly successful, today's hottest books for men."
—*The New York Times*

"Anyone who stands against the civilized forces of truth and justice will sooner or later have to face the piercing blue eyes and cold Beretta steel of Mack Bolan, the lean, mean nightstalker, civilization's avenging angel."
—*San Francisco Examiner*

"Mack Bolan is a star. The Executioner is a beacon of hope for people with a sense of American justice."
—*Las Vegas Review Journal*

"In the beginning there was the Executioner—a publishing phenomenon. Mack Bolan remains a spiritual godfather to those who have followed."
—*San Jose Mercury News*

"Mack Bolan stabs right through the heart of the frustration and hopelessness the average person feels about crime running rampant in the streets."
—*Dallas Times Herald*

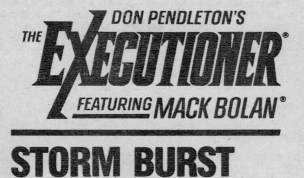

DON PENDLETON'S

THE **EXECUTIONER**®

FEATURING **MACK BOLAN**®

STORM BURST

A GOLD EAGLE BOOK FROM

WORLDWIDE®

TORONTO • NEW YORK • LONDON
AMSTERDAM • PARIS • SYDNEY • HAMBURG
STOCKHOLM • ATHENS • TOKYO • MILAN
MADRID • WARSAW • BUDAPEST • AUCKLAND

First edition June 1992

ISBN 0-373-61427-6

Special thanks and acknowledgment to
Jerry VanCook for his contribution to this work.

STORM BURST

Printed in U.S.A.

War is at best barbarism.... Its glory is all moonshine. It is only those who have neither fired a shot nor heard the shrieks and groans of the wounded who cry aloud for blood, more vengeance, more desolation. War is hell.

—from a graduation address at
Michigan Military Academy,
June 19, 1879

The hell comes after the war, when innocent civilians are forced to rebuild shattered lives. But make no mistake. When some madman finally pushes the button to start a nuclear war, there'll be no rebuilding, no starting over.

—Mack Bolan

CHAPTER ONE

To the battle-trained ear the sudden explosion was unmistakably Soviet—115 mm U-5TS smoothbore, which meant a T-62 Main Battle Tank. It sounded dull, distant.

But it was close enough.

Mack Bolan dived from his chair at the head of the conference table as shards of razor-edged glass blew from the windows. From the corner of his eye he saw Yakov Katzenelenbogen roll under the table on the other side of the room.

Automatic rifle fire—Russian Kalashnikov—erupted from the front of the two-story headquarters building. Bolan wrapped his hands around the M-16/ M-203 assault rifle-grenade launcher combo leaning against the wall. Rolling beneath the window, the warrior heard return fire from below as what remained of Colonel Joshua Eldridge's Seventh Special Forces Group entered the fray.

Bolan took time for a quick glance over his shoulder. The five warriors of Phoenix Force needed no orders. Katz had already drawn his Beretta 92-F and joined the Executioner at the window.

Calvin James and Rafael Encizo had taken up positions at the door leading to the staircase. Bolan heard the bolts of their M-16s slide home simultaneously, jacking 5.56 mm hollowpoints into the chambers.

Gary Manning and David McCarter, their assault rifles extended arm's length in front of them, crawled across the floor, coming to a halt at opposite sides of the window at the far end of the room.

Bolan rose cautiously above the sill as the autofire continued below. Sharp fragments of glass still clung to the bottom of the frame, extending up into the blown-out cavity like an uneven forest of transparent trees. Peering through the clutter, he saw the bodies of gate sentries littering the front of the compound.

Beyond the closed gate hundreds of dark shadows sprinted toward the Special Forces compound perimeter fence. The features of the advancing soldiers were indistinguishable under the faint light of the quarter moon. But the Executioner could see two common, contradictory denominators—the attacking enemy soldiers all wore traditional Iraqi combat gear, but they were tall. Too tall to be Iraqi.

As the first attacker reached the chain-link fence, fell to his knees and yanked a pair of wire cutters from his fatigues, Bolan caught a glimpse of his face—hard, Slavic features, light, ruddy skin.

Russian.

Spetznaz.

Bolan aimed the M-16 and fired. The man with the wire cutters fell forward into the fence, then rebounded to his back in the sand. Three more Soviets moved in to take his place.

The warrior fired another burst. Next to him Katz began picking off the enemy with a steady stream of shots from his Beretta.

The Executioner's mind raced back to the meeting he'd had the day before with the Soviet "advisers" in Iraq. General Gennady Kaganovich hadn't lied. The Soviet Union intended to back the United Arab Republic with whatever it took to make sure the "One Arabic Nation" movement was successful.

"We support the Arab people in their quest to become independent," had been Kaganovich's words.

"The Soviet Union will finally secure warm water ports in the Persian Gulf," had been what the man meant.

A volley of 7.62 mm rounds flew through the window, forcing Bolan back below the sill. More soldiers arrived at the fence. Cutters and heavy combat blades began to snip through the wire. The Executioner sighted down the barrel of his M-16 and squeezed the trigger, spewing brass casings across the conference table behind him. But for each of the enemy that fell, four more moved in to replace him.

"Katz, take everything to the right of the gate!" Bolan ordered. Immediately the Israeli fired off a triburst, and two Spetznaz fighters dropped to the ground. The Executioner emptied his own magazine into a trio of men to the left.

Glass broke, and Bolan cast a glance over his shoulder to see the last window blow at the rear of the room. The steady pounding of 5.56 mm rounds deafened him as the men of Phoenix Force returned fire.

Bolan rammed a fresh magazine into his weapon as ten more Spetznaz soldiers leaped over the bodies along the fence and went to work on the chain links. Behind them the human wave of their compatriots continued to cross the sands toward the compound.

The Executioner glanced at the M-203 mounted beneath his rifle. He could take out half the would-be fence cutters with one twitch of the trigger, but the grenade would also indiscriminately destroy a large section of the fence. Bolan had no intention of opening the gate and doing the Soviets' work for them.

He fired, reloaded, fired and reloaded again. Men dropped along the fence like insects caught in a cloud of noxious vapor.

Calvin James's excited voice rose suddenly over the deafening roar of the M-16s. "Twelve o'clock high! Chutes!"

Bolan looked skyward to see the silhouette of dozens of Soviet paratroopers descending through the moonlight.

Then, across the desert, two tiny flames suddenly flickered. A second later the boom of the smoothbores roared above the small-arms fire. The Executioner felt his stomach sour as he sent another burst into the attackers along the fence. Then he waited, knowing full well what was about to happen.

The first 115 mm round hit ten feet in front of the fence. Pieces of Spetznaz bodies flew through the air. The second round landed in the northwest corner of the compound, more of the enemy disintegrating before his eyes. As the smoke cleared, and the flying sand and gravel returned to earth, Bolan saw the ten-foot hole in the fence.

He watched helplessly as hundreds of Soviet special forces began pouring into the compound.

THE MOOD OF CONGRESS could be summed up in one word—tense. Carl Lyons stood against the wall to the left of the stage, staring at the assembled politicians. Whispers and nervous laughter issued forth from the congressmen as they made their way to their seats.

And why shouldn't they sound nervous? Lyons thought as he moved closer to the podium at the front edge of the stage. In the past few days terrorists backed by the United Arab Republic had turned the U.S. and Europe into a shooting gallery. Politicians had been assassinated, government buildings bombed and civilians had been taken hostage or gunned down in the streets. Worst of all, nuclear weapons had been stolen from Israel.

America was at war—one she was losing.

Lyons stopped near the front of the room and stared at one of the men seated in the journalists' section. Robert Koffman.

Intel from Stony Man Farm, the 160-acre command base in Virginia's Blue Ridge Mountains and home base for Mack Bolan, Phoenix Force and Able Team, had alerted Lyons that Koffman was a new face in the chambers. The sandy-haired *New York Times* Capitol correspondent was a last-minute replacement for Melvin Ogle, the eighty-eight-year-old reporter who'd covered the Hill during seven different presidential administrations. Ogle had passed away late that afternoon.

In addition to Koffman, two of the CNN cameramen were new. All had passed rigorous background checks, but that didn't seem to satisfy Lyons.

The Able Team leader let his gaze leave Koffman and roam over the enormous chamber room, his thoughts returning to the United Arab Republic.

In all his years of law enforcement—both official and covert—he'd never seen anything like it. The UAR didn't just plan and carry out their terrorist strikes; they had backup plans as well as contingency plans. They also had split-second timing, which spelled communication with a capital *C*.

How did they do it? A centralized communications command post, Lyons concluded. But where?

The big man cleared his mind. He had a job to do—protect the President—and speculation on the UAR communications command would have to wait. The Man had ignored Secret Service requests that he cancel this address, or at least restrict it to a televised speech from the White House, which meant security had been beefed up to a point never before seen in the history of America.

Would the UAR take a shot at the President tonight? Able Team had no special reason to believe they would, yet no special reason to believe they wouldn't.

Lyons took a deep breath, then saw Dwight Stover, the head of the Secret Service Presidential Protection Team, enter the room. Because of the confidential nature of all Stony Man operations, Lyons and the other two members of Able Team, Hermann "Gadgets" Schwarz and Rosario "Politician" Blancanales, were working under U.S. Department of Justice credentials. Direct orders from the President had ensured a warm reception and "no questions asked" from the Secret Service.

The Able Team leader scanned the rear entrances again. Schwarz, dressed in a conservative blue suit, white shirt and burgundy "rep" tie, stood near the metal detector, talking with a first-term congressman from Florida. Rosario Blancanales was moving into a seat two rows behind Robert Koffman. Able Team's undercover specialist wore a flowing white caftan. The tails of a red-and-white-checkered keffiyeh fell around his neck, and in his hands were a notebook and pen. Lyons knew that both Able fighters were well armed and ready for anything.

He turned his attention to the stage as a thin grayhaired man set a pitcher of ice water on the shelf behind the podium. The aide turned and disappeared again behind a curtain.

The speaker of the House suddenly appeared at the podium, and the congressmen still standing scrambled for their seats. A moment later the white haired, square-jawed speaker said, "Ladies and gentlemen, the President of the United States." He turned away and took his seat behind the podium next to the vice president as "Hail to the Chief" began to play over the loudspeaker.

The President crossed the platform amid the applause from the chambers. Reaching the podium, he shuffled the index cards in his hands, adjusted his glasses and waited for the clapping to die down. Lyons noted the new wrinkles creeping from the corners of the Man's eyes. Over the past few months the President's face had been marveled at in the press. Even while guiding the nation through the Gulf War he'd seemingly escaped the "Presidential syndrome" of visibly aging twenty years for every four in office.

In the past seventy-two hours that situation had been reversed. The eyes that now looked out over the chamber were tired, worried. "My fellow Americans," he said, "ladies and gentlemen of the Senate and House. The war has come to our shores."

The chamber fell into silence.

"Hostilities continue to rage in the Gulf, but we face a more direct threat on the home front. Three days ago a senator of the United States of America was assassinated. Two days ago a major airport was bombed. Other men and women have been slaughtered or taken hostage." His voice rose slightly in tone. "We can no longer regard terrorism as an overseas phenomenon that only indirectly affects our country."

The President went on, listing a dozen more outrageous acts of the UAR. As he listened, Lyons saw one of the new CNN cameramen reach into his jacket.

The Able Team leader's hand shot automatically to the Colt Python beneath his arm. From the corner of his eye he saw Schwarz turn toward the camera and reach into his coat. In the journalists' section Blancanales turned his head, his hand disappearing under the caftan.

A small screwdriver appeared in the cameraman's hand. He tightened the camera grips, then returned the tool to his pocket.

Lyons breathed a sigh of relief.

"The United Arab Republic, they call themselves," the President said. "Terrorists, *I* call them. Anarchists, murderers, men and women bent not on improving our new world order, but on destroying it. Bloodthirsty, ruthless barbarians whose victims are the weak and helpless." He paused as emotion threatened to overcome him. Then, after another sip of water, he said, "But I promise you they will not succeed!"

The last statement brought a burst of applause.

The President closed his speech and announced he'd take questions. Hands shot up.

"Mr. President, will we invade Iraq?"

"I will not rule out any possibilities at this time."

"Mr. President, is there really any way to combat the terrorism we're now seeing, or must we simply..."

The questions continued. The President's response to each was professional, but evasive. Anyone reading between the lines realized there was much he simply couldn't—or wouldn't—discuss.

Lyons felt his hand move involuntarily under his coat again as Robert Koffman stood. "Mr. President, how much is the United States willing to sacrifice?"

The President paused, frowning. "Could you be more specific, Mr.—" he glanced down at the rostrum "—Koffman, I believe it is?"

"Let me rephrase it," Koffman said, his voice growing cold, hard. "Are we willing to sacrifice to help our Arab brothers? Or will America continue its policy of exterminating all dark-skinned people?"

Murmurs of displeasure circulated throughout the chamber.

The President started to respond, but Koffman spoke up again. "Because I for one," the reporter said, his voice gradually rising to a scream, "am prepared to sacrifice all!" A SIG-Sauer 9 mm pistol suddenly appeared in his hand.

Lyons's hand shot to the grips of the Python as Secret Service-issue Glocks and Uzis appeared throughout the chambers. Koffman's pistol began to rise as the ex-cop jerked the Colt from shoulder leather.

Even as he struggled to drop the sights of the Python on the reporter, Lyons saw the futility of his efforts. He and the rest of the men assigned to protect the President would be a split second late.

Suddenly a blur of white and red rose in the journalists' section. Like some great bird spreading its wings, Blancanales seemed to fly, the caftan fluttering as he dived over the seats. His outstretched hands caught the back of Koffman's jacket and jerked down. The reporter's arm, and the SIG, shot up toward the ceiling.

A loud roar echoed through the chambers. The shot sailed high over the President's head.

Lyons sprinted forward. As he ran, he saw Blancanales grab Koffman's wrist and twist. A sharp, sickening crack echoed throughout the chambers as the bone snapped. Koffman screamed in pain as his weapon clanked hollowly against the back of a seat and fell to the floor.

Two Secret Service agents leaped on stage and tackled the President in a defensive maneuver. Three more piled on top, shielding the Man with their bodies as Lyons left his feet, diving over a row of seats and grasping Koffman by the throat. Using his descending body weight to wrestle the reporter to the floor, the Able Team leader rolled the guy onto his back, straddled the man's chest and drove a hard right down into the would-be assassin's jaw.

Koffman blinked twice, then closed his eyes and went limp.

Pandemonium ruled the chambers as an army of Secret Service men joined them. More agents mounted the stage, formed a protective ring around the President and hustled him offstage through a rear door.

Lyons rolled Koffman onto his stomach, ripped a set of handcuffs from behind his back and clamped them around the reporter's wrists. As he got to his feet, agents jerked Koffman upright and hurried him away down the aisle.

Schwarz joined them as Lyons grabbed Blancanales by the arm and pulled him up from the floor, saying, "Let's go." They hurried up the steps to the stage as more armed Secret Service personnel rushed into the room to maintain order.

A voice roared over the loudspeaker. "Please remain seated. I repeat. Remain seated. Until order is restored, anyone standing may be considered hostile and fired upon."

Hundreds of congressman suddenly lost their curiosity and scampered back to their seats.

A dozen Secret Service men raised their Uzis as Lyons, Schwarz, and Blancanales reached the door at the rear of the stage, then lowered them as the Able Team warriors were recognized. The men raced past and into the "safe room."

The President, visibly shaken, stood next to Dwight Stover in the middle of fifty men with machine pistols. He grinned nervously as the staff makeup artist brushed his suit with a whisk broom. "That was a close one, Dwight," he said.

"Are you all right, sir?" Stover answered.

"A little bruised maybe, but considering what might have happened, I'd say that was a pretty fair trade. Any idea what—"

The President stopped suddenly in midsentence, and his face turned an ashen gray as he struggled for air. Then the eyes of the Chief Executive of the United States closed, and he pitched facedown toward the floor.

LIKE A HORDE of angry bees, the Spetznaz troops stormed through the hole in the perimeter fence. Volleys of gunfire flew through the shattered windows of the HQ room, forcing the Executioner and the men of Phoenix Force back to the floor. Steady streams of automatic rounds ricocheted off the concrete walls, rebounding around the room like ball bearings in some supersonic pinball machine, and sending a fine mist of cement dust raining through the air.

David McCarter lay on his belly next to the field phone in the corner. Bolan scooted along the floor toward him. "David!" he yelled above the maelstrom. "Get Riyadh on the line! Tell them what's going on!"

The former British SAS officer rolled onto his side and lifted the receiver, tapping numbers quickly into the instrument. "Reinforcements?" he bellowed back.

"No time! It'll all be over before they get here!"

Bolan rose to his knees as the onslaught waned momentarily. He heard McCarter make contact as he raised his assault rifle and shoved the barrel through the window.

"Striker!" McCarter shouted. "They want to send air support."

Bolan sighted down the barrel of the M-16/M-203 as he primed the grenade launcher mounted beneath the rifle. Behind him he heard the rest of Phoenix Force resume fire through the side windows. "Negative. The enemy's too close. Riyadh might have 'smart' bombs, but they're not *that* smart."

The Executioner dropped the front sights of the weapon on the hole in the fence. Now he had nothing to lose by using the grenade launcher, and while it wouldn't stop the attack, it might slow it down, make the advancing Spetznaz soldiers a little less anxious to rush through the opening.

Squeezing the trigger, Bolan routed a grenade through the window to the horde of men invading the compound. It exploded on target and sent more Spetznaz bodies tumbling in a cloud of sand and blood. Above the ongoing clamor, screams of shock and anguish drifted up to the HQ room.

Bolan dropped below the window again as return fire answered his attack. Turning back toward the room, he shouted, "Katz! Get below and order a retreat! Take David and Gary with you!" He turned to Calvin James. "Calvin, you stay with me. We'll hold them off up here as long as we can." Turning back to Katz, the Executioner pointed to the watch on his wrist. "Everyone meets at the rear gate in ten. Now get out of here!"

Katz raised his prosthetic arm in a quick salute, then hurried toward the staircase with McCarter and Manning at his heels.

Bolan rearmed the grenade launcher and turned toward James at the side window. "Any gates open your way?"

"Negative."

Across the desert another quick flash appeared in the night, as if some distant soldier might have just flicked a cigarette lighter. But the familiar boom followed, then an explosion sounded on James's side of the building.

The black warrior turned to Bolan. "Let me retract that last statement. Got a hole big enough for a tank to drive through now."

The Executioner tossed the grenade launcher through the air. "Slow them down."

James dropped his M-16 and caught the weapon. He turned back to the window as Bolan dived for another M-16/M-203 that lay in the corner.

Below, the Executioner heard the sounds of vehicles starting as the retreat began. He readied the grenade launcher, fired, loaded, fired again. Beside him James did the same thing. The advance slowed.

But Bolan knew the grenade launchers were a momentary solution to a lethal situation. With each explosion dozens of Soviet troopers were sent to their graves. Dozens more hesitated, dropping back. But each grenade widened the holes in the fence, and eventually the Executioner's battle tactics would begin to work against them.

Another flash in the distance and another boom.

Bolan heard the 115 mm soaring toward them like some predatory bird. "Incoming!" he shouted, and dived to the center of the room beneath the conference table.

James fell to the floor next to him, his shoulder crashing painfully into the Executioner's ribs.

The explosion threatened to deafen both of them.

Then, as if some giant hand from heaven had slapped it, the HQ building began to shake. Fire leaped up the face of the front wall, the flames lapping briefly through the window, then receding. A slow rumble began beneath them, then the second-story office crumbled forward.

The sudden shift in gravity sucked Bolan and James along the floor. The two men slammed against the wall beneath the window as the room continued to collapse, finally settling at a forty-five-degree incline.

The Executioner peered over the window to see a ten-foot crater where the front door had once been. The second story of the headquarters building had become the ground floor.

James pulled himself to his feet. "Troops at the front must have radioed back," he panted. "The shooters are redirecting fire from the fence to *us*."

Bolan nodded. "We've done all we can from here." He turned toward the door that had once led to the stairs. Dislodged concrete blocks now formed an impassable barricade. Looking back to the window, he saw a new wave of Spetznaz troops suddenly burst through the openings in the fence.

"Get ready," Bolan said. "The front's the only way out."

The Executioner primed his grenade launcher, as did James. Taking up positions on both sides of the window, they pulled the triggers simultaneously.

The explosions rocked the front of the compound. Sand, flesh and blood soared through the air, forming a temporary cloud of cover between the HQ building and the fence. "Let's go!" Bolan shouted.

The Executioner dived through the window, firing a steady stream of rounds as he hit the ground. James followed, his own M-16 chattering nonstop in his hands. Three Spetznaz troopers who'd braved the grenades fell beneath the fire.

The two men sprinted for the corner of the building and were met halfway along the side of the building by Gary Manning. The Canadian did a double-time about-face, falling in next to the running men as they sprinted toward the vehicle pool. "Resistance mounting at the rear, Striker," he panted, out of breath. "But it's still lighter than the front."

A sudden, massive explosion sounded behind them. The concussion drove all three warriors into the air, then onto their faces in the sand. Bolan turned as he sprang back to his feet, his ears ringing.

The left side of the HQ building had fallen to the cannon fire of the T-62 MBT in the desert.

As they took off again toward the vehicles, Bolan saw the flashing lights of small-arms fire in the desert past the fence. Next to the open rear gate Katz, McCarter and two dozen other troops were doing their best to keep the attackers at bay as jeeps and personnel carriers raced through the opening.

Autofire suddenly screamed over the Executioner's shoulder. Turning on the run, he spotted three Spetznaz soldiers who'd broken through past the HQ building. "Keep going!" he ordered James and Manning. "Make sure the rest of the troops are out and make a vehicle available for *us!*"

Dropping to one knee, Bolan tapped the trigger and sent a 3-round burst into the Soviet leading the race toward the motor pool. The man twisted a full 180 and fell facedown into the sand.

The soldiers behind him stopped in their tracks. Bolan fired again, this time carving a figure eight back and forth between the troopers, who fell on top of their fallen comrade.

The Executioner was back on his feet and running before the bodies had settled in the sand. The fallen forms of American soldiers littered the grounds as he neared the motor pool. He hurdled the casualties, gritting his teeth as a mental image of Joshua Eldridge entered his mind.

This was Eldridge's fault. All of it. The demented colonel's desertion had left the compound underprotected. The blood of these men was on his hands, and Eldridge would pay with his own blood.

The Executioner would make sure of it.

Ahead, Bolan saw Manning open the door and leap behind the wheel of an M-998 High Mobility Multipurpose Wheeled Vehicle. The HMMWV, or "Hummer" as it was commonly known, was mounted with a .50-caliber machine gun. Manning twisted the key in the ignition as James dived into the passenger's side.

Sprinting past the Hummer, Bolan yelled, "Bring it up to the gate!" He sprinted on to the fence to join Katz, McCarter and the other men as they fired at the shadows across the sand.

Two personnel carriers slowed as they reached the gate.

"Climb on board, soldiers!" the Executioner yelled.

"Sir, we'll stay with—"

"That's an order!" Bolan dropped to one knee, firing through the fence as the troops boarded the vehicles.

He turned, dropping two men who foolishly charged past the vehicle pool into the lights. He saw James jam the barrel of his M-16 through the window of the Hummer and fire into another pair as the HMMWV raced toward the gate.

Manning reached over the seat behind him, opening the rear door as the Hummer slowed. Bolan grabbed Katz, throwing him up into the back seat as McCarter jumped in on the other side. With a final burst at a trio of Soviets sprinting past the motor pool, the Executioner slung his rifle. Leaping into the air, he grasped the machine-gun turret and hauled himself up on top of the vehicle.

Grasping the grips of the .50-caliber gun, Bolan pulled himself to his knees. From out of the darkness came a new barrage of small-arms fire, the muzzle-flashes looking like firecrackers exploding in the darkness.

The Executioner lowered the barrel. As the Hummer bounced across the rugged desert terrain, he pressed down on the trigger button, answering the fire with a steady stream of .50-caliber rounds.

"Where are the troops headed?" James yelled out the window.

"Kuwait City," Manning shouted back as another assault began from the darkness. "*If* they can get there!"

Far away in the distance the Executioner could just make out the shadowy forms of the fleeing jeeps and personnel carriers. He let up on the trigger. "Katz!" he shouted.

Katz stuck his head out the window as the Hummer raced on.

"Tell Gary to follow the other troops."

Katz's head disappeared again as Bolan tapped the trigger on the big machine gun, aiming at the "fireflies" that popped out in the darkness.

The HMMWV fell in behind the other retreating vehicles on the rough trail through the sands. Bolan continued to fire, and slowly the "fireflies" dissipated. Ahead, the fleeing convoy topped a hill, then disappeared over the ridge.

Three rounds skidded off the roof of the Hummer to Bolan's left. Twisting the turret, he aimed toward the muzzle-flash and fired as the vehicle topped the hill.

Suddenly Manning stomped on the brake. The Executioner flew forward, grabbing the turret as the vehicle skidded sideways through the sand and threatened to overturn. Bolan's legs flew into space off the side of the vehicle, then the Hummer rocked to a halt.

He looked up and saw the reason for Manning's sudden stop. A hundred yards down the road the fleeing American troops were being systematically gunned down by a new Spetznaz assault. Soviet light armored vehicles and personnel carriers had emerged from the shadowy desert to converge on the retreating Americans from all sides.

Manning stuck his head out the window, his troubled eyes showing his turmoil as he stared up at the Executioner. "Forward, Striker?"

Bolan stared at the fighting in the distance, knowing what he had to do. A few of the men ahead might escape. But most were about to die.

And they would die regardless of what he and Phoenix Force did.

The warrior's heart screamed for him to answer Manning with a yes—to command the Canadian to press forward into the battle and join the Americans who were falling to the Spetznaz attack. But Bolan's brain ordered restraint, commanding him to use common sense and to realize that the best revenge was to live to fight another day, taking more of the enemy with him than he could possibly hope to take under the present conditions.

Reluctantly the Executioner shook his head. "There's nothing we can do," he heard himself say.

Ahead, a detachment of Soviets spotted the trailing Hummer. They broke away from the battle and started down the road.

"Throw this thing in reverse, Gary," Bolan commanded. "We'll have to cut around the compound on the east."

Katz poked his head out the window. "The bulk of the rear attack came from the southeast, Striker."

Bolan nodded. "We'll turn north as soon as we've passed the compound."

James stuck his head out of the Hummer on the other side. "If we head north, we'll be driven straight into—"

"Iraq," Bolan finished for him. "We've got no choice."

Manning threw the HMMWV into reverse, backed up and slammed the gearshift into first.

As they started forward, Bolan's mind raced ahead to what they were about to face. Somewhere, between here and the Iraqi border, there had to be a hundred places to hide. The problem was, he wasn't familiar with the terrain, and in the darkness he wouldn't find them.

The Executioner wished briefly for Talia Alireza, the half Jew, half Arab mercenary they'd hired as a guide, then forced his thoughts away. Alireza knew the territory like the back of her hand, but the confused woman had switched sides, gone over to the UAR. The Executioner could wish Alireza had listened to reason until hell froze over if he wanted to. That fact wouldn't change.

Wind whipped through Bolan's hair as the Hummer picked up speed. Sand flew from under the wheels and then, as they topped the ridge again, the burning Special Forces base appeared across the desert in the night.

Bolan watched the flames leap into the blackened sky and thought once more of Joshua Eldridge. Then he turned back toward the pursuing Spetznaz vehicles as their first rounds sailed past the Hummer.

CHAPTER TWO

The city of her birth looked more like the site of a random natural disaster—a tornado came to Talia Alireza's mind—than a town that had been continuously bombed for six weeks in the greatest air strike in the history of mankind.

The destruction in downtown Baghdad was far from total, and visible only to the trained eye that looked closely.

Buses and automobiles hurried past sidewalk carts, where merchants sold fruits, vegetables and pastries. The streets, alleys and parks were alive once more with children playing tag, soccer and, of course, *army*, reenacting the fictitious victories of which Saddam Hussein had boasted throughout the Gulf War.

As she walked along the street disguised in the long black dress and veil of a Shiite woman, Alireza saw an occasional building in shambles, as if the tornado in her mind had arbitrarily touched down, done its damage, then risen into the air to scout out another target.

She hurried on, passing several burned-out buildings. The untrained eye might have wondered why the Allies had targeted a florist shop, a meat market and an Arab international insurance company. But Alireza's eyes had been trained, and she knew that remnants within the back rooms of the buildings would answer that question.

Within the crumbling walls of the florist shop one would find the scraps of ignition components more consistent with the manufacture of electronic explosives than with the keeping of roses and carnations. On the floor of the meat market would lie charred pieces of implements once used in chemical warfare experimentation. And while the citizens of prewar Baghdad had never known just what the international insurance company really did, they'd known it *didn't* write insurance policies. Anyone who'd been in Alireza's business knew it had been a front for a massive telephone backup system that connected Saddam Hussein's palace with major military installations throughout the country.

As she walked past the former communications center, Alireza saw both the obvious and that which the obvious attempted to conceal. Like the chemical laboratory and the explosives factory, the backup phone system had been taken out with what the Americans called their "smart" bombs. She gritted her teeth, thinking that they shouldn't be called "smart." The bombs could be better described as being only "borderline retarded." True, the new explosives had spared the surrounding areas. But what of the many citizens who'd been in the wrong place at the wrong time? They'd been vaporized.

The dejection gnawing at Alireza's heart turned suddenly to anger.

She turned away from the downtown area and started the half-mile walk that led to the residential section where her mother lived. She passed an old woman who sat on the front porch of her house, gazing blankly into space with hollow eyes. The elderly matron looked as if a "smart" bomb had bull's-eyed her soul and destroyed all that was within the shell, but left the walls standing intact outside.

More people puttered through the neighborhood as Alireza lugged her suitcase along the street. In her Shiite woman garb she received no more second glances than she would have in camouflage fatigues back at the American Special Forces compound. Both outfits were disguises. And as she walked along, she suddenly realized for the first time that her clothing had always been a disguise of one sort or another.

First had been the disguise of the Arab schoolgirl. That had been changed the night the tough-looking men awakened her, when she learned that her father was a Mossad agent. His cover had been compromised, and before she had time to put things into perspective, she'd found herself uprooted and transplanted in Tel Aviv.

In Israel she'd worn the disguise of a Jewish girl. She was never more than half accepted by the other children, and she'd spent the rest of her childhood years wondering just who she really was.

Next had come adulthood, and her own training and employment as a Mossad operative. Her father had been a hero within the ranks, and she'd been treated well—until his death.

After her father's death, Alireza's mother had returned to Iraq. That act had caused the bureaucrats within the Mossad to focus more on Alireza's Arab half, and the paranoid suspicions as to her true loyalty had finally resulted in an assassination attempt that drove her from Israel. Her training and talents had soon found her leading a band of international mercenaries in order to survive. She'd been a woman without a country, and as she had as a child, Talia Alireza had again begun to wonder just who she was.

For a fleeting moment, during the last days of the Gulf War and afterward, the mercenary woman believed that question had been answered. While she hadn't condoned the Allied bombing, she'd tried to look past it to a greater good. She'd seen Saddam Hussein's ruthless efforts to destroy the Iranians, his attempts at genocide with the Kurds, and the inexcusable annexation of Kuwait and the torture, rape and murder that had followed.

The Americans had given her a chance to fight such evil, and for a brief, shining moment in time she'd felt as if she belonged somewhere.

Alireza turned the final corner and there, at the end of the street, she saw the house where she'd lived as a child. She stood frozen for a moment, then forced her legs to move forward, a new and different fear filling her soul.

Just when she believed she'd found a home with the Americans, just when she suspected that the man known as Colonel Rance Pollock was a man she could trust, in one lightninglike moment, things had changed again. First, she'd seen the moronic destruction the so-called "smart" bombs had done. And then the United Arab Republic had been formed, with a promise of One Arab Nation. She'd become confused once more, finally realizing that her destiny lay with the UAR—a government that would unite the Mideast once and for all.

Alireza came to a halt in front of her mother's house. Her hand rose to finger the veil that covered her face. Why was she still in disguise? Was she hiding from her mother?

Yes. In a sense, she was. Alireza knew what her mother's reaction would be when told she intended to offer her services to the United Arab Republic. The woman would smile and echo what Pollock had said—that the UAR would profess one people, but that they intended to destroy the Jews and many others. Just as Pollock had, she'd cite the acts of terrorism as irrefutable evidence.

And that would be the logical part of Amilah Alireza's argument. Then would come the visions, the supernatural insight she'd claim to have.

And all of it would make the young woman wonder.

Alireza prepared to knock when the door suddenly swung open.

An elderly woman wearing a rumpled warm-up suit smiled through the screen. The wrinkled face showed no surprise. "I knew you would come," Amilah Alireza said, opening the screen and stepping back.

Alireza embraced her mother in the doorway. Amilah reached up, a liver-spotted hand gently removing Alireza's veil, an impish smile curling the wrinkles at the corners of her mouth. "What is this?" she asked. "You've converted?"

Alireza shrugged self-consciously, suddenly feeling like a child playing dress-up. "A disguise," she muttered.

Her mother's eyebrows rose in mock furtiveness. "Then, quickly, come inside. Who knows what eyes may be watching?" She ushered her daughter down the hall into the living room. "I've made tea," she said, and hurried out of sight into the kitchen.

Alireza dropped down onto the couch, the fatigue of the past several days suddenly catching up to her. She stared at the Persian carpets covering the floor, the brass bowls and other works of Arabic art that sat on the end tables by the couch.

The photograph of her father on the wall.

Amilah returned a moment later. She carried a tray holding two small glasses of hot tea and a bowl of sugar. She sank down next to her daughter, set the tray on the coffee table in front of them and lifted a spoon. "Sugar?"

Alireza took the tea. "No, thank you." She balanced one of the glasses on her knee, curling her fingers around the edge, trying to draw strength from the warmth. "You said you expected me, Mother. Why? No one knew I'd come here."

Amilah smiled. "A dream."

The younger woman suppressed a sudden desire to roll her eyes toward the ceiling. Instead, she said, "Tell me about it."

The old woman carefully measured out two spoonfuls of sugar, then dropped them into her glass. "I don't understand it. You were being chased through the desert by a large, ferocious black bear. As you ran, I could see fear and confusion in your eyes. I wanted to help you, but my arms and legs wouldn't move." She slowly stirred the sugar into her tea.

Alireza waited impatiently.

"Then I looked closely at the bear. I knew he didn't normally live in the desert. The heat was hard on him, and he went thirsty much of the time. He had large, powerful claws that were good for climbing trees, but held little use where trees didn't exist.

"The bear survived only because of his strong will, Talia. And I wondered why he wanted to eat you so badly that he'd be willing to suffer the desert." She took a sip of her tea, then returned the glass to the tray.

"Then I looked back to where you ran, and suddenly I saw a wolf crossing the sand, preparing to attack you from the side. You couldn't see him, but I could. His long, sharp teeth dripped with saliva, and his eyes were wide with the lust of the kill. You tripped and fell. Both the bear and the wolf overtook you." The old woman's eyes brightened. Her face began to glow. "But instead of attacking *you,* the bear ripped the wolf apart with his claws, and I suddenly realized that this had been his intention all along. He didn't wish to harm you, Talia. He had come to protect you."

"I don't need protection," Alireza said, irritated. No matter how old she became, regardless of her training and skills, her mother would always consider her a helpless little girl.

Amilah smiled. "Perhaps not," she said, "but in my dream you did. And you were hungry. The bear offered to share the meat of the wolf with you. And the two of you ate."

For a long moment the room remained silent. Alireza fought the temptation to laugh. She loved her mother, but the silly woman had begun to believe the neighbors when they told her she had the powers of a psychic.

Finally Alireza said, "An interesting dream, mother, but I'm sorry, I can't help you interpret it. I'm sure it means nothing."

Amilah Alireza shook her head and smiled. "It means *something*," she said with assurance. "All dreams do."

STAFF SERGEANT JERRY PECK wedged his entrenching tool into the sand and pulled the green beret from his head. The undefinable anxiety that had permeated his soul for the past several days swept over him as he squinted up into the blazing Iraqi sun.

Peck wiped the sweat from his eyebrows with the back of his hand. He wasn't sure when the uneasiness had started; it had crept gradually through his body, sometimes lying dormant, other times shooting through his system in a sudden surge. He didn't know what caused it, but he knew it had something to do with religion.

The sergeant replaced his beret and picked up the shovel. Across the trench he saw Corporal David Lee Collins throw a shovelful of sand behind him, then stop. "Don't know what all this digging's about, do you, Sarge?" Collins asked. "So far we haven't stayed in one place long enough to take a peaceful dump."

Collins shrugged. "Guess we're digging in for a while. Can't 'hit and git' forever without getting caught by the enemy. Got to let things cool off once in a while."

The corporal grinned. "Nothin' cools off when it's 120 degrees outside."

"No kidding."

Both men resumed digging.

As the small OD green shovel stabbed in and out of the desert sand, Peck let his eyes wander across the camp to where more Special Forces soldiers dug other trenches, unloaded trucks and staked out tents. Eldridge's dozen personal staff officers were busy constructing a platform out of map tables. A rostrum had already been set up in the center of the makeshift stage.

Peck watched the men—the "Mysterious Twelve," as he'd begun thinking of them. Every one of them was, well, weird. Eldridge had chosen his new staff from all nine of the company's B-teams when he restructured his command. The reorganization had come as soon as Colonel Pollock and his force had departed the compound in northern Kuwait.

Collins leaned forward on his shovel to catch his breath. "What the hell do you think they're up to now, Sarge?" he asked. "Is Eldridge going to give another patriotic speech?"

Peck paused again, his eyes returning to the make-shift stage. He shrugged. "Maybe. Not that I'd call them patriotic anymore. They're getting to be more like sermons."

Collins chuckled. "No shit. I mean, the colonel's always been a little strange."

To Collins's rear Peck saw Lieutenant Ferguson, one of the "Twelve," approaching. He tried to get Collins's attention—shut him up—but the corporal was staring down into the trench.

"But now Eldridge is beginning to sound like Jimmy Swaggart or somebody," Collins finished.

Ferguson cleared his throat. Collins jerked around, dropped his shovel and saluted.

"You were saying, Corporal?" the lieutenant prompted.

"Er, nothing, sir."

Ferguson nodded and walked on.

Collins waited until the lieutenant was out of ear-shot, then whispered, "You think he heard me?"

Peck nodded.

"Damn. I'll get written up for that one, sure." He paused. "What'd you think of Eldridge's question-naire?"

"Weird," Peck whispered back.

Collins nodded. "No shit." He picked up his entrenching tool, and the two men went back to work.

The sun continued to beat down on Peck's nape. The blisteringly dry desert wind battered his face. Then, for no reason he could put his finger on, the fear streaked suddenly through his testicles to his stomach.

What was it? Peck wondered.

It was religion, all right. But how? Why? He hadn't had religious fears since he'd been a kid in Sunday school and the teacher had taught a section on the Book of Revelation.

Peck continued to dig as he struggled to get a grip on his emotions. He forced himself to think. He was raised in a Christian church, grew up believing in that religion. Then, when he got older, he questioned Christianity, rejected it, then went back to it. Did he go back to it because he really believed, or because it was the path of least resistance? Was it a true conviction, or just a way to answer some universal questions that bothered everybody?

Did he *really* believe there was a God?

Peck threw another shovelful of sand to the side of the trench and paused, pulling his canteen from his web belt and lifting it to his lips. He thought of Eldridge and the strange things that had been happening the past few days. Lots of commanders sprinkled biblical quotes through their speeches. That was no big deal. But with Eldridge it had become a little too frequent. Was that what had spawned the religious confusion he was now experiencing?

Peck drove his entrenching tool into the sand with a vengeance, using his nervous energy on the task at hand. He thought of the chaplain who'd been assigned to Eldridge's Seventh Special Forces Group. The whole deal had been the first of the weird occurrences. One day the chaplain had been there, the next day he was gone.

The sergeant loaded another shovelful and threw it over his shoulder. Then had come the questionnaire. The *religious* questionnaire. The Mysterious Twelve had circulated it to all troops, along with the flimsy story that the chaplain had been suddenly transferred and mistakenly taken his records with him. New files had to be made.

But the information on the questionnaire demanded bore little resemblance to the Army's usual inquiries like "Christian or Jew," "Catholic or Protestant." The questions dealt with each soldier's personal belief about strange, obscure prophecies that Peck recognized as coming from the Book of Revelation.

And now that he thought of it, Peck realized that the colonel's restructuring of the command, and this strange hit-and-run mission into Iraq led by Eldridge himself, had come almost immediately after the questionnaires had been collected.

Was there a connection? Peck didn't know. It was all too confusing.

The sounds of the wind and the digging were suddenly broken by the static of a loudspeaker system scratching on. The two men turned toward the noise.

A moment later Peck recognized Eldridge's gravelly voice. "This is the group commander. All personnel, assemble in the parade area on the double. Sentries remain at your posts." The mike clicked off.

Peck threw his entrenching tool into the hole. "Thank God," he said as he forced his weary muscles to follow Collins toward the center of the camp.

As the men assembled in front of the podium, Peck saw the twelve staff officers finish arranging the chairs behind the podium. Then they dropped into the seats like a panel of judges, staring down at the men.

Eldridge emerged from his command tent. His prematurely white crew cut glistened under the sun as he climbed up onto the stage and crossed in front of the staff officers to the podium.

The colonel took his place behind the rostrum, his huge, blocky shoulders stretching the material of his dress uniform. The sunlight sparkled off the medals on his chest. He smiled. "At ease, gentlemen."

There was a shuffling among the troops as they shifted to more comfortable positions.

Waving a hand over his shoulder toward the desert, Eldridge said, "Moses wandered through this region for forty years before God led him to the Promised Land. But the Lord has brought us here in two days." He paused, pulled a handkerchief from his pocket and wiped sweat from his forehead.

Peck stared at the colonel's shining face as the man continued. "We've found our home, gentlemen. All further strikes will begin and end at this camp. It will be our Alpha and our Omega—our beginning and our end.'' Eldridge looked up toward the heavens as he went on. "The war will soon be over, and when the great battle comes to end it, we'll see a victory far greater than the earth has ever known. It won't be simply a victory for America, although America will be at the forefront. It will be a victory for all. And when it's over, a reign of peace the likes of which mankind has never known will begin.''

Peck heard a voice mutter, "What the hell's the man talking about?'' He turned to see Theodore Lassiter, a black demolition sergeant.

Eldridge's eyes turned toward Lassiter, burning holes through the man. Lassiter clamped his jaw tight.

Peck shifted uneasily. Lassiter was right. There was something different—something unsettling—about Eldridge's tone. It was different than the countless other Bible-sprinkled speeches he'd heard from senior officers over the years. The words seemed almost meant to be taken literally.

Eldridge's face suddenly took on the same iconoclastic expression Peck remembered on the face of an evangelist an old girlfriend had once dragged him to hear. "Who is our enemy?'' the colonel shouted, his tanned face turning a deep red, his eyes burning suddenly with fire. "Our enemy has been the same since three thousands years before the birth of Christ! Our enemy is no different today in the times of Shawiyya and Jaluwi than it was during the reign of Nebuchadnezzar! Our enemy is still found in the ancient whore city of Babylon, and now also in its sister city Baghdad!''

Peck stood frozen, unable to believe what he was hearing. He heard confused whispers from several of the men around him.

"Thou hast defiled thy sanctuaries by the multitude of thine iniquities!" Eldridge screamed. Then, just as the evangelist had done when he wanted to make a point, the colonel lowered his voice to a barely audible murmur and whispered, "Therefore will I bring forth a fire from the midst of thee. It shall devour thee, and I will bring thee to ashes upon the earth in the sight of all them that behold thee. So sayeth the Lord."

Peck heard more muffled whispers within the ranks. Then, as the shock wore off and his emotional paralysis began to lift, new waves of horror swept over him.

"Our enemy is Satan!" Eldridge screamed at the top of his voice.

And as the words reverberated across the desert, Sergeant Jerry Peck's religious confusion suddenly came into perspective. He realized for the first time since childhood, without reservation and with complete conviction, that, yes, he was indeed a God-fearing man.

And with no less certainty he understood that Colonel Joshua Eldridge was irreversibly mad.

Peck stood in a half daze as Eldridge concluded his address. He had to get out of there. He didn't know what the madman was planning, but he knew that he had to get out of there.

Eldridge dismissed the men and ordered them to return to their tasks. Peck turned away, his eyes moving toward the motor pool, his mind racing, weighing the odds, wondering if he might be able to steal a vehicle and escape back to Kuwait—to reality.

As he stared at the parked vehicles, he saw Lieutenant Ferguson walk past him. The staffer locked his fingers around the arm of Corporal Collins, and the man looked up in surprise.

"Corporal Collins," the lieutenant said.

"Yes, sir?"

"Come with me, Corporal. The colonel wants to speak to you."

Peck watched the two men start toward the colonel's tent.

LYONS LUNGED FORWARD, catching the President in his arms as the man fell toward the floor. Two Secret Service men moved in and grabbed the Man by the arms. Together they laid the limp body on the floor.

The Able warrior pressed a forefinger into the President's carotid artery. "Pulse is weak," he pronounced, "and too fast."

A short, squat man with a receding hairline knelt next to Lyons. He pulled a stethoscope from his pocket, shrugged into the earpieces and placed the disk on the President's chest.

Lyons glanced up and saw a thin man in a dark suit moving casually toward the door.

The aide, Lyons thought, the man who'd brought out the president's water....

"Grab him!" Lyons shouted, pointing at the man.

The aide's head jerked around. Turning, he bolted for the door.

Two huge Secret Service men were on him in a flash, grabbing him as he reached for the knob. The taller of the two agents grasped the aide's right arm in a painful "come along" hold.

Lyons leaped to his feet and grabbed the man by the lapels. "What was it?" he demanded, shoving his nose into the man's startled face.

"What? I don't understa—"

Lyons swept the Python from under his jacket and shoved the barrel into the man's nose. "We don't have time to play games," he snarled. "And if you even *say* the word Miranda, I'll blow your fucking head off." He cocked the revolver for emphasis.

The aide went suddenly limp, supported by the two Secret Service men. "I don't know," he said defiantly. "I was just paid to—"

"Gadgets," Lyons called. "Get the glass and pitcher from the rostrum."

Schwarz scrambled back through the door to the chambers.

Lyons turned back to the President. The short man—the staff physician, he assumed—was directing two medics to load the President on a stretcher. One of the men placed an oxygen mask over his face while the other slipped a blood pressure cuff onto his arm.

The Able leader turned to Stover. "Which hospital?" he asked.

"Walter Reed. Security's always set up—just in case."

Lyons nodded. "We'll follow in the van."

Stover reached out, grasping the ex-cop's arm. "No. Normally I'd never dream of doing this, but nothing is normal these days." He cleared his throat nervously. "There's already been two attempts on the President's life tonight, and God only knows...there could be a third."

Lyons was distracted by a side door opening suddenly. He looked up in surprise to see a man who could have been the President's twin walk into the room.

"I want you to take the President in your van," Stover went on. "We'll take the double in the ambulance as a decoy—just to be safe."

Lyons nodded. He turned toward Blancanales to tell him to bring the van to the rear exit, but Pol was already on his way.

The presidential double lay down on a second stretcher and was carried from the room.

The Able Team leader exited the building to the secured parking area and waited by the van as Blancanales and three Secret Service agents loaded the President inside and climbed in after him.

Lyons slid behind the wheel of the van as Schwarz, the President's water glass and pitcher clutched in his arms, took the passenger seat.

The van followed two escort cars and four motorcycles out of the parking area. Three more automobiles fell in behind, then the decoy ambulance and a half-dozen more Secret Service vehicles.

Lights blazing and sirens piercing the night, they raced down Georgia Avenue toward the hospital.

A few minutes later Lyons pulled to a halt at the emergency-room entrance of Walter Reed Army Medical Center. Three dozen Secret Service personnel crowded around the van, shielding it from the street and the parking lot. The agents carried the President inside.

Lyons, Blancanales and Schwarz stopped in the waiting room as he was transferred to a gurney and wheeled into one of the emergency rooms. Through the door, Lyons watched doctors and nurses scurry back and forth.

A young doctor in surgical greens ripped the pitcher and glass from Schwarz's hands. "Is this it?" he asked, already disappearing through a swinging door marked Lab by the time Schwarz nodded.

Stover, grasping a walkie-talkie in his hands, joined Able Team, his face almost as gray as the President's. He looked as if he'd aged ten years in the ten minutes it had taken to get to the hospital. "Thanks," he murmured weakly, "I—"

The walkie-talkie in his hand suddenly crackled to life, a voice calling, "943...943."

Stover raised the radio to his lips. "Go ahead, 943."

"Ten-twenty?"

"Walter Reed. Emergency room."

"Ten-four, 943. Ten-twenty-five the Justice agents assigned your team?"

Stover glanced at the three members of Able Team. "They're right here."

"Advise them ten-twenty-one headquarters immediately. Ten-thirty-three and thirty-five."

Stover started to translate the ten-code, but Lyons was already reaching for the nearest phone.

A ten-thirty-five meant confidential information. Ten-thirty-three meant it was an emergency.

Under the present circumstances the two numbers together could mean only one thing: another terrorist strike was in progress.

Barbara Price, Stony Man Farm's mission controller, answered the phone on the first ring.

"Lyons here."

"Temple B'nai Israel," Price said without formalities. "It's a small synagogue on Missouri Avenue. All hell's broken loose. Police and FBI Hostage Rescue are on the way, but they'll need all the help they can get. You need air transport? Mott's waiting with the chopper."

Lyons hesitated as Blancanales shoved a city map of Washington, D.C., in front of him. Next to Jack Grimaldi, Charlie Mott was the best wingman Stony Man had. Before being recruited by the Farm the former Marine fighter pilot had divided his post-Vietnam War time between clandestine CIA missions and commercial cargo deliveries into the remote Alaskan badlands. Like Grimaldi, he could fly everything from a kite to the space shuttle, and if he had to, Lyons suspected Mott could get a Volkswagen Rabbit airborne.

The ex-cop squinted at the map, locating the address. "Negative on transport," he finally said. "It'll be faster to drive.'' He started to hang up, then said, ''But tell Charlie to stand by just in case.''

''Affirmative.''

Lyons hung up. ''We're gone,'' he said, and raced back to the van, Schwarz and Blancanales at his heels.

Gadgets drove, guiding the van around the busy Washington traffic as Lyons and Blancanales changed into combat dress in the back.

Schwarz suddenly hit the brake. The van skidded, and Lyons and Blancanales slid forward against the seats.

''What's going on?'' Lyons stuck his head between the bucket seats and looked through the windshield, answering his own question.

The van had come to a halt behind an aging Ford LTD. Ahead, traffic was backed up for two blocks. The flashing red lights of squad cars and ambulances were visible in the distance.

''What is it?'' Blancanales asked. ''A wreck?''

''It doesn't matter,'' Lyons growled. ''Whatever it is, it's holding us up.'' He squinted at the bumper-to-bumper jam ahead. ''Get in back and get changed, Gadgets,'' he said. ''I'll take the wheel.''

The two men exchanged places. Lyons reached under the dashboard, switching on the police scanner as they waited.

''Ten-four, John 14. Shots fired. Backup on its way.''

''Officer down! Ambulance requested immediately.''

''All units en route.''

"Any hostages, David 4?"

"Don't know yet, Base."

As the seconds ticked away, Blancanales finished dressing and slid up into the passenger seat. "Sounds like all hell's broken loose," he said. "You say the cops and Feds were already there?"

Lyons nodded. His heart felt as if it were about to jump out of his chest. He fought an irrational urge to throw the van into gear and plow through the LTD. Instead, he leaned back against the seat and gripped the steering wheel.

Mentally the Able Team leader kicked himself. He should have had Mott pick them up at the hospital. But they were less than a mile from the synagogue now, and it was anybody's guess whether or not the Stony Man pilot would be of any help at this point. Still, if traffic didn't start soon...

As if in answer to his thoughts, the LTD began to inch forward. Lyons threw the van into gear and crept after it, breathing a sigh of relief.

Then the traffic suddenly screeched to a halt again. Lyons jammed on the brakes, the front fender of the van stopping and bobbing up and down an inch away from the rear of the LTD. "I've had all of this I can handle," he said. Twisting the wheel, the ex-cop peeled rubber across the oncoming lane, jumped the curb and came to a halt in the parking lot of a darkened supermarket. He reached for the cellular phone mounted next to the scanner. "I'm going to call Mott and have him pick us—"

The clipping sound of helicopter rotors suddenly penetrated the closed windows of the van. Lyons leaned forward, looking up to see the chopper descending toward the parking lot. He traded the phone for the programmable two-way radio mike and tapped in the Stony Man frequency. "That you, Charlie?" he asked.

Mott's voice came back. "That's affirmative, Able One. Mott to the rescue. I knew you guys would get lost without me."

Through the window the men of Able Team watched the Stony Man pilot set the chopper down in front of the supermarket. Grabbing their weapons, they raced across the lot and climbed up into the aircraft.

No one spoke as the bird rose once more into the air and turned toward the synagogue.

THE HUMMER RACED through the night, dodging boulders, sandbanks and the refuse of the ground war that had occurred only months before. Bolan swiveled the .50-caliber machine gun to the rear of the vehicle, laying down a steady stream of fire behind them. Two Soviet personnel vehicles fell to the Executioner's barrage. The rest sped on.

As they drew even with the southern boundaries of the compound, Bolan saw a sudden flash of light to the north, which was followed by a dull thud. Then flames leaped high into the air, illuminating the desert, as the last of the headquarters building exploded and clouds of smoke began to rise.

A beam of light suddenly shone down from the sky, revealing the Hummer's position. Bolan looked up to see a Soviet helicopter hovering overhead.

Manning swerved instantly off the road, sliding through the sand and out of the spotlight's lethal beam as a volley of gunfire from the chopper's multibarreled gun stitched the road. The Executioner dropped the grips of his machine gun. Swinging the M-16/M-203 from behind his back, he loaded the last of the grenades, aimed up into the light and pulled the trigger.

The sudden explosion rocked the Hummer. Fiery scraps of the chopper rained down over the vehicle, which skidded onto two wheels and spun back onto the road, threatening once more to overturn.

Bolan lunged forward, hugging the machine gun turret as the Hummer spun to a 180-degree halt. The engine choked, then died.

Facing the oncoming convoy of Spetznaz vehicles, the Executioner opened fire once more, sending an onslaught of .50-caliber missiles toward the approaching enemy force. Below, he heard the starter grind as Manning twisted the key, trying desperately to fire the engine.

The Hummer sputtered back to life on the third attempt. Bolan hung on again as Manning spun the vehicle around and took off once more down the road.

The Executioner slowed his rate of fire as the ammo began to dwindle. He sent sporadic bursts into the oncoming personnel carriers, more in an attempt to slow their pursuit than to disable the vehicles.

A mile past the compound the Hummer topped another hill. A quarter mile to the east Bolan saw a new contingent of Spetznaz troops racing forward to head them off. Leaning down over the side of the vehicle, he shouted through the driver's window, "North!"

Manning took a side road, turning toward Iraq as the two Spetznaz detachments cut across the sands to close them off.

Rifle barrels extended through the windows of the Hummer as the warriors of Phoenix Force joined the Executioner's barrage of fire toward the oncoming trucks. In return the Hummer was subjected to waves of return fire from the new convoy of Spetznaz hunters. Soviet bullets sailed past the HMMWV as red-tailed rockets lit the sky from the slower moving tanks at the rear of the column.

Somewhere along the road the Hummer left Kuwait and entered Iraq.

Bolan fired until the well of his weapon ran dry, then shoved his last mag of 5.56 mm rounds into the M-16, using it to blow the tires on yet another Soviet personnel carrier.

Gradually the Hummer began to outdistance the slower moving Russian vehicles. Phoenix Force's return fire dwindled as the last of their ammo was expended.

"Save your pistol ammo!" Bolan ordered. "Gary, get us off the road!"

The Canadian cut the lights, pulled off the road and navigated through the sand by the light of the moon. Bolan lay spread-eagled on the roof, gripping the struts to the turret as they bounced over the rugged terrain.

They'd gone a half mile when disaster struck. The wing of a half-buried, burned-out Iraqi MiG-29 Fulcrum appeared in front of the Hummer a split second too late.

"Turn!" Bolan shouted.

Manning swerved the wheel, but the Hummer's right front tire hit the wreckage peeking out above the sand. The vehicle flipped up into the air.

The Executioner tumbled through the darkness, slamming into the sand and rolling onto his stomach in a storm of pebbles and grit. His nostrils filled with gravel, he looked up in time to see the Hummer roll twice, then come to a halt on its side.

As the sandstorm settled, the left rear door opened slowly at the top of the vehicle. Rafael Encizo pulled himself up out of the Hummer and staggered toward Bolan. Blood covered the Cuban's face. With a deep, rumbling gasp he collapsed to the sand, two feet from the Executioner.

CHAPTER THREE

Joshua Eldridge pulled the white handkerchief from his uniform blouse and blotted the sweat on his eyebrows. The heat made his skin feel as if demons were tickling it with feathers. Wiping more moisture from his cheeks and neck, he dropped the damp rag onto the map table and glanced toward the tent flap.

It would be cooler with the flap open. Cooler yet outside the tent.

Eldridge turned back to the table, opened a manila file and shuffled through the papers inside. No, he couldn't conduct this interview outside, or even with the entrance uncovered. He needed privacy, privacy in which he could meditate, search his soul and listen for the Voice.

The flap flew suddenly back. Lieutenant Ronald Ferguson stuck his head inside. "Permission to enter, sir?" he asked.

"Permission granted."

Ferguson stepped inside, followed by Corporal David Lee Collins.

Eldridge frowned, glancing down at Collins's questionnaire. The corporal had made subversive statements about him—Ferguson had overheard them. That, in itself, didn't necessarily mean the corporal was in league with the Evil One. But combined with the unenthusiastic responses Collins had given to his questions . . .

Eldridge smiled as both men saluted. "Dismissed, Lieutenant."

Ferguson exited the tent, reclosing the flap.

"Take a seat, Corporal," Eldridge said. He leaned back in his chair as Collins lowered himself into the one across the table. The colonel glanced down at the questionnaire, then looked back up. He forced a fatherly smile onto his face. "Please," he said. "Relax. This is an informal interview. Simply a few things that need to be clarified." He cleared his throat. "Tell me, Corporal. What did you think of my questionnaire?"

Collins hesitated, stiffening again. Looking down at the table, he asked, "Permission to speak freely, sir?"

"Certainly."

"I didn't understand it."

"The questions? I tried to make them as rudimentary as possible."

"No, sir, the questions were clear. The *purpose* of the whole thing was . . . was what threw me. I couldn't understand why you did it in the first place."

Eldridge chuckled. "I work in mysterious ways," he said. "Tell me, Corporal. Are you a religious man?"

Collins nodded, then stopped and shrugged. "Well, yes. I mean, I think so. I mean, I believe there's a God and all that."

"Really," Eldridge said, trying to keep the sarcasm out of his voice. "Exactly *when* did you start believing in God?"

Collins shrugged. "I don't know for sure, sir. I . . . I grew up in a churchgoing family."

"Church attendance and faith are hardly one and the same, Corporal."

"No, sir, I realize that. What I meant was, I was taught the Bible from the time I was a kid. It's like . . . like I've *always* believed it."

Eldridge felt himself frown again. Just as he had been on the questionnaire, Collins was being evasive. Another bad sign. "Have you ever read the Book of Ezekiel?" he asked.

"Yes, sir. I mean, not straight through. But I'm sure I've read *from* it. In church and stuff."

"The Book of Revelation?"

"Sure. I mean, yes, sir."

"And what were your feelings about it?"

"Well, sir, I'll have to admit I don't really understand it. But I don't guess anybody does, really."

That was where he was wrong, Eldridge thought.

Collins looked up to the top of the tent. "It's some pretty weird stuff. Scary."

"Yes." Eldridge nodded, his smile returning. He stared hard at the corporal, and suddenly the Voice in his head said, *In the final days even the evil of the earth shall call, "Lord, Lord."* He leaned forward and almost whispered, "What are your feelings about the Arabs and the Jews, Corporal?"

Collins hesitated. Eldridge saw that the man was trying to read the correct answer from his eyes. "Well, sir," he finally said, "I've got some Jewish friends at home. Grew up with them. They're a little different in some ways, I guess, but aren't we all?'' He waited for a response.

Eldridge gave him none.

"I mean, we're all different, yet we're all the same,'' Collins went on nervously. "If you know what I mean.'' He stopped again, waiting for a reply. When none came, he said, "As for Arabs, I feel sorry for the ones in this country. Most of them didn't want war. The only Arabs I was ever around back home in Kansas City were some guys I worked construction with one summer when I was in high school. I liked some of them, didn't like others. They're pretty much like any other group of folks, too, I guess.''

Eldridge's eyes narrowed. He felt the anger rise in his chest. He listened closely for the Voice, but it didn't come. "You don't really know what you believe, do you, Corporal?''

"Well, yes, sir, I think I do. I mean, I don't have all the answers to all the questions. But I don't think anybody does.''

Eldridge had heard enough. He had passed judgment. Now it was time for sentencing.

The colonel stood. "Corporal Collins, you are what the Bible calls lukewarm. You are neither cold nor hot in your convictions.'' Flames of righteous indignation filled his breast. "'So then because thou art lukewarm, and neither cold nor hot, I will spew thee out of my mouth.'''

Collins watched curiously as Eldridge summoned Ferguson back into the tent. As soon as the lieutenant had thrown back the flap and stepped inside, the colonel nodded toward Collins, then closed his eyes, bowed his head and shook it.

Ferguson produced a set of handcuffs.

Eldridge watched with satisfaction as the expression on Collins's face shifted from curiosity to concern.

"Sir?" he said as Ferguson cuffed his hands behind his back. "What . . . what did I do?"

"Silence!" Eldridge shouted, standing up. He turned to Ferguson. "You know what to do. Send Lieutenant Lindley to take your place while you're gone."

Ferguson grasped Collins's shoulder and shoved him roughly through the tent flap. "What's happening?" Eldridge heard the corporal say as the two men's footsteps faded away. "Tell me what I did! Please!"

Eldridge dropped back into his seat. He opened the manila folder again, spreading the questionnaire across the table until the name Lassiter appeared at the top of one of the forms. In the distance he heard Ferguson's jeep start and pull away.

Lieutenant David Lindley, another of the twelve men he'd picked to be his personal staff, stepped through the flap and saluted. "Yes, sir?"

"Bring Corporal Lassiter in next," Eldridge said. He glanced down at the page in his hand. "Theodore M." He paused, staring down at the table. "You know. The man who tried to start the disturbance during my speech."

THE FIERCE WIND above Washington, D.C., shook the helicopter like a rag doll as it hovered a block south of Temple B'nai Israel. Carl Lyons spotted the small one-story synagogue below, standing alone on a well-kept lawn between a three-story office building and a shopping center.

Police cars and wooden sawhorses ringed the synagogue, isolating the building from the rest of the block. Plainclothes men, as well as officers in SWAT and police blues, scurried between the vehicles wielding shotguns, AR-15 assault rifles and two-way radios.

Near the front of the ring Lyons saw the dull gray panel truck that belonged to the FBI Hostage Rescue Team. "You got contact, Charlie?" He pointed to the radio mounted in front of him.

Mott didn't answer. He lifted the mike from the hook and handed it over. As Lyons took it, the Stony Man pilot leaned forward, punching the FBI frequency into the program.

Lyons hesitated. He couldn't use his usual call number, which was Able One. No one below would recognize it.

From the seat behind him Blancanales read his mind. "Call yourself Justice 307," Politician suggested. "It sounds impressive."

Lyons thumbed the mike button. "Justice 307 to FBI Hostage Team," he said. "Come in." He slipped his thumb from the key.

Below, a tiny figure leaned into the driver's window of the truck. "Bureau 714 here. Go, Justice."

"What's your situation?" Lyons asked. "We're a fully equipped rescue team, ready to go in."

The man standing next to the FBI truck looked up into the sky. "Negative, Justice. You'd better come on down."

Lyons stayed on the radio as the helicopter began to descend. As they neared the street, he saw a half-dozen bodies littering the ground in front of the temple.

"Fill us in, 714."

"This thing started out as another 'shoot and scram,'" the FBI agent replied. "D.C. cruiser stumbled onto it and blocked them off. The terrorists moved inside and took hostages."

The chopper touched down. "How many have they got?"

"Four, total. Two women—sisters—and the daughter of one of the women. Six years old. And a rabbi."

"Ten-four, Bureau." Lyons clipped the mike.

Able Team jumped out of the helicopter, heads bowed low under the twirling blades. They jogged to the van.

Scattered around the FBI van, their Colt 9 mm assault carbines aimed toward the synagogue, were a dozen men in FBI Hostage Rescue Team coveralls. A man of medium height with near-black hair stood next to the window. He tossed the microphone back through the truck window and stepped forward. "Special Agent John Bishop." He indicated the nearby men in coveralls with a sweep of his hand and added, "My team."

In less than a heartbeat Lyons had Bishop pegged. Long black hair curled from under the SWAT-style cap and fell over the agent's ears—a direct violation of FBI policy. Combine that with the years of experience etched on Bishop's face, and his rank as an HRT team commander, and the ex-cop could come to only one conclusion: Bishop was more than just a competent leader. He was good—good enough that the pencil-necked bureacratic "suits" running the FBI over-looked his minor infractions.

"You running the dog-and-pony show, Bishop?" Lyons asked.

The agent shook his head. "Just the assault, if it comes. Ratskowski, the special agent in charge, is handling negotiations."

Lyons frowned. "Negotiations? He's not planning a deal with these bastards, is he?"

"Yeah, for what good it'll do."

Schwarz took a step forward. "What do they want?"

The agent scowled. "The usual. A 747 with full tanks at National. City bus to get them there."

Bishop turned and pointed to a dark blue sedan, where a young agent with short brown hair and a carefully manicured mustache sat speaking into a cel-lular phone. "That's Ratskowski. Bet you a Bud-weiser he can recite the policy manual forward and backward. But it hasn't sunk in yet what we're deal-ing with." Bishop took off his cap, ran his curled fingers back through his hair, then replaced it and shook his head in disgust. "The guy's over there right now arranging for the bus and plane. I never met him before tonight, but I've met plenty like him in my fifteen years with the Bureau.''

"I've known a few myself," Lyons said. He shrugged. "You've just got to circle them." The Able Team leader turned back to Bishop. "How many terrorists inside?"

"Six, maybe more." He pointed to a small man wearing a yarmulke who sat in the back seat of the Washington squad car. "That's Rabbi Wilenzick. He was on his way inside to help set up for a bar mitzvah when the shooting started. He saw the UAR go in."

"You try to get them to release the little girl yet?" Blancanales asked.

Bishop snorted. "Ratskowski got them to agree to let her go after they're on the bus. Then, once they've reached the plane, they'll release one of the women."

Lyons frowned. He was afraid he already knew the answer to his next question. "How about the other woman and the rabbi?"

"They go along for the ride. The terrorists promise to release them as soon as they're out of the country."

"Right," Lyons said. "A Jewish woman and a rabbi? These are Arab fanatics, Bishop. Muslim extremists. If those two hostages get on that plane, we better have the graves ready. No, forget that. We'll never find the bodies."

The agent nodded. "No argument from this quarter. If it was up to me, we'd already be inside. But I've got my orders. I don't move unless I hear shooting."

Lyons glanced back at Ratskowski. Turning to Blancanales, he indicated the SAC with a jerk of his head. "Stall the boy wonder if he gets off the phone."

Blancanales grinned and started toward the sedan.

"Come on," Lyons told Bishop. With a puzzled look the agent followed Lyons and Schwarz to the car where Rabbi Wilenzick sat. The ex-cop tapped on the window, and the old man rolled down the glass. "Rabbi, tell me about the roof of the building."

Wilenzick looked as puzzled as Bishop. "The roof?"

"I need a way to get in. Any ventilation shafts? Things like that?" Lyons heard a car door open behind him and he glanced over his shoulder as Ratskowski got out.

Blancanales stepped in front of him, cutting him off.

"There's a skylight over one of the classrooms," Wilenzick told him.

Ten yards away Ratskowski extended a hand impatiently to Blancanales. Politician reached in his coveralls and pulled out his Department of Justice credential case.

Lyons turned back to Wilenzick. "The skylight, Rabbi. Is the hole big enough for a man to squeeze through?"

Wilenzick's eyes dropped to Lyons's boots, then traveled back up the ex-cop's body to his face. "You or me?" The rabbi grinned, then turned serious again. "It'll be a tight fit, but, yes, I think you could do it."

Behind him Lyons heard a throat clear dramatically. He turned and came face-to-face with a belligerent Ratskowski.

"May I presume you two are with the Justice Department, as well?" the young man said tightly.

Lyons nodded.

Ratskowski sighed and held out his hand. Lyons and Schwarz fished out their phony credentials. The young SAC squinted, studying the two men's pictures with exaggerated importance, then handed the cases back. "We appreciate your interest, gentlemen," he said condescendingly, "but the Federal Bureau of Investigation has the situation well under control." He indicated the helicopter with his head. "Yours?"

"Yes, sir," Lyons replied.

"Please move it. The bus will be here any moment. The helicopter is in the way."

Lyons fought an urge to throw a mock salute, but what he'd planned hinged on letting the arrogant young SAC believe he'd been intimidated. He settled for another subservient "Yes, sir."

Ratskowski turned away and strode off in the other direction. Bishop walked the Able Team warriors to the chopper.

"Guess there isn't much point asking you what a guy like *Rat*skowski's nickname is," Schwarz said.

Bishop laughed. "Yeah. And 'pompous' is his middle name. Hope you won't judge us all by him." He extended his hand to Lyons.

Lyons shook the man's hand. "Get your team ready, Bishop."

Bishop frowned. "My orders are—"

"To move in if you hear shooting," Lyons finished for him. He followed Schwarz and Blancanales on board the chopper. Leaning out through the open door, Lyons glanced down at his watch. "And in about five minutes, my friend, you'll hear all the shooting you need."

BOLAN KNELT over Encizo as the rest of Phoenix Force climbed out of the Hummer. A steady stream of blood coursed from the Cuban's nostrils and dripped off his jaw.

The Executioner jammed a finger into the man's neck. The pulse was strong, steady.

At best the Phoenix Force warrior had only a broken nose; at worst he had a concussion to go with it. Bolan thumbed one of Encizo's eyelids upward. The pupil looked slightly dilated.

Katz approached the two men, followed by Manning and McCarter. They each held an arm of a limping Calvin James.

The Israeli looked down. "Concussion?"

Bolan rose to his feet. "Too early to tell. See if you can rouse him with some water."

Katz pulled a canteen from his hip and knelt next to Encizo as the Executioner turned to James.

The black warrior looked down at his ankle. "Just a sprain," he said. "Nothing serious."

Bolan turned to face Manning. "Wrap it for him, Gary." Turning to McCarter, he said, "David, dig through the truck. Strip it of everything we can use."

The Executioner looked down to where Katz knelt next to Encizo. A stream of water poured from the Israeli's canteen had done little to bring the Cuban around. "Yakov, what does the ammo situation look like?"

Katz stood up. "We're down to side arms, Striker."

Bolan trudged through the sand and climbed over the side of the Hummer. He found McCarter sitting cross-legged on the broken side window that faced the ground. Digging through the scattered refuse, they found two more canteens, a tin of combat makeup and a box of 9 mm rounds someone had left in the glove compartment.

McCarter looked up at the starry sky outside the vehicle. "Not much to start this nature trek on," he observed as they climbed back out. "Any idea where we are?"

Bolan scanned the arid land around them as he opened the makeup can and smeared his hands and face with the black-and-tan grease. "Few miles west of the Euphrates. We'll have to head that way." He flipped the makeup through the air to McCarter. "We're too easy to spot out here."

Faint lights appeared across the steppes to the south as the Briton caught the can. "We'll have company soon," he said. "They're bound to see the tracks where the Hummer left the road."

Bolan nodded. He turned back to the others. Katz had knelt next to Encizo again. The Israeli held the canteen to the Cuban's lips. James stood gingerly on his good leg. He was nearly bare-chested, his ankle wrapped in shreds of cloth torn from his fatigue blouse.

"Calvin, get your boot back on before it swells," the Executioner ordered. He pointed toward the lights. "Let's get ready to move out. Bring the rifles. I don't want the enemy knowing they're dry." He hurried back to Encizo and hoisted the man across his shoulders. "David, you and Gary help Calvin if he needs it. Let's go!"

Bolan led the way toward the nearest sand dune, glancing over his shoulder as the lights suddenly halted on the road. "They've made us," he shouted. "Double time!"

The team broke into a trot, plowing through the sand as the lights turned off the road and started toward them. The Executioner looked down at his feet as he ran. Good. The sand slid back into place beneath his boots almost as quickly as he lifted them. Their prints would be covered.

He reached the top of the dune as the headlights of the lead Spetznaz vehicle fell on the wrecked Hummer. "Drop over and dig in!" he ordered.

The rest of the team reached the crest and dived over the other side into the sand.

Hurriedly the Stony Man warriors burrowed through the grainy earth. Bolan positioned Encizo next to him, pulling the bill of the Cuban's boonie hat down to shield his nostrils before shoveling sand over both of their heads.

They waited.

A few moments later the sound of jeep doors opening and closing pierced the night. Muffled voices rose from the other side of the dune, drifting toward them in the still desert air.

Bolan stared up, hoping the sand and makeup hid his face. He and Phoenix Force would be dead if the Spetznaz soldiers stumbled onto them.

Footsteps sloshed up the side of the dune. A head, then shoulders, then the legs of a tall, light-skinned soldier in an Iraqi uniform appeared at the top of the dune. Bolan saw the yellow insignia on the man's sleeves—the badge worn by soldiers of the countries that had joined the United Arab Republic.

The soldier scanned the desert, then looked down.

Bolan closed his eyes to prevent the whites from giving him away, and held his breath.

A voice called out in the distance. "Search the area!" it shouted in Russian. "They can't have gone far!"

Bolan heard the man above him forge back through the sand the way he'd come. He opened his eyes again. As he did, Encizo began to stir.

The Executioner shifted under the blanket of sand, clasping a hand over Encizo's mouth. He pressed his face against the Cuban's ear. "Quiet."

Encizo recognized the voice and nodded slowly.

The sound of boots wading up the dune filled the air. Bolan and Phoenix Force held tight, hoping against hope that none of the Soviets would stumble on top of them.

Five, ten, then fifteen minutes went by. The Executioner breathed shallowly through the sand in his face. Boots, both in front and back of the buried team, swamped through the loose earth as the Spetznaz troopers continued to search. Flashlight beams stabbed through the darkness.

Soft movements next to Bolan told him that Encizo was fully awake. The Cuban couldn't know the situation, or even where he was. But that didn't worry the Executioner. Encizo was a well-trained member of one of Stony Man's most elite corps. He'd follow the order of silence and take further cues from the Executioner's own movements.

A set of boots started up the dune from the rear. Labored breathing issued forth from the same direction. As they drew nearer, Bolan realized the Soviet had inadvertently determined a path directly toward them. Slowly the Executioner shifted his arms through the sand, gripping the butt of the suppressed Beretta, and held his breath.

The breathing grew louder as the enemy soldier approached. Then, suddenly, a boot sank through the sand onto the Executioner's shoulder.

Bolan reached up and wrapped steel fingers around an ankle. A surprised shriek echoed over the sands as he pulled down, jammed the Beretta into the enemy's chest and pulled the trigger, using both the suppressor and the soldier's own flesh to muffle the sound.

"What was that?" an anxious Russian voice shouted from the other side of the dune.

"Nothing!" Katz answered in Russian. "I stumbled."

Quickly Bolan and Encizo rose from the sand, buried the body, then dug back down.

By the sounds, it appeared that several dozen of the enemy were on the scene. As the search continued, the Executioner prayed silently that the dead man next to him wouldn't be missed.

Ten minutes later the footsteps began moving back to the wreck. Muffled voices sounded again, then the vehicle doors opened and closed. Engines started, and the Spetznaz troops pulled away.

Bolan and the rest of the men stayed put.

A half hour later, when he heard no signs that any of the searchers were still at the scene, the Executioner stood. He saw taillights in the distance as Phoenix Force rose to join him. His eyes made a full 360-degree sweep. The lights shone back to him from all four sides.

"They gone?" Encizo asked softly. A gritty mixture of blood and sand covered his face.

Bolan shook his head. "They're just beginning."

The Executioner didn't kid himself. The Spetznaz hadn't abandoned the search. The Soviet special forces soldier knew that their prey had to be somewhere in the area, and on foot. They'd set up bases surrounding the wreck.

The men from Stony Man were in the eye of the storm.

AARON "BEAR" KURTZMAN grabbed the arms of his wheelchair and shoved away from the computer. Spinning to face the glass wall that separated the intel room from the mission-control center, he stared intently at Barbara Price. Stony Man Farm's mission-control chief had bent over the radio console, the heel of her hand pressed on the table radio microphone key. Kurtzman watched her lips move as her words drifted faintly to him. "Temple B'nai Israel. It's on Missouri Avenue...."

The Stony Man computer wizard turned back to stare blankly at his screen. It would be Able Team Price was talking to, which meant another terrorist attack somewhere in the D.C. area. He'd get the details soon enough—when it was time for Tokaido or one of his other assistants to add them to the growing computer file of seemingly unrelated facts that he prayed would eventually mold into something that made sense.

Kurtzman glanced down from the raised platform on which he worked to the long bank of computers below. Akira Tokaido sat pounding rhythmically away at his machine, the samurai-style topknot at the rear of his punk-cut Mohawk bobbing up and down as if he were the organist in a rock band. A thin wire ran from the portable CD player belted around the young Japanese's waist to the earphones wrapped around his head. Kurtzman winced, wondering what thunderous, unintelligible, new-wave noise must be blaring into Tokaido's brain. The young man was shirtless beneath a rhinestone-encrusted leather vest, and the cheap stones sparkled brightly under the room's overhead track lights.

Kurtzman choked back a moment's disgust at Tokaido's appearance. Regardless of how he looked, the young Japanese was good at what he did. A grin crept from the side of Kurtzman's mouth. And twenty years ago they'd called *Bear* a hippy!

Next to Tokaido was Carmen Delahunt. Kurtzman took in her conservative red skirt-suit and pearls. Delahunt's fingers were as flamboyant as Tokaido's as they flew over her terminal keys. And Huntington Wethers, on the other side of Delahunt, was letting no grass grow on his hands, either.

Two questions currently plagued the computer staff at Stony Man Farm—where was Hamoud Jaluwi, the leader of the UAR, and how were the terrorists in the U.S. able to get the detailed, up-to-date info that kept making their strikes successful.

Kurtzman turned back to his own computer. Slowly, his brain working simultaneously with the machine, he typed the details of several bombings and assassinations, his thoughts becoming words on the screen. Then, pressing the appropriate buttons, he sat back and clasped his hands behind his head.

A few seconds later the screen lit up in yellow-orange letters: ALL AVAILABLE DATA SUGGESTS HIGHLY SOPHISTICATED COMMUNICATIONS SATELLITE.

"Thanks, you damnable bag of wires and bolts," Kurtzman muttered. "I'd have never thought of that on my own." He tapped more keys, entering the fact that the U.S. Air Force had already swept the earth's satellite area three times and come up with nothing.

SUBSTANTIAL MARGIN FOR ERROR came back on the screen. SATELLITE SWEEPS NOT EFFECTIVE IF... "I knew *that*, too," Kurtzman growled as he struck the Enter button, blanking out the screen.

What it boiled down to, he thought as he leaned back in the wheelchair, was that until he had some new outside information to add to the file, the magic machine just wasn't going to give him any answers.

Price's voice continued to drift through the glass. "Affirmative, Able One. Will you need air transport?"

Kurtzman sighed. The terrorists had to be using a satellite somehow. But that didn't necessarily mean the UAR had its own orbiting space station. In fact, he'd bet the ability to walk again that they didn't. Iraq, Syria, Iran—none of them had the technology yet. The Soviets did, sure. They could have launched a satellite into orbit for their new best friends, but somehow Kurtzman's instincts said no. The cost would have been enormous, and right now the boys in Moscow were having enough trouble putting borscht on the table.

There had to be a much simpler answer. Okay, given: none of the countries making up the United Arab Republic could launch their own orbiter. But they weren't in the Dark Ages, either. They *did* have what it took to link into an existing satellite, and if they used it only when they needed to transmit and receive, and cut the power off the rest of the time...

Kurtzman sighed again. Tracing it would be tough.

Leaning forward again, he began to add these suspicions to the file. As he was about to hit the Enter button, the intercom on his console suddenly buzzed.

Reaching for the receiver, Kurtzman glanced into the control room. Barbara Price still stood next to the radio console. She stared back at him through the glass, her own receiver pressed against her ear.

"Bear, check flight schedules in the D.C. area. Able needs to know of any low-flying craft that would have passed over their site in the past two hours." She gave Kurtzman the coordinates of the synagogue.

"How low is low?"

Price hesitated. "Anything the terrorists inside the building could have heard. Able One wants to know how they've reacted to the noise."

Kurtzman hung up and returned to the keyboard, tapping into the flight schedules of the surrounding airports. When the data was available, he hit the Print Control key. The laser printer kicked on and began rolling out a hard copy.

Grabbing the page out of the printer tray, Kurtzman lifted the receiver. "Plenty of action in the area," he announced as soon as Price picked up the other end. "But it's all high. Nothing anybody inside the synagogue would have noticed. You need the copy?"

On the other side of the window Price shook her head. "No. Just keep it handy." She hung up and

Kurtzman heard her relay the information to Able Team.

Staring at the screen again, Kurtzman let his mind return to the satellite. The bottom line was this: he wasn't going to locate the UAR communication base until he had more information to feed the computer, which meant he could do one of two things. He could keep going over the same data he already had—and come to the same dead ends—or move on to the other problem at hand.

Where was that bastard Jaluwi, who was in charge of the whole show?

With a determined scowl on his face Kurtzman took a deep breath, typed Jaluwi's name into the computer, and hit the return key.

HAMOUD JALUWI FORCED a smile as General Gennady Kaganovich entered his office. Jaluwi didn't like Soviets—Russian Soviets, in particular—and he hated Russian Soviet army officers most of all, particularly opinionated, obnoxious bores like Kaganovich.

But for the time being the Soviets were a necessary evil.

"Any further developments in America?" the Russian asked abruptly.

Jaluwi shook his head. "The President is still at the hospital. Doctors pumped his stomach, and after identifying the ethylene glycol in the water, administered an antidote. He's expected to be back in the White House tomorrow."

"Any chance of attacking him again while he's at the hospital?"

Jaluwi snorted. "Our communications center reports that the Secret Service and U.S. Marines are practically arm in arm around the building."

Kaganovich nodded. "There'll be other chances. What about the synagogue?"

"Ibrahim and his men are still trapped inside. The authorities have agreed to provide them with a plane and safe transport to the airport."

"And you believe they will?"

Jaluwi shrugged and swiveled in his chair, facing a side wall. "Who knows? Our men made a serious and unforgivable error in timing. They should have destroyed the synagogue and been gone before the police even learned of their deed." Turning back to the Russian, he leaned over his desk and clasped his hands in front of him. "But it doesn't matter. Ibrahim and his men are expendable. And what of your men in Kuwait?"

The general's bloated pink face puffed further with pride. "The American Special Forces compound in northern Kuwait has been destroyed. Rance Pollock and his band of brigands have been chased north into the desert. It's only a matter of time until they're found and executed."

Jaluwi had started to inquire how the general could be so sure when the phone on the desk suddenly rang. He lifted the receiver to his ear. "Yes?"

"President Jaluwi," the voice from the UAR's American communications post said, "there appears to be no change in the situation at the synagogue."

"Do you have it in sight?"

"Yes. Ibrahim reports that the Americans have promised that the bus is on its way."

"Put Ibrahim through. And stay on yourself."

Jaluwi heard a series of clicks, then Ibrahim's voice came onto the three-way line. "Yes, Mr. President?"

"Are there any changes?"

"No, Mr. President. The bus is on its way. We've agreed to let the young girl go before we board."

"What!"

"It was the only way they would negotiate," Ibrahim said quickly.

Jaluwi snarled. "The girl was your best shield. The American fools value children's lives above all others. You should have demanded to trade one of the old women instead."

Ibrahim cleared his throat nervously. "I'm sorry. It's done."

There was a long pause. Wind and a series of muffled, flapping noises in the distant background were the only sounds on the line.

"What's that noise?" Jaluwi demanded.

Ibrahim's voice rose an octave. "I don't know! Wait!"

Jaluwi heard the receiver crash down. Footsteps receded from the phone, returning a moment later. "A helicopter flew over the synagogue!" Ibrahim shouted.

"Prepare to execute the hostages!" Jaluwi ordered. "Does the synagogue have more than one telephone line?"

"Yes!"

"Then get whoever you've been dealing with on the phone, you fool! Find out about this helicopter. And tell them what will happen if it doesn't go away!" As he waited, he turned to Kaganovich and cupped a hand over the mouthpiece. "If the Americans don't kill Ibrahim there, I'll do it myself when the fool returns."

The general nodded his approval.

Jaluwi turned back to the phone. He heard Ibrahim speaking on the other line. "Liar!" the strike leader screamed.

"Put me through to the authorities," Jaluwi ordered.

A moment later the link was switched and a voice said, "Special Agent in Charge Ratskowski."

"You'll deal with me from this time forward, Ratskowski."

"Who are you?"

"It doesn't matter. What's the helicopter doing over the building?"

"I don't know," Ratskowski replied, "but I promise you, it's not ours. Wait a second."

In the background Jaluwi heard Ratskowski say, "What, Bishop?"

More unintelligible speech followed.

"One of my men thinks it's a news chopper," Ratskowski said, coming back on the line. "I don't know for sure. I can't see the markings in the dark. But I promise you, it's not one of ours."

"Get it away from the synagogue!" Jaluwi screamed.

"I'll do my best."

Ibrahim came back on.

"Switch back to the secure line," Jaluwi directed.

A second later the voice at the post said, "It's done."

"Tell me what you can see."

"The helicopter flew over the roof several times, but I can't see what they're doing in the dark."

"Could it be from a news station?"

"It's possible. I can't be sure."

"Ibrahim?"

"Yes?"

"Are there any entrances into the building from the roof?"

"No. Only a skylight in one of the large classrooms. I have men guarding it."

Jaluwi paused, thinking. His thoughts were interrupted by Ibrahim again. "Wait!" the UAR strike leader said. "The bus has arrived. It's out front now."

The UAR leader felt himself relax. "Do nothing until you're certain it isn't a trap. Relay any new developments back to me immediately. Don't release the little girl until I give the order."

"Yes, sir."

Jaluwi turned back to the Russian. "There's nothing to worry about, General," he said, smiling. "Everything is under control."

CHAPTER FOUR

Lyons twisted the dial, turning up the volume on the police band scanner. A muddled series of messages squawked from the frequencies being swept. He leaned forward, looking down through the chopper's bubble windshield at the roof of the synagogue. "You see any reaction?" he asked as they passed over the building.

Charlie Mott shook his head. "Uh-uh."

"That's the problem," Schwarz said behind him. "It's too dark to see anything until we drop down. But you can be sure they've heard us."

"No way to avoid it," Lyons replied. "So the next best thing is to make lots of noise. Be obvious, and hope they figure we're a TV station or something."

The police scanner locked in suddenly on a transmission from below. "Federal Bureau of Investigation to unidentified news helicopter over Temple B'nai...FBI to helicopter...respond immediately."

Blancanales smiled. "At least we fooled Ratskowski."

"Ratskowski's not who I'm worried about." Lyons turned to face Mott. "Get us as low as you can, Charlie. We don't want them hearing our boots hit the roof. Pull out as soon as we're down.'' He looked back over his shoulder. "Everybody ready?''

Schwarz and Blancanales nodded. "How many terrorists did they say were inside?'' Politician asked as they made ready to jump.

"The rabbi counted six,'' Lyons replied, "but be ready for anything.''

Mott guided the chopper over the center of the synagogue, cut the engine and hovered. Assault weapons slung over their backs, the members of Able Team jumped simultaneously from the chopper, falling to the end of the thick rubber bungee cords attached to their shoulder harnesses. Jerking skyward again like puppets, they bounced up and down until the force of their fall had dissipated.

Disconnecting their lines, the three Able warriors dropped quietly to the gravel-covered roof. Lyons lifted his black combat boots high over the gravel, lowering them quietly with each step. He knelt next to the translucent skylight, careful to keep his shadow out of sight. Through the smoky plastic he saw the indistinct forms of two men. Both cradled assault weapons of some kind in their arms. One of the men stood just to the left of the window, the other to the right.

The Able Team leader rose to his feet, drawing the suppressed .45 from his belt. "On three,'' he whispered to Blancanales, who was already threading a sound suppressor onto his Beretta. "You take the one on the left.''

"Got ya.''

Gripping the .45 in his right fist, Lyons dropped the luminous front sight on the shadow beneath the skylight. His left hand rose into the air. One, two, three fingers flipped up, then he squeezed the trigger.

The .45 and Blancanales's 9 mm coughed as if from the same gun. A pair of perfectly round holes appeared in the hard plastic, two narrow shafts of light from the room below streaking up into the night. The shadows below the skylight sank to the floor.

The Able Team warriors dropped to their knees. Lyons yanked a lock-blade from his coveralls, flipped the thumb stud and began slicing through the caulking around the skylight. Schwarz and Blancanales did the same with their own knives, then the three men lifted the skylight from the hole and set it softly on the gravel to one side.

Schwarz stuck his head through the hole and scanned the room. His head popped back out, and he flashed the okay sign with his thumb and forefinger.

Grasping the edge of the roof, Lyons lowered himself into the classroom, followed by the other two Able warriors. The ex-cop led the way across the slick tile floor to a partially closed door, peering through the crack to see a semilit hallway that dead-ended ten feet away. A cross hall extended both ways from the wall in front of him.

Maintaining a precarious balance of silence and speed, the Able Team leader moved along the wall toward the connecting passageway. At the corner he dropped to one knee, the .45 hugged tightly to his body. Nosing past the wall, he saw two more doors, one to the left, the other to the right. The faint light that had filtered down the hallway came from both doors.

So did voices—speaking Arabic.

Lyons turned back to his team. "Two doors." He nodded at both men and pointed to the right.

As Gadgets and Pol tiptoed silently into the hall, Lyons holstered his handgun and unslung his Atchisson Assault 12 shotgun. He moved to the door on the left, taking up a position next to the frame. Dropping below eye level, he peered around the corner.

The large room he saw was a reception hall. Metal folding chairs ringed the walls, and just inside the door stood a long buffet table covered with white linen napkins. A crystal punch bowl and cups had been stacked on top of the long counter set into the far wall. Beyond the counter was a darkened kitchen.

Seated in the corner farthest away from the Able Team leader were the hostages, their chairs turned to face the wall. The little girl, wearing a pale blue ruffled party dress, sat closest to the corner. Next was the rabbi, then the two women. All had been bound and blindfolded.

A UAR terrorist wearing gray "urban" camouflage fatigues stood beside the rabbi, his AK-47 resting on the man's nape. Another, similarly dressed gunman stood at the end of the line, bearing an Uzi. Three more UAR men stood talking in the center of the room. All wore the same gray cammies and held some sort of automatic weapon.

Another trio stood at the windows at the front of the building, while a man bracing a Remington pump-action shotgun scanned the dark backyard of the synagogue.

Lyons counted them off mentally. Eleven. The rabbi had been more than a little off, meaning some of the men had probably entered the building from the other side. The ex-cop's mind whirled. It also meant even more terrorists might be scattered throughout the synagogue, or hidden in the shrubbery that surrounded the building outside.

The loud whoosh of air brakes sounded suddenly through the front window. The terrorists turned toward the noise.

Lyons jerked his head back into the hall.

"Ibrahim!" he heard a heavily accented voice say, followed by what sounded like orders in Arabic.

Lyons glanced back down the hall to where Blancanales and Schwarz were poised on both sides of the other door. At the angle they'd be entering they'd have to shoot through some of the hostages to get to the terrorists next to them. That meant it would be up to him to take out the men against that wall, as well as the shotgunner at the back window. It would be close shooting with little room for error.

It wasn't work that the Atchisson was designed for, and Lyons dropped the scattergun to the end of the sling and drew the big Colt Python from his shoulder rig.

Schwarz and Blancanales both nodded to him as if they'd read his mind, and even with the mounting tension Lyons felt sweeping through his body, he had to smile. Able Team had been through far too many battles together to need their orders verbalized.

The shrill ring of a telephone from inside the reception hall suddenly broke the silence. It stopped abruptly in midring. "Yes," a gruff voice said. A long pause, then, "Yes. Don't forget. If you try anything, they'll be executed. The girl will die first."

Lyons turned back toward Schwarz and Blancanales, who'd readied their M-16s. The ex-cop held up a finger, then two fingers and three.

The Stony Man warriors burst into the room. Lyons locked the Python's front ramp sight on the chest of the terrorist next to the little girl. The explosion from the big Magnum ricocheted off the walls as he double-actioned a 125-grain, semijacketed hollowpoint from the cylinder, through the barrel and into the terrorist's breastbone.

The M-16s rattled off sustained bursts before the .357's booming noise had a chance to die down. From the corner of his eye, Lyons saw Pol enter high and send a steady stream of rounds into the three men in the center of the room. Gadgets went in low, crouching, tapping the trigger of his assault rifle and shredding more flesh along the front row of windows. Glass shattered behind the surprised terrorists as they fell to the floor of the reception hall.

Lyons aimed his Python at the UAR gunman with the Uzi as the man turned toward the hostages. A double-tap of Magnums burst from the big revolver and knocked the terrorist against the wall. He slithered to the floor, leaving a trail of bloody skid marks in his wake. Grimacing, he struggled to raise the machine pistol again. Another turn of the Python's cylinder sent a hollowpoint drilling through his brain. The terrorist twirled sideways, away from the wall, then crashed through a window.

Outside the front windows Lyons heard John Bishop's HRT team open up. The ex-cop jammed the Python into his belt and brought the Atchisson Assault 12 into play. He'd been right. Some of the UAR men *had* hidden outside. They'd been waiting...just in case.

A terrorist with a short, curly beard bolted for the kitchen counter. For a moment it looked as if he'd make it over the top. Then his boot slipped on the slippery surface. He fell to the floor, turned and brought his AK-47 up to fire.

The Atchisson boomed twice as Magnum buckshot sprayed the man's gray camouflage fatigues. Several of the triple-aught pellets spread to the side, and the punch bowl and crystal cups exploded in a brilliantly sparkling cloudburst of glass.

The shotgun still vibrated against Lyons's wrists as the final gunman at the front of the room fell under a combined onslaught of 5.56 mm rounds from Schwarz and Blancanales.

The room turned suddenly quiet, but for the ongoing battle outside. Screams of terror from the women and little girl replaced the roar of the firearms.

"Gadgets! Pol!" Lyons barked. "Get them into the kitchen!"

The two men rushed to the row of chairs. As Lyons moved to the center of the room where he could cover both doors, he saw the blade of Schwarz's Cold Steel Terminator flash under the lights. A second later the rabbi's feet were free, and Gadgets was shoving him toward the door next to the counter. "Run!"

The rabbi hobbled forward on stiff legs.

Blancanales had freed one of the women when the first set of boots came pounding down the hall. A foolish terrorist turned the corner and ran straight into the room. "Ibrahim!" he shouted. "Ibrahim—"

A 12-gauge blast from the Atchisson cut him off in midsentence.

More boots sounded as Lyons saw Schwarz free the other woman. The little girl's feet were still bound, a napkin knotted around the white anklets above her patent-leather party shoes. Blancanales whisked her into his arms and dived over the counter.

Two more gunmen in gray cammies burst into the reception room. Lyons's shotgun boomed twice and they fell in the doorway.

Schwarz and Blancanales joined him in the center of the room. Lyons moved to the front row of windows and dropped to his knees. Pol and Gadgets could hold off any more attackers who came through the doors. He'd concentrate on the terrorists on the outside who battled Bishop and his crew and see if he could catch them in a cross fire.

A muzzle flashed suddenly below him, two feet from the window. Lyons leveled the Atchisson on the light and pulled the trigger.

The muzzle-flashes halted abruptly.

Behind him Lyons heard the staccato sounds of the M-16s. He looked over his shoulder to see another terrorist fall on top of his comrades in the doorway.

Suddenly the gunfire outside halted.

Lyons moved to the telephone on the wall above the kitchen counter. Sometime during the melee it had been knocked off the hook. The receiver dangled from the end of the spiral cord, swaying back and forth across the top of the counter through a carpet of ragged glass. Pressing the hook down, Lyons got a dial tone, then realized he didn't know the number to call outside.

Rehooking the receiver, he waited. Ten seconds later he heard the ring.

"What the hell's going on?" Ratskowski screamed. "Is this the Justice team? I gave orders . . . you bastards just wait until I get hold of your superiors!'

"Oh-oh," Lyons said with feigned concern. "Whatever you do, don't ask for Brognola." He hung up.

Swinging his legs over the counter, the Able Team leader dropped into the kitchen and saw the hostages sitting against the wall next to a large stainless-steel refrigerator.

Lyons squatted next to the little girl. Gently he raised her chin with a forefinger and smiled.

The tear-streaked eyes opened wide. And smiled back.

A LONELY, EMPTY STILLNESS filled the desert night. For all he could see, feel or hear, Mack Bolan might have been the only human being on the planet.

The Executioner's other two senses worked overtime as he crawled through the sand on his belly. The odor of hot sand filled his nostrils as his nose moved along an inch from the ground.

Bolan paused to rest, letting his cheek fall against the sand. He closed his eyes, regathering his strength, calling on the willpower that had seen him through countless similar survival situations over the years.

With a surge of determination the Executioner pushed his head back up off the ground. The Spetznaz forces were only one of the dangers that now plagued him. Exhaustion and dehydration were others. Time was a third.

Bolan glanced at the luminous hands of his watch. If he and the men of Phoenix Force didn't reach the cover of the river before sunrise, they'd be spotlighted on the white sand like blemishes on the nose of a beauty contestant.

Reaching forward, the Executioner resumed his crawl. Earlier he'd watched the Spetznaz soldiers set up their containment guard. The Russians knew their enemy couldn't have gone far on foot, and they'd divided into five teams, setting up base camps three miles away and circling the wrecked Hummer. From where he and Phoenix Force had watched, the lights of each camp had looked like the glowing tips of a five-pointed star.

With them trapped in the star's hot core.

The Executioner had known that by the time they reached the containment lines, Spetznaz forces would have spread across the desert on foot, linking each camp. Their strategy had left the Stony Man warriors only two choices.

Buck the odds and attempt to get through, anyway, or stay where they were and die of dehydration the next day in the desert.

The choice had been easy. Bad odds were better than none. Grasping another handful of sand, Bolan crawled on.

The Russians had been smart in the way they'd set up their enclosure. On the assumption that the Americans would try to return to Kuwait, the majority of vehicles had headed south. Two of the star's points now blocked that pathway, which was another reason the Executioner had chosen to head east toward the Euphrates and the relative concealment the river's banks would provide. To avoid detection Bolan had ordered Phoenix Force to spread out over a half-mile area before starting their slow crawl through enemy lines.

The grade turned upward. Bolan's crawl became more of a climb. Good, he thought as the sweat poured from his forehead. Another dune—more high ground. He could get his bearings, see how far from the camps he now was, and—

The sand in front of him suddenly hissed with movement as something slithered forward. The Executioner froze, staring ahead.

Dull, lifeless eyes set in a table-flat head stared back at him, an inch away. Two dark bands converged into a V on the top of the head. A pair of needle-point fangs fell backward toward the throat within the open mouth.

The Executioner's mind raced, trying to recall what he knew about the Palestinian viper. It was poisonous. That much he remembered. Did its venom kill? No, not usually. Not if the bite was immediately drained.

It just made the victim so sick he *wished* he were dead.

Man and snake continued to stare at each other as the Executioner held his breath. It made no difference, he realized, if the venom itself was fatal. Not under the circumstances. The bite would be to his face—impossible to suck out. If the snake struck, he'd lie here in the desert, unable to continue until the Spetznaz assassins found him.

The seconds became a minute. The minute became two. Then three. Bolan's lungs threatened to burst within his chest as his body screamed for oxygen. Finally, unable to hold it any longer, his dry, cracked lips parted and he let the air slowly out.

The frightened snake jerked back, then slithered away into the darkness.

The Executioner pulled himself to the top of the dune and peered over the sand. A half mile to his left he saw the dark outline of vehicles under the moon. Turning his head, he saw the next base camp several hundred yards to his right.

Bolan reached back, unhooking the canteen from his belt and holding it to his lips. He drank sparingly, knowing the night wasn't over yet, and the river was still several miles away. Returning the canvas-covered container to his hip, he reached up to the suspender strap of his webgear, his fingers closing around the checked rubber grip of his SOG Pentagon dagger.

The Executioner drew the five-inch dagger blade from the sheath and crawled on. From here on in it would be touch and go. He might encounter a roving patrol at any moment.

The warrior moved slowly, cautiously, the tiny "swishes" his body made as it rubbed the sand sounding like thunder to his own ears. He drew abreast of the camps, passed the imaginary line joining them and moved on.

The sudden sound of boots shifting through the sand made Bolan halt again. He rolled onto his side toward the noise, the dagger clutched tightly in an ice-pick grip. With his left hand he quietly unholstered the suppressed Beretta.

The footsteps drew closer, and the dark silhouette of a man appeared against the sky, an assault rifle dangling at his side on a sling. Bolan held his breath.

The man's path would bring him directly to the Executioner.

As the Russian neared, Bolan thumbed the Beretta to semiauto. The 93-R might be equipped with a suppressor, but that didn't make it silent—particularly in the utter hush of the desert. If the Spetznaz trooper got close enough, he'd use the Pentagon. If not, one well-placed 9 mm round was all he could risk.

As the enemy continued to stalk forward, Bolan's left index finger snaked inside the Beretta's trigger guard. It was then that he heard the footsteps on his other side.

Bolan's finger froze on the trigger. He saw the man in front of him stop in his tracks, the AK-74 jerking up into assault mode.

A voice behind the Executioner called out in Russian. "Sergeant Amalrik? Is that you?"

The assault rifle lowered. Bolan heard a nervous sigh. The Executioner's command of the Russian language was rudimentary, but he picked up enough to get the two men's meaning. "Yes, Lieutenant. It's me."

"Have you seen anything, Sergeant? Any sign of them?"

The man in front of Bolan took another step forward. "No, no sign. I don't think they've come this way."

Bolan waited. Neither man had seen him. If they came no closer to continue their conversation, it was unlikely they would. He wouldn't have to risk either the hush of the Beretta, or the sound of bodies tumbling to the sand.

But if they decided this was a good time to get together and take a break . . .

Behind him Bolan heard the Spetznaz lieutenant take another step forward. The soft rustle of canvas clothing carried to him on the breeze.

The man had reached into his pocket. What was he getting?

A soft, metallic sound behind the Executioner.

What was it?

The answer hit the Executioner as the flame from the cigarette lighter glowed suddenly over his shoulder. He twisted onto his back in time to see the lieutenant's hand freeze in front of his mouth, his eyes staring down at Bolan's prostrate form illuminated in the light.

Bolan squeezed the trigger, sending a 9 mm round past the flame into the face behind it. The man slumped to the sand.

As he twisted back, the Executioner heard the voice on the other side say, "Lieutenant, what...?" The man with the AK-74 hurried forward.

Bolan sprang to his feet, bringing the Pentagon around in an arc. The serrated side of the blade caught the Spetznaz trooper under the chin and slashed jaggedly through his throat, a fire-hose spray of blood shooting out from the carotid artery.

The warrior dropped back onto his belly, waiting, listening. When he heard no more footsteps, he hurried toward the body in front of him. Stripping the man of the AK-74 and two extra magazines, he dug down in the sand, scooping handfuls over the body until the Russian had disappeared.

The lieutenant carried only a Makarov pistol and one extra box mag. Bolan stuffed them into his waistband and took the canteen from his belt before burying him, as well.

The Executioner squinted into the darkness, scanning the desert toward both camps. Anyone within hearing distance would have already arrived at the scene. Shouldering the AK-74, he hurried away from the containment line. Ten minutes later he slowed to a walk. Kneeling in the sand, he pulled the luminous compass from his pocket and charted a course toward the prearranged coordinates where he'd meet Phoenix Force.

It took another ten minutes to reach the site in the barren desert. Bolan topped another in the seemingly endless series of sand dunes at a jog, then slowed to a walk, the AK at the ready.

Suddenly the sand erupted in front of him. The barrel of the AK-74 fell automatically to the spot. Bolan started to squeeze the trigger, then stopped. Calvin James's face smiled back at him from the hole where he'd been hiding.

Bolan knelt again as James climbed out of the hole. "Any of the others here yet?" he asked.

James shook his head. "Not yet."

No sooner had he spoken than footsteps sounded behind them. Both men turned, their weapons in front of them.

David McCarter strolled in as if he owned the desert.

"Any problems?" the Executioner asked.

"A couple," the former SAS man answered. He tapped the Sykes-Fairbairn stiletto hanging upside down from his webgear. "But I'll be the last person they ever bother."

Fifteen minutes later Manning topped the dune. "Imagine, meeting old friends halfway around the world in the middle of nowhere," he quipped weakly. The Canadian looked as if he'd been through the wringer. His desert cammies had been almost ripped from his body, his skin was scratched and torn and his lips had split from the dry air.

Bolan handed him his canteen as they waited for the others. "Drink up."

"I had mine," Manning protested.

"It wasn't a request. It was an order," Bolan replied. "You're even closer to dehydration than the rest of us. And none of us wants to carry you the rest of the way."

"But—"

"It won't matter," Bolan said, anticipating Manning's next protest. "We should be at the river in a few hours. If we aren't, water will be the least of our worries."

Manning drank deeply.

A half hour went by. Bolan stared up at the sky. Dawn was approaching. As soon as it was light, the Spetznaz troops would canvas the area between them and the wreck. When they didn't find the Americans, they'd realize their prey had slipped through their net and turn their search outward. If Encizo and Katz didn't show up soon, he'd have to assume they'd been captured and go on without them.

Finally Bolan heard the soft sound of footsteps across the sand. A moment later two heads, one on top of the other, appeared on top of the dune behind them. Then both men fell to the ground.

The Executioner and the rest of Phoenix Force rushed forward to where Katz and Encizo lay in the sand. The Cuban's legs were still locked around Katz's waist, but he was unconscious.

Bolan opened the canteen he'd taken from the Spetznaz lieutenant and held it to the Israeli's lips.

Katz's breathing came in short, raspy pants. "Found...him...just this side of...the containment line. Passed...out."

Bolan stared at Encizo. The Cuban's head injury had opened up again, bleeding through the field dressing the Executioner had applied. He'd lost more blood, and his body had gone into shock.

Helping Katz to his feet, Bolan lifted Encizo for the second time that night. "Let's go," he ordered. "We'll tend to him when we reach the river."

Led by the man who had created their team and steered their missions so many times in the past, Phoenix Force started across the desert again toward the river. Gradually the terrain began to change. Here and there, stubborn, scraggly bushes and patches of tough grass began to poke out of the sand, fed by the underground water. A faint humidity began to replace the dryness in their nostrils. Little by little the vegetation thickened as they neared the Euphrates.

They were still a half mile away when the sun began to peek over the horizon, casting an eerie, moonlike twilight over the newfound grasslands. Bolan broke the team into double time, forcing their depleted bodies toward the water.

Bolan reached the top of the last dune first, and the sparkling river beckoned up to him.

A tiny speck along the shore to the south caught his eye, and he dived to the sand. Encizo fell on top of him. Following his lead, Phoenix Force hit the ground behind him.

The Executioner stared through the dawn toward the camp a quarter mile away. His weary vision finally focused on the line of tents, the American M-2 Bradley Fighting Vehicles and M-109 howitzers parked to the side of a series of tents.

"Eldridge," the Executioner said.

Katz crawled to his side, pulling a set of compact binoculars from his web belt. He glanced through the lenses, then passed them to Bolan.

The Executioner adjusted the focus ring and aimed the binoculars on the camp. He saw men moving out of the tents, stretching, stiff from the night's sleep.

"No chance to take them on now," Katz said, verbalizing the Executioner's own thoughts.

Bolan shook his head. "Not with one assault rifle and pistols."

Manning crawled next to them, exhausted. "So much for heading back south to Kuwait," he whispered.

Bolan turned back to the other men. "We'll head back a half a klick, then cut north another mile before we turn back toward the water. After we're rested, we'll head north."

"You mean…" James said, letting his hoarse voice drift off without finishing.

The Executioner nodded. "We're going to Baghdad." As they moved back down the sand dune, he felt fiery anger overcome the fatigue that threatened to drop him in his tracks.

Eldridge. The man had deserted, stealing armor and troops, leaving the Special Forces compound all but defenseless. And the nuclear weapons stolen from Israel? Bolan couldn't see them below at the camp. But that didn't mean they weren't in Eldridge's possession. The renegade colonel might or might not have the rockets. But even if he didn't, he was responsible for every dead American who'd fallen in the previous night's surprise attack.

And there was nothing the Executioner could do about it. At least not for now.

With Encizo over his shoulder, Bolan led the men back into the desert. Following the route he'd outlined, they finally collapsed at the edge of the river and replenished their water-starved bodies.

Bolan placed Encizo in the weeds next to the water and bent to fill his canteens. Returning to the stricken Cuban, he poured water over the man's closed eyes, keeping one of his own eyes on the terrain behind him as he held the canteen to Encizo's lips.

Eldridge. So close, yet so far away.

As Encizo opened his eyes, Bolan made a silent vow to return to destroy the man who had destroyed so much himself.

AARON KURTZMAN FOUGHT the temptation to drive his fist through the computer monitor. He stared at the screen.

ACCESS DENIED: PETITIONER ID REJECTED flashed in front of his eyes.

Kurtzman hit the escape button before the tracer that would have already started from Damascus could pinpoint Stony Man Farm. He sat back, rubbing clenched fingers across lifeless thighs in frustration.

The computer wizard had spent the past two hours trying to break into the files of Syria's Deuxième Bureau, better known as G-2. But each time he found a way to bypass one security check, three more had arisen to stop him cold. The bottom line was that the trail he had hoped to follow from Jaluwi's home country to the UAR president's present location continued to dead-end.

Could he eventually break the codes and gain access to the information he knew Syria would have?

Yes. Definitely. But it would take time—time that he, Bolan, Phoenix Force and the world didn't have.

Kurtzman ran a hand through his hair. There had to be a shorter route to the UAR leader. He looked up as Barbara Price entered the room and mounted the ramp to his console. The mission controller carried a steaming cup of coffee in each hand. She didn't speak as she handed him one, then took a seat in the swivel chair beside him.

"Any luck?" Price asked.

Kurtzman shook his head. "I feel like I'm fishing without a hook. Synagogue deal over?"

Price nodded as she sipped her coffee. "More or less. FBI took one of the terrorists alive. The SAC is on the phone to Brognola, bitching about interference from the Justice Department." She shrugged. "Just your typical petty bureaucratic jealousies."

Kurtzman chuckled. "Hal could fade the heat on that one with half his brain tied behind his back. Lyons must have had a field day out there. He's never liked suits, anyway. Anybody more concerned with how they look on paper than who goes to jail doesn't cut it too well with Ironman."

"Heard from Striker and Phoenix Force?"

A flash of concern crossed Price's face, then disappeared. She shook her head again. "Nothing since they left the compound. An Army lieutenant who escaped saw them being chased north. That means Iraq, which means the odds aren't good."

"The odds are never good," Kurtzman said. "I think that must be in their job description." He saw the worry lines etched in the corners of Price's eyes.

The computer man knew she and Bolan had some sort of personal relationship, but it didn't appear that they were in love. It was more like a mutual attraction, affection, and two adults in need of comfort from the high level of stress in their profession. Still, it meant Mack Bolan held a special place in Barbara Price's heart.

Kurtzman twisted in his chair and patted her knee. "Nothing to worry about," he said in a fatherly tone of voice. "Striker always finds a way out. Like the camel in the Bible, he can slip through the eye of a needle when he has to. Katz and his crew of misfits aren't too shabby, either.''

The woman forced a smile. ''I know, Bear. I'm not worried. According to Lieutenant Jordan, they had a pretty good lead on the Spetznaz troops when they—''

A sudden surge of adrenaline shot through Kurtzman. ''Who?'' he nearly shouted.

Price looked stunned. ''Lieutenant Jordan. The officer who saw them escaping north.''

Kurtzman swiveled in his chair to face the screen again. She'd given him the magic word.

Jordan.

The impoverished country wedged between Syria, Israel and Iraq had been trying to straddle the fence between its more powerful neighbors for centuries. Jordanian intelligence would have Jaluwi's history on file. They might even be able to provide the catalyst to launch Kurtzman on his search for the UAR base.

And they'd be a far easier nut to crack than the Syrian Deuxième Bureau.

Kurtzman barely noticed Price rise from her chair and leave the room. His eyes were locked on the screen.

As his fingers flew across the keyboard, Stony Man Farm's top intel officer was already considering various methods by which he might bypass Jordanian computer security.

CHAPTER FIVE

The Executioner led Phoenix Force across the river into the bulrushes along the bank. They'd drunk heartily from the waters of the Euphrates, the moisture bringing new strength to their spirits as well as their bodies. Now, refreshed, they began the long trek toward Baghdad.

Bolan's decision to head deeper into Iraq hadn't been made lightly. He'd have preferred to return to Kuwait, reequip and come back to end the threat Eldridge represented once and for all. But that would mean sneaking through whatever guard the traitorous colonel had posted. And even if they were successful, the Spetznaz would be massed along the border by now, realizing their prey had escaped the trap.

Continuing west, deeper into the area between the Tigris and Euphrates rivers, was equally out of the question. Iraqi forces—primarily elements of the Republican Guard—had long held that position.

The Americans trudged on through the mud. The Executioner wondered briefly how they'd infiltrate the city once they arrived, then pushed the concern from his mind. Right now just getting there was their goal. He glanced over his shoulder at the men behind him.

Rafael Encizo had come back to life. He was still weak but able to walk. James, whose ankle sprain wasn't as bad as first thought, and McCarter were taking turns helping the Cuban along the path.

James and McCarter appeared no worse off for their waterless night in the desert, and Gary Manning, who was recovering quickly from his own dehydration, had taken to calling them the "human camels."

Katz brought up the rear. The Israeli was tired from carrying Encizo on his back half the night, but otherwise in good shape.

Bolan led the men around a slow curve and started down a straightaway of several hundred yards. He glanced to the east, where the Tigris meandered slowly away before bending back toward its sister river near Baghdad.

The Tigris and Euphrates. Somewhere in this region civilization had begun. It had been a bed of war and turmoil ever since.

Bolan came to another bend in the river. A random noise ahead caught his ear. He froze, holding up a hand to halt the men of Phoenix Force. "Wait here," he whispered over his shoulder.

His fingers wrapping more firmly around the pistol grip of the captured AK-74, the Executioner moved toward the bend. More sounds drifted from around the curve. Dropping to the ground, he pressed his cheek against the sandy vegetation. A soft rumbling met his ears.

Hooves. In this area that meant sheep. And sheep, in turn, meant Kurds.

The Executioner rose to his feet, rounded the curve and saw a small herd drinking and grazing along the bank. A half-dozen sheepskin tents had been staked out a short distance from the river. Men, women and children in tattered clothes went about various tasks at the camp.

Bolan dropped the assault rifle to the end of its sling. He wasn't likely to need it—the Kurds weren't big fans of the Iraqi government. He'd be more likely to encounter trouble by looking too aggressive.

A small child turned toward him as the Executioner walked into view, then hurried, shouting, toward a man building a fire in front of one of the tents.

The man turned.

Bolan saw the blisters on the man's face as a scarred hand fell to the rusty Webley revolver in his belt. The Executioner stopped in his tracks. He swung the rifle slowly over his back, then walked forward, his hands in front of him, palms out. Other Kurds hurried toward the tent as Bolan neared. He stopped again ten feet from the man, whose hand remained on the revolver.

"I'm not an enemy," the Executioner said.

The man frowned.

"English?" Bolan asked.

The man shook his head.

"Spanish?"

No.

They settled on French.

"I'm American," Bolan stated.

The Kurd's voice was harsh, raspy, his throat as well as his face a victim of Iraqi mustard gas. But the grim smile of the survivor peeked through the painful grimace his speech produced. "That much I can see."

"We need food. Clothes. Can you help us?"

The man shook his head again. "I would like nothing better," he croaked. "But Shawiyya—" he turned and spit onto the ground before continuing "—has taken almost everything. And I can't take what little we have left from the mouths of my people and give it to you."

Bolan nodded. He understood. The genocide of the Kurds that Saddam Hussein had started, and Shawiyya had carried on, hadn't ended. Jaluwi had simply picked up the gas and continued.

"Do you have anything to trade?" the Kurd rasped. Speech obviously pained him, and his hand rose to rub his throat.

Bolan shrugged out of the AK-74 and saw the old man's eyes light up. "This rifle," he said. "For whatever clothing you can spare. And we'll give you our clothes. As for food, we can scavenge along the river until we reach Baghdad."

The Kurd nodded.

The warrior turned, holding his fingers to his lips and whistling. A few moments later Phoenix Force rounded the curve and started toward the tents.

Twenty minutes later the Executioner led his men from camp. A frayed sheepskin tunic and baggy black pantaloons hid the Beretta and Desert Eagle, and a black-and-white-checked keffiyeh shaded Bolan's head and neck from the climbing sun. The members of Phoenix Force were dressed with equal shabbiness, their pistols, ammo mags and knives hidden beneath long, flowing cloaks and caftans.

Even with the heat of the day setting in, the Stony Man warriors' strength continued to return. Manning's pace quickened, and Encizo began to walk on his own. All seemed well.

Until the Iraqi patrol from the north suddenly rounded a bend in the river.

THE MIDMORNING SUN shone brightly around the curtains on the bedroom windows. Talia Alireza felt beneath the clothes in her suitcase to make sure the Bernadelli 16-shot 9 mm and extra magazines were in place. Her fingers brushed the grips of the American Derringer Model 3. She hesitated, then pulled the four-inch minipistol from a pile of underclothes and drew it from the garter holster.

Thumbing the latch at the top of the barrel, Alireza broke the weapon open and made sure the twin 410 shotgun shells were in place. Returning it to the holster, she raised the hem of her long black dress and slipped the garter up her thigh. As she pulled the dress back down, the woman mercenary heard footsteps in the hall behind her. She ran her hands down her thighs, smoothing the skirt back in place as the door opened.

Amilah Alireza entered the bedroom, smiling. The smile faded as her eyes fell on the suitcase. "You're leaving so soon?" she said.

The words were more statement than question, and they sent a chill of guilt flooding through the younger woman. Before she could answer, her mother added to the guilt. "You don't visit your mother for over five years. Not even a telephone call. And now one night is all you can spare?"

"I have things I must attend to, Mother."

"Really! What's so important that you can't stay another day? Will you miss the war? Will fighting that has gone on for thousands of years suddenly stop if you aren't there? If it will, then stay forever."

Alireza started to answer, then stopped. She closed the suitcase and fastened the clasps.

Amilah took a seat on the edge of the bed, gently placing a hand over her daughter's. "Stay, Talia," she pleaded. "One more day. It's important. I...somehow I feel it." She clasped both hands against her breasts. "I feel it *here*."

Alireza didn't turn around. She opened the front door. "I'm sorry. I must go."

"Then give your mother a farewell kiss," Amilah said. "I'm getting old, and we aren't likely to see each other again."

Alireza turned, embracing her mother, and felt tears forming in the corners of her eyes. She pushed her mother to arm's length, and for the first time noticed the deep wrinkles that now covered the woman's tired face.

"One more day," she said, setting the suitcase down. "But one more only."

Amilah Alireza smiled.

CHARLIE MOTT LANDED the chopper in the parking lot next to the Able Team van.

"Thanks, Charlie," Lyons said. He dropped down and walked to the driver's side of the vehicle while Schwarz and Blancanales led the handcuffed terrorist to the sliding rear door.

The UAR gunner had surrendered outside the building. The FBI had quickly cuffed him and placed him under guard in the back seat of a Bureau sedan. Knowing Able Team would have trouble even talking to the prisoner after bucking Ratskowski's orders, Lyons had quickly decided to "circle" the young SAC again.

The Able Team leader had stood meekly in the front yard of the synagogue, his eyes on the grass, trying to suppress a laugh while Ratskowski had verbally ripped him up one side and down the other. Meanwhile, the Stony Man warrior so aptly named Politician had distracted the agents guarding the terrorist with a barrage of double talk. And Schwarz had whisked the man from the car to Mott's waiting chopper.

"What's your name?" Lyons heard Blancanales ask the terrorist as the rear door slid shut.

"I have not to answer," the terrorist said defiantly in broken English. "Is America. I have rights."

"Oh, brother," Lyons muttered under his breath as he started the van. "Are *you* in for a surprise."

The vehicle pulled back onto Missouri Avenue as Schwarz and Blancanales positioned the man between them on the floor. "Okay," Politician replied. "But what should we call you?"

The terrorist snarled.

"Okay, for convenience's sake we'll call you Hamid." In the rearview mirror Lyons saw Blancanales grin at Schwarz. "Hamid's got a point, you know," he went on. "It *is* America. He's got rights. A trial and all that."

The terrorist grinned smugly.

"So what do you say we give him his trial right here?"

Hamid's smile suddenly vanished. "What...what is this? I demand lawyer. Now."

"Gadgets," Blancanales said, "you had a year of law school, didn't you?"

"Well, no," Schwarz answered. "But I thought real hard about taking the LSAT one time. Does that count?"

"Good enough for me." Blancanales nodded. "Hamid, meet your court-appointed attorney, Mr. Gadgets."

Schwarz grinned. "My advice, Mr. Hamid," he said, "is to throw yourself upon the mercy of the court immediately."

Hamid stared at Schwarz in wonder.

"Hey, Ironman," Blancanales called to the front. "Back when you were a cop, and all the judges were letting the bad guys walk, you ever wish it was *you* up there on the bench?"

"More times than I can count."

"Then you got it, Your Honor."

Hamid's eyes flickered to each of his captors. "This is not trial," he said nervously. "And you . . . you are not police."

Blancanales shook his head and smiled. "Not by a long shot."

The terrorist visibly shrank, his shoulders rising to meet his chin. "Then you are American . . . gangsters?"

"What do you know about American gangsters, Hamid?" Schwarz asked.

Hamid raised his handcuffed hands to mimic a machine gun. "Bang! Bang! Bang! Al Capone. Lucky Luciano. Al Pacino."

"Yep, that's us." Schwarz nodded. "Particularly Al Pacino."

An idea suddenly hit Lyons between the eyes like a baseball bat. He had interrogated thousands of suspects in his time. Every prisoner had a weakness. The trick was to find it, then exploit it. And he'd just found Hamid's.

The frightened man's concept of America had come from television and movies. Well, good. He could play that one to the hilt.

As he slowed for a stoplight, Lyons twisted in his seat and looked at Blancanales. "Excuse me, Mr. Luciano."

Blancanales stared at him, deadpan. "Yes, Mr. Pacino?"

"I'm going to go ahead and start for the river. Just in case the verdict's guilty."

With the word *river,* Hamid's eyes opened wide in fear.

Lyons turned the corner and started across Washington toward the Potomac as Blancanales spoke again. "You've been charged with terrorism, Mr. Hamid," he said. "How do you plead?"

"Not guilty! I am not a terrorist!" He looked hopefully toward the front seat. "I am a freedom fighter!"

Blancanales shook his head. "You know what Shakespeare said—rose fertilizer by any other name would smell . . . anyway, the charges still stand."

In the mirror Lyons saw Blancanales lean forward and press into Hamid's face. "And the penalty is just what you think it is, pal. The only way you might get your sentence reduced is to tell us what you know about future UAR activity."

Hamid's chest caved in as he tried to shrink farther away from the men in the back of the van. "But I know nothing," he whimpered.

"I don't think His Honor believes you," Blancanales said. "Do you believe him, Judge?"

"Nope." Lyons stopped at another light and spotted a hardware store on the other side of the intersection. A modification to his plan suddenly hit him.

The light turned green. Lyons pulled into the parking lot and parked the vehicle. "I'll be right back."

Inside, Lyons located the garden section and hefted a fifty-pound sack of dry cement to his shoulder. He found a ten-gallon aluminum bucket in an adjoining aisle and a row of five-gallon jugs of Sparkling Ozark Spring Drinking Water near the checkout stand.

He paid for the items, exited the store and walked back to the van. Handing his teammates the purchases, Lyons returned to the driver's seat and pulled back into traffic. They continued toward the river as Gadgets and Pol began mixing the cement.

"What you are doing now?" Hamid whispered.

Blancanales shrugged. "Just getting ready for the inevitable. You aren't cooperating, Hamid. The sentence will have to be carried out."

The Potomac appeared in the distance. Lyons pulled down a pier and parked overlooking the water. He got out, walked around the vehicle and slid the door open again so the terrorist could see the river.

Schwarz and Blancanales shoved the terrorist's trembling feet into the bucket of wet cement.

Blancanales looked at his watch and sighed. "You buy the quick-drying kind, Judge?" he asked. "I've got a date in an hour."

Sweat poured from Hamid's forehead as the seconds turned to minutes and the cement hardened around his ankles. Schwarz gave a minute-by-minute update on the time, and with each announcement Lyons saw Hamid's dedication to the UAR slip further.

Schwarz leaned forward and tapped the hardened cement. "Time."

Lyons reached inside the van and grabbed Hamid's legs as Blancanales and Schwarz each took an arm.

"Wait! Stop!" the terrorist screamed at the top of his lungs. "I do not know much. But if you will not throw me in the river, I will tell you what I do know."

He did.

And when Lyons heard what Hamid had to say, he came very close to dropping him into the Potomac, anyway.

THE IRAQI PATROL looked almost as disheveled as the Kurds. Their uniforms were torn and soiled, and many of the men looked half-starved.

The Executioner would have been tempted to sympathize with them had the evidence of war crimes not been so manifest throughout their ranks. Here and there he could see carefully carved wood-and-ivory fetishes hanging from the men's necks. One man wore gold bracelets. Another, near the front, had tied the cords of a canvas bag to his web belt. Clinks and tinkles echoed softly toward the Executioner's ears as the wind swayed the bag back and forth.

The gold bracelets were hardly Iraqi army issue. The sounds coming from the bag were made by soft metal objects—gold and silver—scraping against each other. And the fetishes were the good-luck charms worn by local Kurdish tribes.

They might be tired and hungry, but the men of this patrol had killed Kurds and looted their camps.

Bolan counted eighteen soldiers as a man wearing sergeant's stripes on his sleeves walked forward. His eyes were narrow, cruel and suspicious as they darted over the men behind the Executioner.

Without being told, Katz stepped forward to take charge. While his Arabic wasn't impeccable, it would pass.

The sergeant barked a question at the Israeli, and Katz shrugged, pointing at the river as he answered. He'd taken on a posture of weary respect, and Bolan hoped it would have the desired effect, prompting the Iraqis to continue on their way.

The Executioner let his right hand slide casually closer to the bottom of his tunic. From the corner of his eye he saw James do the same. As Katz and the sergeant continued to converse, he scanned the rest of the Iraqi patrol. The AK-47s the soldiers carried were gradually lowering. A good sign.

As the discussion wound down next to him, the Executioner continued to watch the rest of the men. All wore the yellow UAR patches sewn onto their uniforms.

Katz lifted his prosthetic arm and pointed behind him down the river. Bolan saw the Iraqi sergeant's eyes rise, following the finger that hid the .22 Magnum in the Israeli's false finger. He said something else, then turned back to his troops and waved them forward. The men reshouldered their weapons and walked on.

Katz led the men a few hundred feet north until the patrol was out of sight, then turned to Bolan. The rest of the men gathered round.

"They thought we were Kurds," Katz said. "I told the sergeant we were looking for a spot to ford the river with our flock."

Bolan nodded. "Then they know about the camp to the south?"

"Yes. It was unavoidable. I told them our brothers would give them a sheep when they got there."

"Damn," James said. "They'll take *all* the sheep and kill the people." He paused. "After they've raped the women."

"No, they won't," Bolan told him.

Katz grinned. "That's what I figured."

The Executioner didn't have to give any orders. The men of Phoenix Force knew their duty as well as he did. Without being told, they began taking inventory in preparation for the ambush.

Manning drew his Browning Hi-Power. "Three 13-round mags and a full gun. Fifty-three rounds, total."

James lifted his caftan. "Got a full sixteen in my 92 with the one up the pipe. Two extra mags. Forty-six."

The rest of the Force was carrying Berettas like James. Each had two to four magazines, except Encizo, whose pistol had been lost somewhere during his delirious night in the desert.

Bolan handed him the Makarov he'd taken from the Spetznaz trooper the night before. The men from Stony Man Farm broke into double time, hurrying back in the direction they'd come. When the Iraqi troops appeared ahead, they slowed to a walk, keeping well behind. It would make no difference if they were spotted. The Iraqis would simply assume they'd found the site where they planned to cross the river and were returning for the flock.

Bolan remembered the small rise they'd climbed shortly after leaving the Kurds. When it appeared in the distance, he said, "Get ready. As soon as they're out of sight, we go."

When the last soldier dropped over the rise, Bolan and Phoenix Force drew their handguns and broke into a sprint. They flopped to their bellies in the sand at the top of the ridge, peering over in time to see the Iraqis move into the camp, their assault rifles aimed at the startled Kurds.

The sergeant's voice barked in the distance. The Kurds began to form a line in front of the tents. The old Kurd with the scarred face was conspicuously absent.

"Where do you suppose their chief is?" Katz asked.

Bolan shrugged. "Inside one of the tents, maybe. He's got the AK."

As the Kurds continued to line up, Katz shook his head. "I can never get used to it. I've killed many men in my life, and perhaps someday I'll have to explain each one to God. But to do it like this in cold blood..."

Bolan cocked the sound-suppressed Beretta as rifle bolts slid home in the hands of the soldiers below. "I should be able to take out a couple of them before they figure out what's happening. But as soon as they do, or if they look like they're ready to start shooting the Kurds, the rest of you open up."

Five heads nodded.

The Executioner thumbed the selector switch to semiauto and sighted down the barrel. The front sight locked in on the back of the soldier wearing the gold bracelets. The 93-R coughed softly, and the man folded forward.

Before the soldier could hit the ground Bolan swung the Beretta toward the man with the canvas sack. Another quiet 9 mm round hissed through the air to sever the soldier's spinal cord. The sergeant stopped speaking and turned toward the rise.

Bolan continued to fire as Phoenix Force opened up, 9 mm Parabellums exploding from the barrels of the Beretta 92-Fs and Manning's Browning. The Soviet Makarov popped steadily in the hands of Encizo.

Below, the wall of one of the tents began to billow out. Small holes appeared through the sheepskin side curtain as the Iraqi soldiers continued their dances of death, 7.62 mm slugs sputtering impotently from their weapons into the air and ground.

One by one the Iraqi soldiers who had thought they faced just another helpless tribe of Kurdish shepherds fell to the sand, dead. The sergeant dropped his assault rifle and sprinted toward the water. Bolan turned the Beretta his way, leading the man slightly with the sights. As he started to squeeze the trigger, he saw the old man with the scarred face emerge from the tent, the AK-74 gripped in his fists.

The Executioner relaxed his trigger finger. He let the man who had suffered so much from the Iraqi army drop the sergeant with a steady stream of fire. The sergeant fell forward, facedown, into the shallow water along the bank of the Euphrates.

Bolan and Phoenix Force rose to their feet and started down the slope as the Kurds turned toward them. The old man raised his rifle, then recognized their clothes and lowered it again. The scarred face twisted into a smile.

Silently the Stony Man warriors stripped the bodies of rifles, pistols and ammunition, dividing the take with the Kurds.

Bolan heard a sudden squeal. He turned to see one of the Kurdish men standing next to a lamb that hung upside down from a naked tent post. Blood gushed from the severed throat of the animal. The man began skinning the sheep as the women stoked the fire.

Kurdish children crowded around the Stony Man warriors as they began burying the Iraqi bodies near the river. The women not preoccupied with cooking the lamb brought more clothes, amulets—anything the impoverished tribe still had that might serve as gifts.

A dark-skinned girl of eighteen or so extended another tunic to Bolan.

"No," the Executioner said, shaking his head. "You need it more than we do."

When the bodies were hidden, Bolan and Phoenix Force squatted around the fire with the men of the tribe. They cut chunks of the mutton from the spit above the flames with their knives and ate, conversing in a hybrid vernacular of French, Arabic, English and Kurd.

"Thank you," the Executioner said when the meal was finished. He rose to his feet, and Phoenix Force prepared to move out. As they turned toward the river, the tribal chief grabbed him by the sleeve of his tunic.

Looking up into the eyes of the Executioner, the scarred man lifted the AK-74 in one hand. With the other he tugged the sleeve of Bolan's tunic. Then, pointing the rifle toward the shallow graves where the bodies of the Iraqi soldiers lay, the Kurd nodded vigorously.

"A good trade," he said in French. "A good trade."

COLONEL JOSHUA ELDRIDGE leaned forward in the open jeep and tapped the driver on the shoulder. "Stop," he ordered.

The jeep pulled to a halt along the curb.

Eldridge stood up in the back seat, squinting against the sun as he surveyed the ruined village. Dust and smoke still rose from the rubble the howitzer's 155 mm main gun had produced during the hour and a half he'd shelled As-Samawah. Ravaged bodies littered what remained of the streets. Eldridge's troops moved in and out of the few dwellings that remained standing, and an occasional shot told the colonel that even the massive ground-to-ground bombardment he'd launched had left a few survivors.

"Wars and rumors of wars," Eldridge muttered under his breath.

"Sir?" the driver asked.

"The Scriptures, Sergeant. In the end times there will be wars and rumors of wars." He frowned at the man. "You aren't familiar with the verses?"

The driver grinned sheepishly. "Uh, yes, sir. I remember now. I'm sorry. I guess I was busy scanning the streets for the enemy."

Eldridge braced a hand on the man's shoulder and stepped down from the jeep. "Exactly what you should be doing, son. Exactly what you should be doing."

As the colonel's feet hit the cracked asphalt, Ferguson came out of a partially demolished house. The first officer hurried toward the jeep. "All dead inside, but we didn't do it."

Eldridge ran a hand over his short-cropped hair and frowned. "Explain."

Ferguson removed his beret and wiped the sweat from his forehead with the back of his wrist. "The people inside the house have been dead some time. Some kind of illness, sir."

The colonel felt his lips curl up into a grin. He looked out over the village. Waste—both human and animal—had backed up in the sewers that had been bombed out during the war. Other long-dead bodies of man and beast rotted where they'd fallen in the streets. "Disease," the colonel said. "In the end times, diseases will spread. Don't worry, Ferguson. The plague shall not be upon you...Exodus 12:13."

Eldridge walked past the man and strolled down the street, stepping over bodies and rubble as he surveyed the damage. "I will bring them against thee on every side, the Babylonians," he said under his breath, and frowned when he couldn't remember the book and verse to which to attribute the scripture.

A personnel vehicle carrying several men passed. The soldiers saluted from the truck's open bed. Eldridge watched them—they weren't of his chosen Twelve, and their faces reflected a mixture of fear, confusion and loathing. He squinted into the sun, trying to catch a glimpse of their name tags, but by then the truck had passed on down the road.

To his right Eldridge saw a flash of sudden movement. Turning toward a demolished house, he saw a disheveled Arab wearing a caftan and keffiyeh shoot out from under the rubble. A split second later three of his chosen Twelve appeared in pursuit.

Eldridge drew the nickel-plated Government Model .45 from his hip and aimed at the Arab as he limped across the street. The pistol boomed, and the man fell in his tracks.

The three soldiers ground to a halt. "Good shot, Colonel!" one of them shouted.

Eldridge nodded as he holstered his weapon. *I have overthrown some of you, as God overthrew Sodom and Gomorrah,* he thought, and the two ancient cities of sin sent his mind suddenly reeling back thirty years.

A hot, sweaty night. Somewhere in the southwestern United States. Texas? Oklahoma? Eldridge couldn't remember. What he did remember was the large circus tent the Reverend Joshua Eldridge, Senior had used for his revivals, and the impoverished farmers in overalls, their wives in faded floral-patterned dresses and bonnets, who attended the camp meetings.

Sodom and Gomorrah had been a favorite theme for his father's sermons. The traveling minister would scare the congregation half to death with stories of the tortures of hell, then order them to cast their worldly goods into the pit he'd dug in front of the pulpit. Joshua Eldridge, Senior's words still rang in his son's ears: "Let the riches of God replace your earthly treasures! Be saved, and escape the fires of everlasting damnation!"

The words would send gold watches, diamond rings, emerald brooches and stickpins flying into the pit.

Eldridge's face stiffened as he continued along the street. He remembered one night in particular. It had been the last night of a week-long camp meeting between De Queen, Arkansas, and the Oklahoma state line. Unable to sleep, he'd arisen from his bed in the back of the Eldridge family bus and gone for a walk.

It was during that walk that he saw his father.

Digging. Digging up the treasures he'd called upon the people to fling into the pit.

The colonel halted at the corner of the street, his eyes staring sightlessly past the ruins of a mosque. From the moment he'd first learned of his father's deception, for the next thirty years, he'd rejected the message the charlatan pastor had preached. By the time he'd graduated high school, his mother had drunk herself into an early grave. He'd left for West Point, and the Army had become his god.

Eldridge gazed up at the clouds, trying to see beyond them, to the heaven he knew lay somewhere beyond. Had he died during the past thirty years he had no doubt he'd have been eternally damned. The thought brought a smile to the colonel's face. Eternal damnation hadn't been God's plan for his life.

Ferguson appeared at Eldridge's side, breaking into the colonel's memories. "Sir, the village has been canvassed. All of the enemy are dead. Some of them are wondering if we'll be going on to Babylon."

"Not yet," Eldridge said. "I have special plans for the city of whores."

Ferguson nodded. "Yes, sir. Can I tell the men where we *will* be heading from here?"

Eldridge sighed. "Must ye know each step? Can you not trust me to lead you?"

Ferguson shifted his feet. "I don't think it's that, sir. Not all of the men are as dedicated as *we* are. I think they're just anxious. Curious."

"Tell them we'll be returning to the base camp," Eldridge said. "Our detachment to Israel should arrive soon. But we have a little task to do on the way back." He paused, scratching his arm in the heat. "Do you remember the three oil wells we passed on the way here?"

"Yes, sir."

"I've decided it's time the Iraqis learned how the Kuwaitis felt when their country was put to the torch."

Ferguson grinned. "Yes, *sir,*" he said, saluted again and turned an about-face to spread the word.

Eldridge held up his hand, stopped the jeep, climbed back on board and resumed his thoughts. No, eternal damnation for Colonel Joshua Eldridge hadn't been part of the Lord's plan. God had big, *big* things in mind for him. Things that had been revealed to him thirty years later when he gave up all hope in the desert.

As the driver continued down the street toward the edge of the village where the troops would regroup, Eldridge's mind flashed back again. This time only a few short months.

The Iraqi desert. Only a few miles from here. Still a major, Eldridge's promotion to colonel would take effect in thirty days.

In his mind's eye Eldridge saw the remnants of the downed American plane, and the other Special Forces men he was leading on the search-and-rescue mission for the pilot. A chill swept over him as he recalled the horror he'd experienced when they encountered the battalion of Iraqi infantry.

They'd run and hidden throughout the night. Each time they'd believed they'd escaped, they'd come face-to-face with new resistance. Artillery shells had fallen close enough that the concussion had knocked them from their feet into the sand.

One by one the men of his team had been killed.

Then, as he'd sprinted frantically through the darkness for his life, the only man left, Joshua Eldridge had seen the tree in the distance. A bright, beautiful cedar tree sprouting from the sand. The terror had suddenly left his soul as he'd marveled at the tree. How had it gotten there in the desert? How did it survive without water?

He'd been drawn inexplicably toward it.

As he'd neared, the tree had burst into flames. Then the Voice had called down to him from the heavens: *Why have you rejected me?*

Eldridge had stopped in his tracks, then walked slowly toward the tree, heedless of the bullets that were flying around him, knowing beyond doubt that they could no longer harm him.

The Voice had spoken again: *Trust not your earthly father, but your Father which art in heaven.*

It was then that Eldridge had realized what he'd seen before him was the same burning bush Moses had seen four thousand years earlier.

The driver of the jeep slowed. Ahead, Eldridge saw several other vehicles already parked at the edge of the village. The driver pulled to a halt in the middle of the group. Silently the colonel waited for the rest of the men to report, his mind returning to that fateful night in the desert.

As soon as he'd heard the Voice the second time, Eldridge had collapsed. He'd awakened in a field hospital to learn that he'd been found in the middle of the desert the next day by another Special Forces rescue team.

The rescue team had seen no signs of shelling. They'd claimed there were no Iraqi forces anywhere nearby. The doctors had assumed the tree Eldridge had spoken of in his sleep had been a hallucination brought on by dehydration.

But Joshua Eldridge had known better.

The colonel watched as the rest of the troops appeared at the edge of the village. More vehicles pulled in next to the jeep.

Ferguson approached. "All present and accounted for," he reported.

"Then let's move out." Eldridge smiled. The driver threw the jeep into gear and they drove away from As-Samawah.

That the rescue team hadn't seen the burning bush, or the signs of shelling, didn't surprise Eldridge. God, in His wisdom, hadn't seen fit to appear to them. God had chosen to reveal His plan only to Joshua Eldridge. And that plan had progressed on schedule—until Colonel Pollock had been sent to the Special Forces compound.

Eldridge felt the skin around his lips tighten as he thought of Pollock. If not for that bastard, he could have stayed at the Kuwaiti compound, carrying out the Lord's work from behind the fences.

Then Joshua Eldridge felt his face relax again, and he gave way to a smile. It made no difference. Not Pollock, not the UAR, and not even the United States could stop him. They might cause minor delays and make him alter his strategy slightly. BUT THEY COULDN'T STOP HIM.

He'd been chosen by God. Chosen to begin the End.

CHAPTER SIX

High above the horizon to the northwest, the snow-capped crest of Pike's Peak protruded at the top of the Rocky Mountains. Lyons's stomach jumped as the Lear Jet descended, and he wondered if the nausea came from the sudden change in atmospheric pressure or from what Hamid had told them on the dock of the Potomac River.

The United Arab Republic was about to machine-gun children at Belmont Grade School, Pueblo, Colorado.

Lyons unfastened his seat belt as the tires hit the runway. Charlie Mott slowed the jet to a crawl, then taxied toward the terminal of Pueblo Memorial Airport.

"Anybody ever been here before?" Lyons asked. "Know anything about the town?"

Schwarz and Mott shook their heads as the plane neared the terminal. "All I know is what I see on TV," Blancanales replied. "Pueblo's where you write to get federal brochures on things like raising mushrooms in your basement."

The plane halted. Followed by his teammates, Lyons dropped to the ground. He reached back into the cockpit, passing the canvas luggage bags out to the men. "Gadgets, I saw a rent-a-car sign as we landed. Go inside and see what kind of wheels you can come up with."

As Schwarz headed toward the terminal, Lyons turned to Mott, still behind the controls. "Take care of the paperwork," the ex-cop said, indicating the terminal building with a jerk of his head. "And stay ready, Charlie. No telling where we'll be going from here."

Mott nodded, then turned to face an airport cart as it approached along the runway.

Lyons and Blancanales hefted the bags and entered the small terminal. They saw Schwarz turn away from a counter in the corner of the room and walk to meet them, a set of keys in one hand, a city map of Pueblo in the other.

"Four-wheel-drive Bronco," Gadgets stated as he fell into step with the other members of Able Team. "The side lot."

Lyons led the way to the brown-and-tan vehicle parked just outside the terminal. He slid behind the wheel, took the keys from Schwarz and started the engine as Politician got in back and Gadgets took the shotgun seat.

He turned from the lot onto Kellar Parkway and headed toward Interstate 50. Schwarz unzipped a padded nylon case and pulled a portable police scanner from the foam rubber inside. He had it mounted beneath the dash and was reaching for the programmable two-way, by the time the Bronco reached the highway.

Lyons turned right at the intersection and leaned on the accelerator, speeding the Bronco toward the city.

"What do you suppose made the UAR pick a town like Pueblo for this?" Blancanales asked.

Schwarz finished mounting the radio next to the scanner, pulled three walkie-talkies with headsets out of another bag and handed one each to the other men. He shrugged. "What's the population? Maybe a hundred thousand? It's big enough that they wouldn't stand out, but small enough to have a limited number of cops, I guess."

"Yeah, but there are other things that don't make sense," Blancanales said. "It's summer. School's not in session."

"Ever hear of summer school?" Lyons asked. "Lots of places have tutoring for kids who had trouble during the school year. Advanced classes for gifted children. Things like that."

A quarter mile in the distance Lyons saw the Y in the highway and the overhead sign announcing the suburbs of Bradford Park to the south, Belmont to the north. Cutting to the right-hand lane, he passed under the sign. Brightly painted houses appeared in a shallow valley to the north of the road. Farther in the distance on a ridge the buildings of Southern Colorado State College emerged to block the view of the mountains.

Schwarz opened the city map and spread it out on his lap.

Red and blue lights suddenly flashed in the rearview mirror as Lyons pushed the Bronco down the highway. His eyes dropped automatically to the speedometer. Eighty-seven.

"Just what we need," Blancanales said, looking over his shoulder.

Schwarz pulled a small pamphlet from his jacket and flipped through the pages. "Colorado," he murmured, "Lamar... Las Animas... here it is—Pueblo PD." He held a thumb on the open booklet as he leaned forward and tapped the frequency into the radio.

Behind them a siren wailed on.

Lyons lifted the mike and keyed the button. "Justice 943 to Pueblo unit south on 50."

A moment later the radio scratched. "Unit calling Pueblo John 12, go ahead."

"Justice 943," Lyons repeated. "That's us in the Bronco right in front of you, 12, and we're ten-six at the moment. How about a break?"

"Ten-four Justice," the voice came back. The siren stopped and the lights flashed off. The pursuit car slowed and pulled back onto the shoulder.

As more buildings sprang up around them, Lyons passed through a green light. He saw Schwarz return the pamphlet to his pocket and glance down at the map in his lap.

"Next intersection, Ironman. Cut a right."

Lyons took the bypass curve just before the next light, and the Bronco cruised north on Bonforte. They passed a shopping center on the right, then Belmont Park on the left, before turning left to McNaughton just beyond a church. A few blocks later a one-story school building appeared in the distance.

Lyons tapped the brakes, slowing and letting his cop mind take in the layout of the school grounds for future reference. The building had several wings. Outside doors led from the playground and parking areas into the classrooms. A half-dozen cars were parked along the chain-link fence that surrounded the grounds. "Looks like summer school was right," he observed.

Drawing abreast of the playground, the men of Able Team saw a group of kids playing soccer, another hanging from the bars of a jungle gym. As they turned left to circle the block, a dark blue sedan pulled up to the fence and parked.

Two dark-skinned men got out of the car and entered the school through the front entrance. Both wore coveralls. One carried a toolbox.

Lyons frowned, his police instincts going on alert. He circled the block, passed the sedan and parked the Bronco a half block up, across the street.

Blancanales twisted in his seat to look over the rear dash. "I didn't see any machine guns," he said. "Maybe Ingrams or Uzis under their coats, in the toolbox. But you'd think they'd have more men. And those guys went right in the front door. Looked like they belonged there."

"Looking like he belonged there worked for the Boston Strangler," Schwarz said. "Seems like we've gotten through a few doors the same way."

Lyons killed the ignition. He pulled a pair of mini-binoculars from the breast pocket of his sport coat and turned in time to see the back of Blancanales's head nod agreement.

"There's a heavy Hispanic population here," Pol said. "Anybody with dark skin could probably pass as a Mexican."

"Could be a recon team," Schwarz added. "Getting the layout down. Then they come back later with the heavy guns."

Lyons focused the binoculars on the sedan's license tag. "PB-1821," he said out loud. "Get a twenty-eight on it, Gadgets."

Schwarz lifted the microphone from the hook. "Locals or Stony Man?"

"Stony Man will be faster."

Schwarz replaced the mike and opened another padded case, producing a cellular phone. A moment later he had Barbara Price on the line. "Ten-twenty-eight," he said. "PB-1821...Colorado." He hung up.

As they waited, the two men came back out and got into the sedan.

Lyons studied them through the binoculars. Hispanic, or Arab? If they were Arab, did that mean they were UAR? At this point it was impossible to know.

The Able Team warriors ducked below the windows as the sedan passed. Lyons rose high enough to see the car turn right into the residential section bordering the school grounds, then fired the Bronco to life. "Get the school on the phone, Pol," he ordered. "Come up with some ploy that won't scare them and find out who those guys were, or at least who they *said* they were.'' He pulled the Bronco away from the curb as Schwarz handed the phone over the seat and Blancanales got Rocky Mountain Bell Information on the line.

''Belmont School Number 31,'' Politician said.

The sedan had turned again by the time the Bronco reached the corner. Lyons leaned forward on the accelerator, raced a block to Dundee and saw the rear bumper round a curve to the left. He heard Blancanales hang up and tap another number into the cellular.

''This is Eugene Frazier, Pueblo Building Codes Office,'' Pol said. ''I need to know—'' He halted in midsentence as Lyons turned the corner after the sedan. ''Okay, thank you,'' he said, and hung up.

Lyons watched the sedan take another right and head back toward Bonforte.

''Sometimes you get lucky,'' Blancanales said. ''Those guys were from Building Codes. I just missed them.'' The phone buzzed suddenly in his hand. He flipped the switch, said, ''Yeah, Barbara,'' listened, then looked up again. ''But their car's as rented as this one, Ironman.''

''No local building inspectors are going to need to rent a car,'' Schwarz said.

Lyons screeched the Bronco to a halt in front of a house with red rocks serving as a front lawn. ''Get back to the school,'' he ordered Schwarz. ''See what you can find. We'll follow them.''

Schwarz grabbed his headset and another of the equipment bags and dived from the vehicle as Lyons pressed the accelerator again.

Racing to the corner of Dundee, Lyons turned in pursuit of the sedan and saw it make another left on Bonforte. He pulled up to the stop sign as a wave of heavy traffic suddenly blocked access to the street.

Blancanales climbed over the seat into the front, staring past the Able Team leader as the sedan disappeared around the curve just past the church. Lyons leaned on the horn, then pulled out into the oncoming traffic. More horns protested the move as the Bronco's tires squealed through the turn. They raced back to highway 50B in time to see the sedan already on the cloverleaf that connected with Interstate 25.

"Keep your eyes glued to them, Pol," Lyons said as he guided the Bronco into the turn. "See if they go north or south."

"North," he replied almost immediately.

Lyons looked up to see the sedan pass under another green-and-white sign, announcing Colorado Springs. The Bronco followed, its tires squealing around the curved ramp that led onto the interstate.

The sedan continued north, a quarter mile ahead. Lyons let up on the pedal, gaining slowly on the other vehicle. With two cars between them he pulled over into the right-hand lane, leaned back against the seat and wrapped the walkie-talkie headset around his ears.

Blancanales rolled down his window, stuck his head partway out and glanced around at the traffic. They passed a shopping mall and several restaurants, then Pol said, "Right-turn signal just went on."

Lyons slowed and followed the sedan onto the exit ramp. Both vehicles made a left, and Lyons saw a sign pointing toward Pueblo West. A short distance later their quarry pulled into the parking lot of a motel.

The Able Team leader drove past the motel to the corner, turned left across the oncoming traffic, parked and pulled out the binoculars.

"Looks like they're planning to stay over," Blancanales observed. "If they were the recon team, they might be part of the hit team, too."

Lyons felt a vibration around his headset, signaling that Schwarz was trying to make contact. He looked down at the walkie-talkie and saw that the volume had been turned off. Flipping the switch, he heard Gadgets say, "Ironman, you there?"

"Yeah." Lyons pointed to his headset and Blancanales slipped his own over his head.

"I'm in the basement of the school," Schwarz said, "and you guys aren't going to like what I've just found."

THE FOOTSTEPS on the riverbank sounded muffled from under the water. The Executioner breathed shallowly through the hollow reed in his mouth, his body frozen among the bulrushes. To his side Bolan saw the watery image of Rafael Encizo, but past the Cuban the rest of the submerged members of Phoenix Force were too indistinct to distinguish.

Bolan had heard voices, and even a few chuckles from above. That meant discipline was relaxed, and the soldiers had resorted to conversation to conquer their boredom.

The Executioner waited. After leaving the Kurds's camp with the captured AK-47s and fresh loads of ammo, he'd sent Calvin James ahead to take point in case more Iraqi soldiers came their way. The Phoenix Force warrior had sprinted back a few hours later with the report that another column was advancing along the river. The Stony Man warriors had barely had time to break off their makeshift snorkels and dive into the water when the first uniform appeared.

The sun had fallen halfway through the afternoon sky when the troops passing their position began to thin. Finally the horizon above the bank cleared altogether. Still, the Executioner didn't move. Any commander worth his salt would have assigned a squad to bring up the rear.

This commander had. Six more soldiers passed five minutes later.

Bolan gave it another ten minutes before his head slowly emerged from the water. Water dripped from his hair as he turned a full three-sixty. Seeing nothing, he reached out and touched Encizo on the shoulder. Beneath the surface he saw the Cuban tap the next man in line. One by one the heads of the five members of Phoenix Force rose above the surface. They moved quietly to the knee-deep water at the edge of the bank.

"We'll stay beneath the ridge line for a while," Bolan told them, "just in case. David, take point."

The former SAS man headed out.

No sooner had he turned than an Iraqi soldier appeared on the ridge to the north. The man froze, his assault rifle hanging at his side.

The Stony Man team stopped in its tracks.

"Just when you thought it was safe to go back in the water," Manning muttered.

The Iraqi turned to shout over his shoulder as Bolan drew the Beretta from his soaked shoulder rig. Water dripped from the weapon as he squeezed the trigger, drilling the Iraqi's chest with 9 mm death. The enemy soldier collapsed on the ridge.

Bolan and Phoenix Force hurried to the rise. Grabbing the man by the boots, they yanked him out of sight and peered over the edge. Three hundred feet to the north an Iraqi jeep led a slow-moving column of transport vehicles along the road paralleling the river. At least a hundred foot soldiers accompanied them, trudging through the wet soil on both sides of the pathway.

The Executioner looked down at the familiar yellow patch on the dead soldier's sleeves. But the man wore another insignia, as well—that of the Republican Guard.

The best Iraq, and now the UAR, had to offer.

The warrior looked out over the muddy ground to the west. Irrigation ditches crosshatched the sector. Several miles away he saw the steel beams and guy wires of an oil rig rising into the air like a modern-day

Tower of Babylon. Ten feet back to the south another narrow road of packed earth cut through the swampy plain, heading off to the northeast.

The Executioner glanced back at the oncoming army. If his calculations were correct, they were only a few miles southwest of Baghdad. Soon they'd have had to leave the cover the Euphrates offered and make their way toward the city, anyway.

Now was as good a time as any.

Bolan turned to the men at his side and saw the same resolved expression on each face. If they had to, the men of Stony Man would die. But they'd take out as many of the enemy as they could before that happened.

"The lead jeep's a good hundred feet ahead of the others," Bolan whispered. "Our only chance is surprise. We grab the vehicle and make a run for Baghdad."

His team nodded.

"I'll take the first shot," Bolan said. "The guy riding shotgun. David, take the man in the back, left. Gary, back, right. Spread out so you can get your angles of fire. The driver's hands will be busy. I'll take him out last." He paused, taking a deep breath. "As soon as we shoot, everybody up and into the jeep."

As the jeep moved closer along the river, Bolan cocked the Beretta. McCarter and Manning moved along the ridge, getting into position.

With the Iraqi vehicle twenty feet away, Bolan locked in on the man in the passenger's seat and squeezed the trigger. A round red hole appeared in the soldier's forehead. Two shots rang out a heartbeat later, and the men in the back of the jeep slumped.

Bolan was over the edge of the ridge a second later, the men of Phoenix Force only a step behind. He sprinted toward the jeep and saw the driver instinctively hit the brake, his face a mask of confusion as he stared at the body next to him.

The Executioner erased the confusion with another silenced 9 mm slug. He then grabbed the driver by the lapels, lifting him up and over the door as the jeep sputtered and died. On the other side of the vehicle Manning, James and Encizo heaved the rest of the bodies out of the way, and the men of Phoenix Force crowded into the jeep.

Bolan slid behind the wheel, twisted the key and brought the jeep back to life. Flooring the accelerator, he raced to the road leading northwest and cut hard on the wheel. The six men were a hundred yards down the road when the first shot skimmed off the rear fender.

GADGETS SCHWARZ SET the equipment bag on the floor of the reception area and pulled the U.S. Department of Justice credentials out of the back pocket of his jeans. Opening the case, he shoved the photo ID across the counter to the Belmont school secretary-receptionist.

The woman's carefully plucked eyebrows rose. "My goodness." She handed the case back. "How can I help you?"

Schwarz stuck the credentials back into his pocket. "I need to know about the two men who were just here."

"The men from the Building Codes Office?" she said. "They were here to—"

Schwarz shook his head. He leaned over the counter, whispering, "They weren't building inspectors."

The woman smiled. "I saw *their* identification, too. It was as authentic as yours."

Schwarz returned the phony Justice ID to his pocket. The irony of one set of false credentials in pursuit of others didn't escape the Able Team electronics genius as he said, "Tell me where they went, what they did."

The secretary shrugged. "I don't know. They said it was just a routine inspection."

Schwarz frowned. "How long have you worked here, Mrs....?"

"Gooch, Marlena Gooch. Almost twelve years. Why?"

"Have you had any other routine inspections during that time?"

"Well, no, I guess not. There was always a specific problem...."

Schwarz looked over his shoulder as a woman he assumed to be a teacher dragged two boys into the reception area by the arms. She directed them toward a vinyl-covered bench along the wall and said harshly, "You two just sit there and be quiet until Mrs. Shades is ready to see you." She stood next to the boys like a guard watching her prisoners.

Schwarz turned back to Marlena Gooch. "Did you happen to see which way they went when they left the office?"

"No, I didn't pay any attention."

A door in the far wall behind the counter opened and a woman in her mid-fifties stepped into the office area. Her gray-brown hair had been tied into a tight bun atop her head, and she reminded Schwarz of his own sixth-grade teacher.

"Is there a problem?" the woman asked.

Mrs. Gooch looked from Schwarz to the woman and then back. "Agent Schwarz, this is Principal Shades. Mrs. Shades, Agent Schwarz of the Justice Department."

"My goodness," Mrs. Shades said, echoing the secretary's earlier words. The principal smiled pleasantly. "How may we help you, Agent Schwarz?"

"Three men posing as building inspectors just came in. Do you know—"

Schwarz heard the voice over his shoulder. "The two guys in coveralls who were in the hall?"

He turned to see the taller of the two boys against the wall looking up at him.

"I told you to be quiet!" the teacher next to him snapped.

Ignoring the teacher, Schwarz walked over to the wall and squatted in front of the boy. He was big for his age. His hair was cut in a long flattop like Arnold Schwarzenegger sometimes wore, and the Able Team man smiled, knowing that must have been what spawned the boy's style. "What's your name, buddy?" Schwarz asked.

The boy looked at his teacher, then his principal. Mrs. Shades nodded.

"Jed."

"Did you see these guys in the hall, Jed?"

The boy nodded.

"What did they look like?" Schwarz asked.

"Both about five-eight, medium build. Dark brown hair, brown eyes. Dark complexion."

Schwarz suppressed a smile. The kid had watched his share of TV cop shows.

"I think they were Hispanic," the boy went on.

The shorter boy next to him shook his head vigorously. "It wasn't Spanish they were speaking, Jed. I know Spanish. That was some other language."

Schwarz felt a chill race down his spine. "Did you see where they went?" he asked the boys.

Jed nodded again. "The basement."

Schwarz rose to his feet. Turning back to the counter, he said, "Mrs. Shades, what's down in the basement?"

"Storage mainly. Extra desks, other equipment. And most of the time a half-tipsy janitor who hides behind the boiler and doesn't think I know what he's doing."

Adrenaline suddenly rushed through the Able Team man's veins. The boiler. An explosive device set next to it could . . .

Hamid had either lied or gotten his wires crossed on the strike at the school. It wasn't going to be another machine-gunning. The two men in coveralls hadn't been an advance party to recon the school.

They were the main event.

"Mrs. Shades," Schwarz said, "you've got to evacuate the school immediately."

"What? Why—"

"I don't have time to explain," Schwarz interrupted. "In fact, I don't know how much time I have for anything. Just get on the loudspeaker and get everyone out of the building."

"But—"

"Do it!" Schwarz shouted. He turned toward the secretary. "Mrs. Gooch, show me where the stairs to the basement are." He grabbed the equipment bag from the floor and followed the secretary toward the door as Mrs. Shades keyed the loudspeaker behind him. "Attention, all students. You will move immediately in an orderly fashion..."

Schwarz followed Mrs. Gooch down the hall to the stairs, then grabbed her by the shoulders. "Thanks," he said. "Now get out of the building. Take the kids to the far side of the playground, and don't come back in until I come out." He shoved her toward the end of the hall, then turned and raced down the stairs three at a time.

When he reached the basement, Schwarz saw an elderly man in striped overalls lying on the floor. But the man wasn't drunk, as Mrs. Shades suspected.

He was dead, his throat slit from ear to ear.

Schwarz charged toward the ancient boiler in the corner. His eyes scanned the tangled mass of pipes, finally falling on the small square metal box half-hidden behind the tank.

As he dived onto his belly, burrowing under pipes and copper tubing, he heard the sound of feet hurrying out of the building on the floor above. He pressed his ear against the box.

Quiet, steady ticks came from under the cover.

Schwarz unzipped the equipment bag. Wrapping the walkie-talkie headset around his head, he flipped the switch on. "Ironman? Are you there?"

Lyons's voice came back a few moments later. "Yeah."

"I'm in the basement of the school," Schwarz said, "and you guys aren't going to like what I've just found." Drawing the Cold Steel Terminator knife from the sheath at the small of his back, the electronics wizard worked the wide leaf-shaped blade gently under the lid of the box.

Lyons's voice sounded in his ears again. "What have you got?"

"Bomb of some kind," Schwarz answered. "Just a second." Slowly he pried the lid off the box, carefully checking for trip wires.

"Are the kids out?" Lyons asked.

Schwarz didn't answer. He stared down at the bomb in horror. The yellow-and-white cake of Semtex looked as innocuous as cheddar cheese on the verge of molding, but there was enough of the plastic explosive in the box to blow up half the school.

"Are the kids out?" Lyons shouted over the air.

"They're on their way."

"Then get your butt out of there, too, Gadgets," the Able Team leader ordered. "The school can be replaced. You can't."

Schwarz studied the timer—a cheap wristwatch. The face read two minutes to twelve—different than the 3:15 his own watch maintained. Unless he missed his guess, the building would go up when the hands lined up on the twelve.

"Gadgets! Did you hear me?" Lyons shouted into the walkie-talkie.

Schwarz switched the radio off. He didn't have time to explain about the children he still heard in the upstairs hall. And he couldn't concentrate on disarming the explosive with Ironman bitching in his ear. He'd deal with the consequences of disobeying orders later.

If he was lucky enough to have a later.

Schwarz's eyes followed the complex system of wires. He saw the actuating coil through which the pulse from the watch would run when the hands lined up. The coil would become an electromagnet, pulling the contact assembly to the pole piece and completing the circuit.

He glanced back at the face of the watch.

One minute.

"Okay," he breathed out loud as sweat began dripping down his face. He started to reach for the coil, then froze as his eyes fell on the backup relay. Connected to the main coil, it would activate the moment he jerked the other wire free.

Gadgets took a deep breath and followed the wire through a bizarre set of twists and turns. Sweat poured into his eyes, blinding him. He took another deep breath as he wiped his face with his shirttail.

Starting from scratch, the electronics expert's eyes moved along the backup relay once more. They stopped suddenly as the relay dead-ended into another actuating coil.

Schwarz gave in and glanced at the watch.

Ten seconds.

It wasn't a backup. It was a dummy.

Or was the system he'd seen first the dummy?

Schwarz's heart hammered in his chest. Which one? He had less than ten seconds to decide.

Reaching into the box, Gadgets caught the second coil between his thumb and index finger. The more complex system had been harder to see. But did that mean *it* was the actual detonator? Had it been meant to be overlooked?

Or had it been meant to be seen and mistaken for the real thing because of its complexity? The bomb could have been designed either way. And he had no more time to decide.

Schwarz grasped the wire and jerked. A sudden, shrill ringing sound, louder than anything he had ever heard, pierced his ears. The Able warrior's eyes slammed shut, and he fell onto his back on the floor.

The cold concrete against the back of his sweat-soaked shirt sent chills racing up his shoulders. Schwarz shivered as he opened his eyes. He stared at the ceiling of the school basement, then a weak smile curled his lips.

The school bell quit ringing.

School was out.

CHAPTER SEVEN

Automatic gunfire slapped the mud next to the jeep as Bolan steered along the narrow dirt road. From the corner of his eye he saw three Republican Guard personnel carriers veer off the road, angling through the soggy earth to cut off the fleeing Stony Man warriors. Six more vehicles stayed on the river road, speeding up as they raced toward the intersecting route that led to Baghdad.

Behind him the Executioner heard Katz, Encizo and James return fire. The windshield of the lead Iraqi vehicle shattered. Mud flew from beneath its spinning tires as the engine stalled and the personnel carrier sank into the dark brown sludge. The vehicle behind it crashed into the rear bumper, tossing guardsmen from both open flatbeds.

The third Iraqi carrier swerved, trying desperately to avoid the accident, but its front fender nicked the side door of the second truck. With a dull thud it spun to a halt, high-centered in the grassy muck.

Bolan leaned harder on the accelerator, trying to coax more power into the jeep's engine. The road curved, heading due west toward the oil well in the distance. The Executioner's heart skipped a beat as the possibility that the pathway might dead-end at the drill site crossed his mind.

No. The workers and equipment would have to be brought out from Baghdad. This road would either continue into the city, or another would lead from the well farther east.

Bolan glanced over his shoulder to see the six remaining trucks racing along the river road toward the intersection. He let out a deep breath. The Iraqi drivers still in the race knew that even with the head start the longer route provided the fleeing jeep, the personnel carriers' larger engines would close the gap before they reached Baghdad.

The mud had bought Bolan and Phoenix Force more time.

But not much.

The Executioner glanced up into the mirror to see the lead truck slow at the turn as the jeep started across an old wooden bridge. The Executioner hit the brakes, skidding to a halt in the packed dirt on the other side of the bridge. "Gary," he said to the man sitting next to him, "blow it!"

The Canadian demolitions expert climbed over McCarter and leaped to the ground. He pulled a clump of carefully wrapped C-4 plastique from his combat vest as he raced back to the bridge. James jumped out of the back seat, following to assist.

By the time the Executioner looked back to the river, all six trucks had made the turn. James's head was visible at the top of the slope leading down into the water, but Manning had disappeared somewhere below the bridge.

James frowned, looking down into the ditch and cocking an ear. Then he turned back to the jeep and shouted, ''Rafael! Bring the rucksack! The detonators—''

Bolan saw that the personnel carriers were picking up speed. ''No time!'' he shouted. ''Get back here! Now!'' He raced the engine of the jeep as James and Manning sprinted back up the slope.

Dirt spun from under the wheels as the six men took off again toward the oil well. As they neared, the tiny objects at the site grew, coming into focus. They raced past the drilling mud house as the pump head rose and fell, looking like some giant prehistoric bird leaning forward to grasp food in its teeth.

The Iraqi trucks continued to close. As they got within range, the shooting from the rear resumed. One round flew through the jeep's windshield, miraculously missing the men crammed into the vehicle.

Bolan raced past the well as a dozen curious oil field workers looked up. Cutting the wheel hard to the right, he guided the jeep through a short jog next to the tanks.

The road angled north again. They sped up a shallow grade, crossed another irrigation bridge and fled past carefully cultivated cotton stalks on both sides. A rolling green hill appeared in the distance as the gunfire from behind continued. The jeep topped the crest, and suddenly the ancient city of Baghdad appeared in the distance.

Empty 7.62 mm brass casings flew from the jeep as Phoenix Force lay down steady cover fire with their captured AK-47s. Bolan heard James shout, "Bingo!" and glanced up at the mirror in time to see the nearest truck swerve off the road on the rims of its front wheels, the black rubber that had once been tires flapping madly. But the remaining five vehicles didn't slow as they maneuvered around their disabled leader.

Scattered outposts—a gas station here, a coffee house there—began to crop up on both sides of the road as the city drew closer.

Soon the selective devastation on the outskirts of the city became apparent. Spotted between houses that showed no signs of damage were the remnants of buildings razed by Allied "smart" bombs.

The rear attack heated up again as the trucks began to close in. Bolan twisted in his seat, shouting over the wind and gunfire. "As soon as we reach the bazaar, scatter! We'll meet tonight at the Mustansiriyah! Everybody know where it is?"

McCarter, Manning and Encizo nodded.

"I'll find it!" James shouted.

The jeep raced on into the city. Bolan spotted a street lined with silversmiths' stands. He hit the brakes, squealed the jeep around a corner and threw the transmission into neutral. "Everybody out!" he shouted as the first of the oncoming trucks slowed for the turn.

A windstorm of automatic rifle fire blew around them as the men of Phoenix Force dived from the jeep and fled in five separate directions. Bolan provided cover fire, sending a volley into the grille of the lead personnel carrier. Then, dropping the empty AK-47, he cut down an alley between two buildings.

The Executioner raced along the brick walls between the buildings, emerging onto a winding street in the noisy coppersmiths' souk. He slowed to a walk, pulled the tail of his keffiyeh across his face, slipped his hand under the tunic to the grips of the Desert Eagle and tried to look casual as he walked past coppersmiths haggling prices with their customers.

Bolan's mind raced as he walked. The Mustansiriyah was the site of the ruins of one of the world's oldest universities. Manning, McCarter and Encizo had been familiar with it. He hadn't caught Katz's reaction, but even if the Israeli didn't know where it was, his command of the language would enable him to find it without drawing undue attention.

Bolan frowned, James hadn't known where the ruins were located, and he spoke even less Arabic then the Executioner.

As he left the souk and passed into a market area of fruit and vegetable stands, Bolan pushed the troublesome thoughts from his mind. Calvin James, like all of the members of Phoenix Force, was the best. He'd be all right. The warrior had other things to worry about, other more immediate matters.

That is, if any of them expected to get out of Baghdad alive.

"GADGETS!" Lyons screamed into the mike. "Gadgets!"

Ripping off the headset, the ex-cop slammed it down on the seat of the Bronco and turned to Blancanales, saying, "He cut me off!"

Blancanales shrugged. "Don't worry. Gadgets is no Wyatt Earp. If he did, he had a reason."

Lyons flopped back against the seat and nodded. True. Schwarz wouldn't needlessly risk anyone's life, not even his own. And this wasn't the Army or the LAPD. If it was, he'd have had a junior officer hanging by the gonads for disobeying an order. In most commands leaders led followers.

But this was Stony Man.

Every member of Able Team, Phoenix Force and the other units working out of the Farm had been a leader to begin with. There wasn't a warrior among them who wasn't capable of taking the reins and making their own decisions. If they hadn't been, they wouldn't have been recruited in the first place.

At Stony Man Farm leaders didn't lead followers. Leaders led other leaders.

Blancanales broke into Lyons's thoughts. "He's a big boy, Ironman." Then, as if he'd read the ex-cop's mind and decided to demonstrate his own command capabilities, he said, "Let's get to the problem at hand."

Lyons nodded and stared at the motel across the street. "We've got to find out which room they're in."

"We can flash the Justice ID."

Lyons shook his head. "They could have slipped the desk clerk an extra fifty to keep his eyes out for something like that."

The other man shrugged. "Well, the desk isn't going to just give out their room numbers to a couple of civilians. Besides, we don't even know what names to ask for."

"Right. Best thing we can do is get a room ourselves. It'll give us a chance to check out the lobby, maybe see something that'll point the way."

"Let's *both* get rooms," Blancanales suggested. "We'll go in separately. It'll double our chances of spotting something."

"Good idea." Lyons frowned, drumming his fingers on the steering wheel as he continued to stare at the three-story motel. "If that doesn't work, we'll at least have a reason to hang out in the halls. And it's not that big a place, maybe forty, fifty rooms." He scanned the nearly deserted parking lot, then looked down at his watch. "It's early yet. Not many civilians inside. We might be able to take them down right here."

The ex-cop's trained eyes continued to study the outside of the building as he twisted the key and started the Bronco's engine. The row of windows at the bottom were half-hidden by the parking lot, meaning the first floor was subterranean.

Pulling the Bronco across the street, Lyons parked along the side of the building as a chartered bus pulled up in front of the door. "I'll go first," he said, watching a gray-haired man in his late fifties step down from the bus. "Give me ten minutes, then tell them you're looking for your business acquaintance, Mr. McFadden." He got out of the vehicle.

"Good Irish name." Blancanales grinned through the window. "I'll register as Laslo and have them ring you when I get in."

Lyons nodded. He rounded the corner and opened the door to the office, letting the gray-haired man enter first. He'd have time to check out the lobby while he waited for this guy to check in.

"Martinez," the gray-haired man said as he walked up to the desk. "Denver Philharmonic."

A youth with a pimple-covered face rose from a chair behind the counter. He smiled cockily, turning to a board filled with keys along the wall. "Yes, sir, Mr. Martinez. You're already VIP express-registered. Sixteen rooms, wasn't it?"

Martinez nodded.

The teenage desk clerk placed a registration card on the counter. "Just sign here, sir. You can park the bus around back on the hill."

The musician lifted a pen attached to a chain and scribbled on the card.

The kid handed him the keys. "Rooms 113 through 128. All downstairs. I figured you'd want them that way 'cause of your instruments and all." He beamed as if the idea had been his own and might be as important to the future of mankind as the invention of electricity.

Martinez snorted, unimpressed, grabbed the keys and left.

The kid looked a little put out as Lyons stepped forward to the counter. "Yes, sir?" he said.

"Patrick McFadden," Lyons said. "Room for one. Tonight only."

The boy nodded, reaching under the counter for another registration card. He made several *X*'s on lines to be filled out, then shoved the card across the desk. "How will you be paying, Mr. McFadden?"

Lyons pulled a credit card issued to all Stony Man personnel from his billfold and dropped it onto the counter as he picked up the pen. The raised letters on the card read simply Bakersfield Industries—a good, nondescript company that might do, or manufacture, anything, and could employ whatever names the members of Able Team happened to choose.

The ex-cop filled in the blanks on the registration card and shoved it back. "A Mr. Laslo will be joining me sometime this afternoon or evening. Give him my room number when he checks in." Behind him he heard the bus pull away.

The kid nodded and handed him the key. "Third floor. Rear of the building."

A few minutes later Lyons opened the door to room 328. He walked past the beds to the window and opened the curtains in time to see the orchestra bus park next to a semitractor-trailer below. The musicians began to get off the bus, their arms loaded with instrument cases and other luggage.

Suddenly Lyons felt the hair on the back of his neck stand up. Something was eating at him.

Two men carrying oboe cases walked below the window into the motel, and the feeling of unease increased.

Suddenly it hit him. Sixteen rooms, the orchestra had rented. But at least thirty men had gotten off the bus.

Since when did an organization like the Denver Philharmonic start making their people double up? For that matter, what was a prestigious group of musicians like this doing at an *economy* motel to begin with?

And every person who'd gotten off the bus had been a man. Why were there no women in the orchestra?

Lyons felt his eyebrows lower as his trained investigative mind went to work, covering all the angles. Okay, maybe donations, ticket sales, whatever, were at an all-time low this season. Anybody, particularly artists, could have money trouble.

And maybe there weren't any women in the orchestra because there just didn't happen to be any women in this orchestra. He'd seen a lot stranger things than that during his years as a cop.

By itself each inconsistency could probably be explained. But together the sum was far greater than the parts.

As he watched the last man leave the bus and carry a large bass case toward the entrance below, the ex-cop's eyes fell on the tiny bulge under the man's left arm.

The bulge didn't look like a concealed flute.

A knock sounded behind him. Lyons crossed the room and opened the door.

"I didn't see anything," Blancanales said as he entered the room. "You?"

"Plenty. More than I'd expected. In fact, more than either of us had counted on."

BAGHDAD HAD ALMOST recovered from the weeks of bombing. The streets had been cleared of rubble, and most of the city looked no different than it had before Iraq had invaded Kuwait.

At least on the surface.

Bolan spotted a phone booth and cut behind a vegetable stand toward the glass door. He'd tried four phones since evading the Republican Guard. In the first he could get no dial tone. In the second and third someone had ripped the receivers from the cords. And in the fourth booth the entire instrument had been removed.

The Executioner closed the door behind him and fished a handful of coins from his pocket. At a market stall several streets over he'd come across an enterprising merchant and traded several Kuwaiti bills for Iraqi dinars. He had no fear that he'd be reported.

The punishment for such a transaction was death to *both* parties.

Bolan was tempted to hold his breath and cross his fingers as he dropped a coin in the slot and lifted the receiver. He was thankful that a dial tone met his ears. Quickly entering the overseas number that would eventually lead back to Stony Man, he waited.

Bolan heard a series of clicks as the call was routed through several other countries before reaching America. Then a low, steady buzz replaced the clicks as a regulator swept the line. If any extra voltage was discovered, the connection would be automatically broken before reaching Stony Man Farm.

As he waited, Bolan watched the people moving up and down the streets outside. Most of their faces reflected a sad resignation as their feet plodded along. The blameless citizens of Iraq were as much victims of the war as the Kuwaitis. They were trying to do the best they could in a country that had been destroyed by the arrogance and insanity of one man.

The Executioner's heart went out to them. They hadn't asked for what had happened, but they'd paid the price. And they'd continue to pay for many years to come.

Finally Barbara Price's voice came over the line. "Yes?"

Bolan turned away from the street. "It's Striker."

There was a momentary pause, then an almost inaudible sigh of relief that was replaced immediately by a tone of professionalism. "Where are you, Striker?"

"In the lion's mouth," Bolan replied. "The cave of Shawiyya and his Forty Thieves."

Another pause. "You're kidding."

"Wish I was."

"Do you always have to do everything the hard way?"

"It was the only way," he said. "But there's no point wasting time with explanations. I'll tell you all about it over a beer when this is over."

Price's voice softened a little. "I'll hold you to that. What can we do on this end to make sure you *do* get back?"

Bolan gripped the receiver tighter. "What SOG groups are still on the ground in-country?"

"Officially none."

"Right," Bolan said. "See if Bear can track somebody down. A unit that could at least hide us out for a little while. Besides Katz, nobody here even speaks the language." The Executioner heard Price hit the intercom button, explain the situation to Kurtzman, then come back on the line. "Any word from Able Team?" he asked.

"They're in Pueblo, Colorado," Price replied. "Attempted bombing at a grade school. Gadgets got it diffused just in time."

Bolan gritted his teeth as a vision of schoolchildren crossed his mind. "How about Alireza?" he asked.

"We haven't heard anything." Price paused, then added, "At least she had the decency to tell us she was switching sides."

"Any idea where she might have gone?"

"Her mother lives somewhere in Baghdad, according to intel."

Bolan heard the intercom buzz again. Price said, "Yes... No... Okay," then returned to the line. "Bear made contact with a Major Steenson through Army Intelligence," she said. "Can you be at the Abbasid Palace Museum in an hour?"

"It shouldn't interrupt my social calendar too much," Bolan answered. "Who do I look for?"

"An Arab named Hasan. He'll be wearing a caftan and checkered keffiyeh."

"That fits three-fourths of the men in this town," Bolan said.

Price laughed. "He'll be looking at a collection of second-century brass work along the east wall in the last room. He'll make an unflattering comment, questioning the works' authenticity when you walk up. You'll agree and say you saw counterfeit pieces like them in Rome. You got it?"

"I got it."

"Hasan will take you to Major Steenson and his crew. But they're pretty much stuck in Baghdad, too, for the time being. They're not going to be much help getting you out."

"We'll have to see."

"Just get back here, Striker," Price said. "I'm holding you to that promise about the beer."

"Right. And thanks." The Executioner hung up.

He glanced at his watch, then opened the door and stepped out onto the sidewalk. He had just enough time to get to the ruins and meet Phoenix Force before he'd be due at the museum.

If they all safely escaped the Republican Guard, and if they all found the ancient university.

Big "ifs," he realized as he started down the street.

A SOFT BREEZE BLEW down the alley, cooling the sweat that trickled from the drenched keffiyeh and ran down Calvin James's neck. At the end of the narrow, semilit passage, past the cages of live pigeons near the street, he heard their footsteps.

James huddled lower behind the trash barrel, pressing his back against the brick wall. The footsteps neared. His hand slipped under the caftan, his fingers encircling the handle beneath the six-inch blade of the Trident fighting knife. His mind flashed briefly to his teenager years.

Navy SEAL training might have helped Calvin James refine his techniques with edged weaponry, but he'd first been introduced to the art of the blade on the streets of Chicago.

The footsteps pounded closer.

James pushed the past from his mind and drew the knife quietly, holding it close to his side to keep the stainless-steel blade from reflecting in the faint light.

The footsteps halted abruptly. Low, whispering voices drifted down the alley. James forced himself to relax, readying himself to spring. He rose slightly over the trash can, risking a look, and saw two members of the Republican Guard.

James ducked again, waiting. If two were in the alley, that meant more would be nearby, searching the streets. They'd followed him as he raced from his last hiding place behind the Iraqi Arms Museum. He'd hidden there, in another alley, after being flushed out of the café.

The voices continued. James listened. The tension built in his chest, threatening to paralyze the muscles he'd soon need to be fluid. In a moment he'd need to react rather than act, let his instincts and training see him through. Conscious thought would only slow him down. He forced his mind from the present danger, reviewing what had happened to him during the past few hours and relying on his subconscious mind to carry on.

When the jeep pulled to a halt, Calvin James had leaped to the pavement with Bolan and the rest of his teammates, firing his AK-47 as he'd fled toward a side street. He'd taken out two of the guardsmen, he knew. Maybe a third. Then he'd turned and raced down the street. Throwing a quick look over his shoulder, he'd seen the Republican Guard forces splintering into groups to chase them. And the majority of the Iraqi troops had chosen to pursue *him*.

Why?

James felt a sardonic grin cover his face. Simple. Because he was black. And it had nothing to do with prejudice or bigotry—he was just the easiest to follow. There were other blacks on the street, sure, but far fewer than lighter-skinned Arabs, and with the deep desert tans the rest of Phoenix Force had, they blended in well.

James had taken refuge first in a crowd, trying to mingle in with a group of similarity clad people in the bazaar. That had lasted all of thirty seconds, when he and the guardsmen realized at the same time that the group had only his and one other black face—and that belonged to a five-foot-one-inch woman.

From there it had been a mad dash through a residential area where he'd found temporary refuge in the garage of an abandoned house. For a moment he'd been safe.

The sounds of the fluttering pigeons resumed as the whispering in the alley stopped and the footsteps headed back toward the cages. For another moment James breathed easy again. Then another set of feet and a new voice joined the two, and the steps reversed direction again and started back toward him.

James shifted the knife into a saber grip. As soon as the guardsmen came into view, he'd spring. If he could take out these three men silently, he might still have a chance to slip through the net he knew would be on the streets.

But the men in the alley would have firearms, and to take them out with a blade would require lightning-fast movement and split-second timing.

James thought once more about his recent flight. From the garage he'd returned to the bazaar area. He'd seen no more signs of his hunters. After several tries, he'd found a shopkeeper who spoke French and had given him directions to the Mustansiriyah. James had worked his way through the crowds, then risked a bus across town.

As the bus had pulled away, he'd seen the soldiers racing toward it. Getting off a stop early had helped, but only a little. Jeeps had screeched to a halt at the bus stop as his feet had hit the ground, and there had been another mad chase through the streets, a chase that led to the café and then the museum, where he was sure he'd lost them again.

Then, with the Mustansiriyah in sight a block away, the guardsmen had appeared again.

The Mustansiriyah—so close, yet so far away.

The footsteps were just the other side of the trash can now. James rose to his haunches, ready to spring.

Suddenly he felt something jab into his ribs from the other side. He turned slowly toward the rifle barrel. Looking up, he saw a half-dozen more Republican Guards, their rifles aimed at his chest.

The man whose rifle pressed against James's side leaned forward and took the knife. Straightening, he barked, *"Kam!"*

James didn't speak Arabic, but he knew that the man wanted him to stand. Slowly he straightened his legs.

A backhanded slap split the Stony Man warrior's upper lip. The soldier stepped forward and pulled the Beretta from under James's caftan, then shoved him toward the street with the rifle.

James walked toward the end of the alley, his thoughts on how he'd survive the interrogation that was sure to follow. He had to get ready, prepare himself mentally. The soldier had yet to be born who could withstand torture forever, but he'd hold out as long as he could—at least long enough for Bolan and the others to regroup and get out of the area.

As the procession passed the chattering pigeons and left the alley, James saw a dozen men in dark caftans in front of a shop across the street. The group split in two as the Iraqis shoved him out of the alley and pointed him along the sidewalk with rifle barrels. One group hurried ahead of them, while the other cut across the street to their rear.

The tails of the men's long, checkered keffiyehs covered their faces, but there was something familiar about the way some of them moved....

As the rifle prodded him onward, James saw the men in front cut across the street, turn and start back toward them.

Suddenly the men threw back their caftans, baring AK-47s.

As James hit the sidewalk, automatic gunfire exploded over his head. Hot brass fell on his arms and legs.

The exchange lasted less than three seconds.

When he opened his eyes, Calvin James saw the bloody, battered bodies of the Republican Guard littering the sidewalk around him. He looked up to see several unfamiliar faces staring down. Then the tallest of the group stepped forward, reaching down for him.

As the man's hand grasped his arm, a light gust of wind blew the tail of his keffiyeh away from his face, and James saw the stony smile that played at the corners of the Executioner's mouth.

"OKAY, I'M CONVINCED," Blancanales said as Lyons stepped back and opened the door.

The ex-cop watched his partner enter the room. Stony Man's ace undercover man had wrapped a tool belt around his coveralls, and where the Beretta 92-F and extra mags usually hung, Pol now sported a hammer, a screwdriver and a tape measure.

"I heard what I'm pretty sure was Arabic before I knocked," he went on, "and there were four of them in the room. They backed up against their instrument cases like kids trying to hide a stray dog from their parents."

"Anything else?" Lyons asked.

Blancanales grinned and patted one of the screwdrivers. "Yeah. Their air conditioner's working fine."

Another knock sounded from outside. Lyons moved to the door and saw Schwarz through the peephole. "Sounds like you had an interesting afternoon," he told Gadgets as he swung the door back.

Schwarz nodded as he entered the room. "You guys, too. What have we got now?"

Lyons and Blancanales took chairs at the table next to the window as Schwarz dropped down on a corner of the bed. "The way I see it," Lyons began, "is Hamid had heard about both a school and a machine-gun attack here in Pueblo. He figured they were one and the same. But the UAR had two separate strikes planned."

"So if the chatterguns don't go to the school, then where?" Schwarz asked.

Lyons shrugged. "Your guess is as good as mine. But it doesn't matter. We aren't going to let them out of the building."

The two other men nodded.

A car engine sounded outside the window. Lyons looked over his shoulder and saw a dark green Nissan Maxima park near the back of the motel. A heavyset man, an equally portly woman wearing a spongy orange pantsuit and a boy and a girl in their early teens got out and began carrying luggage inside.

Schwarz walked to the window and watched them go in. "They're coming up," he said, "away from the UAR rooms."

"They still won't be safe once it hits the fan downstairs," Lyons said. "We've got to evacuate the building, then block off the exits." He stood and moved toward a suitcase on the bed. "Pol, you've already got your coveralls on. There's a maid's closet a couple of doors down. We need a laundry cart."

Blancanales left the room while Lyons and Schwarz changed into battle gear. Politician returned a moment later, pushing the cart.

Lyons and Schwarz dropped the M-16s and Atchisson Assault 12 into the cart and covered them with towels as Blancanales traded his workman's tools for the Beretta. Light raincoats went over the men's shoulders to conceal the weapons at their waists.

"We'll take care of the desk clerk and the lobby first," Lyons said. "We don't need anybody trying to check in when the bullets start flying."

The Stony Man warriors pushed the laundry cart out of the room, down the hall to the front of the building, then carried it down the stairs to the lobby.

The youth who'd been on duty earlier had been replaced by a balding, middle-aged man with heavy horn-rimmed glasses. He sat reading a gardening magazine at the desk behind the counter. His eyes, magnified behind the thick lenses, jerked up nervously as Lyons circled the counter and entered the office through a side door.

"U.S. Department of Justice," the ex-cop said, flashing his credentials. "We're going to have to evacuate the motel."

The desk clerk's bottom lip dropped open. He placed a hand on his chest and shook his head. "Oh, no," he whined. "I don't need this. What's happening? What's wrong?"

"Relax. It's nothing. I need a list of all the rooms currently occupied."

The balding man shook his head. "Oh, no. I can't possibly do that without permission from the manager. It's against all policy." He reached for the phone in front of him.

Lyons caught his wrist halfway there. "Policy has been temporarily suspended." He let go of the man's arm.

The desk clerk became indignant. "I simply *cannot* tolerate this." He reached for the phone again. "I'm calling the manager, then the police."

Lyons sighed. "We are the police. I've shown you my credentials. And given you orders. This is your last chance."

"Hmm!" the clerk said. He began tapping numbers into the phone.

Lyons turned to Schwarz. "Gadgets?" he said.

Schwarz nodded and pulled two sets of plastic cuffs from the back pocket of his coveralls.

The desk clerk's hand froze on the phone. "What are you doing? You can't—" His speech was cut off as Blancanales pulled a towel from the laundry cart and stuffed it in his mouth. He froze like a block of ice as Schwarz wrapped the cuffs around his wrists and ankles.

Lyons reached into the clerk's pocket and found a key ring. ''Take him up to the third floor, Gadgets,'' he said. ''Put him in our room, out of the way.'' He tossed the keys through the air, and Schwarz caught them. ''Then find the guy's car and bring it around front.''

Gadgets nodded. ''Sorry, buddy,'' he said as he lifted the little man into his arms like a baby. ''But it's for your own safety.''

Muffled protests came from behind the towel as Schwarz started up the stairs.

Lyons searched the desk top and found the list of occupants. ''It's still early. Only four other rooms rented so far. Two on the second floor, two on the third.'' He looked up at Blancanales. ''Take the second floor, Pol. Rooms 226 and 232. Get 'em out quiet. Tell them to wait across the street at the restaurant.''

Blancanales turned and started down the hall.

Lyons flipped a switch on the wall, and the No Vacancy sign lit up outside. He glanced over the counter to the door leading outside. Glass. Locking them might slow down an escaping terrorist, but it wouldn't stop him.

Lyons found a passkey on the rack, left the office and hurried up the stairs. He knocked on the door to room 306, and the heavyset man he'd seen in the parking lot opened the door. Flashing the Justice ID, the Able Team leader said, "I apologize for the inconvenience, sir, but we need you to go across the street to the restaurant immediately."

The teenagers and woman in the orange pantsuit crowded around the door. "What's wrong?" the man asked.

Lyons shook his head. "I can't tell you right now. Just get out."

The man nodded knowingly. "Certainly," he said. Then, his eyebrows lowering in a fraternal expression, he said, "I was in the Air Force," as if that meant he had a deep understanding of the need-to-know aspect of clandestine operations.

He led his family quietly into the hall.

Lyons turned, hurried down the hall to 315 and knocked. He heard the rustling of bed sheets inside the room, then faint whispers. Then the room went quiet.

Lyons knocked again, louder. No response.

As he slid the passkey into the lock, the ex-cop's other hand slipped under the raincoat to the grips of the suppressed Government Model Colt. He pushed the door open.

The woman screamed.

Lyons drew the pistol, the sights automatically falling on the two nude figures entangled on the bed. The woman reached down, jerking the sheet protectively to their throats. Shock and fear covered the faces of both the man and the woman.

Lyons tried to hide his smile as the woman said, "Don't kill us. Please don't kill us."

Lyons fished the credentials out of his pocket and held them up. "I hadn't planned to. I just need you to get out of the building."

The man sighed in relief and fell back against the pillow, closing his eyes. "Thank *God*," he breathed. Turning to the woman, he said, "I thought your husband had hired a hit man."

"You can discuss all this at the restaurant across the street," Lyons growled impatiently. "Get dressed and get out. Now."

The Able Team leader's tone shocked the illicit lovers back to their senses. They scrambled from the bed, hurried into their clothes and scurried from the room.

Gadgets and Politician had both returned to the lobby by the time Lyons got back. "All clear?" the ex-cop asked Blancanales.

The men grinned. "Yep. Had a couple of lovers who didn't want to be disturbed, but they got the message."

"You, too?" Lyons grunted. "Pueblo must be one swinging town." He turned toward one of the entrances and saw a six-year-old Toyota through the glass. "The clerk's?"

Schwarz nodded.

"Okay," Lyons went on. "We'll block the doors with the Bronco and Toyota. That'll leave the back entrance open." He turned to Schwarz. "So you'll cover it, and the side windows out of the rooms. Pol and I'll go down and start making the rounds."

Schwarz grabbed one of the M-16s, hid it beneath two towels and took off toward the rear of the building.

Lyons and Blancanales lifted their assault weapons from the cart. The Able Team leader backed the Toyota up against one of the glass doors as Blancanales blocked the other exit with the Bronco. They circled the building outside the motel, nodded to Schwarz at the rear exit and started down the steps to the first floor.

They were halfway down the landing when two men with AK-47s stepped out into the hall.

CHAPTER EIGHT

Angry shouts sounded from farther down the block as Bolan jerked James to his feet. Pushing the black warrior ahead of him, he sprinted after the rest of the Force as they followed Steenson's Green Berets down the street. Behind the Executioner running footsteps joined the shouts, then a rifle cracked as more UAR Republican Guards joined the chase.

"This way!" Steenson shouted as he pivoted around a corner. They cut to the left a half block, then hurried across a street into the dark mouth of another alley.

Steenson and his A-team knew Baghdad's intertwining pathways like the backs of their hands. With Bolan and company at their heels they raced through the confusing labyrinth of tangled alleys and side streets. Gradually the pursuing Iraqi soldiers fell behind.

The warriors emerged from the maze in a darkened industrial area. Rounding the corner out of an alley, they ducked past an auto body repair shop, an electrical supply outlet and a plumbing business before Steenson hurried them down a flight of concrete stairs beneath a deserted building. The major unfastened a padlock and ushered them quickly through a door that led to the basement.

Moldy straw mats covered the cracked concrete floor. More cracks honeycombed the aging plaster and lathe walls, creating an eerie spiderweb effect in the moonlight that drifted through the windows.

The Green Berets knew the drill. Without being told, two soldiers hurried through the room, pulling soiled curtains over the windows and darkening the room further. Steenson lit a lantern, and ghostly shadows danced over the cobwebs on the ceiling as the man took seats on the mats. "Davis," the major said, turning to a tall, angular man, "stand door watch."

Davis pulled the keffiyeh from his head, revealing wild, wavy brown hair. His AK-47 pointed upward, he moved back to the entrance.

Bolan walked to the center of the room and looked down at James. "I didn't get a chance to ask. You okay?"

James nodded. "Thanks."

Bolan continued to stare at the man. "Let me fill you in. Major Steenson's group has been here since the war. They don't have an underground route out of the city because they decided to stay on and create as much chaos for the UAR as possible. They've done a good job, but that doesn't help us right now. Our job is to get out and get to Eldridge." He paused, then turned to address the men as a whole, knowing what he was about to say wouldn't be popular. "We've only got one chance, guys, and that's Talia Alireza."

The Executioner had expected some dissent, and he wasn't disappointed.

Murmurs of disapproval rose quietly from the men of Phoenix Force. Bolan held up his hand for silence. "I know she's switched sides, but it's my guess she's confused." He glanced toward Steenson and said, "The major's men located her mother's house this afternoon. I'm going there now, and I want the rest of you to wait here."

THE WIND PLAYED at the tails of the Executioner's headdress as he jogged through the industrial area to the park. A city transport bus pulled up to a wooden bench on the corner, and he hurried on board.

Bolan gave the driver the fare and took a seat near the emergency exit as they pulled away. Ten blocks later the driver pulled to a halt at the edge of a residential area. The Executioner stepped down, removed Steenson's crude hand-drawn map from his pocket and started down the street.

The warrior didn't even know if Alireza was in Baghdad, let alone at this address, but he had grown to know the woman intimately during their time together, not only as a lover, but as a fellow soldier. He'd learned that Alireza was a complex combination of hard and soft, practicality and romanticism. She could be cold. She could kill without batting an eye when necessary, and the personal hardships of battle washed off her like water.

But Talia Alireza had a sentimental side, as well— the Executioner had seen it—and his gut instinct told him she'd visit her mother before entering a war from which she might not emerge.

Bolan mounted the steps to the door. As he raised his fist to knock, he heard the soft rustle of fabric behind him. Turning instinctively toward the noise, his arm rose in defense.

Stainless steel flashed under the streetlight, and a forearm crashed down into his. The eight-inch blade of a dagger stopped two inches from his face. For a lightning-fast microsecond the Executioner stared down into the hate-filled eyes of Talia Alireza.

Bolan wrapped his fingers around the woman's wrist. With a quick twist against the joint he twirled the black-cloaked figure away from him, then encircled his other arm around her waist and pulled her to him. The knife was still in her hand as he forced the blade to her throat. "I came to talk," he whispered, "not to hurt you."

"I'll kill you!" Alireza snarled.

"Someday, maybe, but not tonight."

The door behind him opened. Bolan turned sideways, pulling Alireza with him as the Desert Eagle leaped into his hand. The woman struggled in his arms as he aimed the big .44 through the opening. He lowered the weapon when he saw the sad smile on the face of the old woman in the threshold.

"Talia," Amilah Alireza said in heavily accented English. "Come in. I don't know this man, but if he wanted to kill you, you'd already be dead."

Slowly Bolan withdrew the knife from Alireza's throat and shoved the Desert Eagle back into his belt.

"She's right, you know," he said calmly. Grasping the knife by the blade, he handed it back.

Alireza grabbed the handle, refusing to look at him as she strode inside.

The old woman looked up into the Executioner's eyes. "Please come in." She waited until he entered, then pointed to a Western-style couch. Bolan took a seat and stared across the room to where Alireza had dropped into a chair. The mercenary woman's eyes still blazed in anger.

The Executioner couldn't help wondering if her rage came from her new conviction to side with the UAR, or from being disarmed by him on the porch.

"I'll fix tea," Alireza's mother said, and disappeared into another room.

Bolan looked across the room and came right to the point. "I need your help to get my men out of the country."

Alireza's expression turned to one of incredulous disbelief. She shook her head. "You Americans are amazing. Do you really find it impossible to believe that anyone can disagree with you?"

"In this instance, yes."

"I made my position perfectly clear when I severed relations with your Stony Man Farm," she said. "I haven't changed my mind again."

"I'm not convinced you ever changed it the first time," Bolan said. "You're confused, Talia."

The woman's eyes widened further. She opened her mouth, but before she could respond her mother brought in a silver tray. The old woman poured hot tea into a small glass, handed it to Bolan, then did the same for her daughter.

Taking a glass for herself, Amilah Alireza sat primly on the edge of the couch next to Bolan and looked her daughter in the eye. "I believe this man, Talia. He's good. I can sense it."

"No. I won't help him destroy more of my people."

"I haven't destroyed *any* of your people," Bolan said simply.

"The United States couldn't wait to bomb my country!" Alireza cried. "Why didn't it wait for the sanctions to work?"

Bolan stared at her. "How much longer should they have waited? The only ones hurt by the sanctions were the innocent citizens who had no say in the matter." He set his glass on the floor next to his feet. "Do you think Saddam Hussein or his family missed any meals because of the sanctions? How about Shawiyya? Jaluwi? No, the only way the sanctions would have worked would have been to starve off everyone from the bottom up."

"Nonsense!"

"Is it?" Bolan said. "Look at the facts. Even after the bombing started it would have ended the moment Iraq withdrew from Kuwait. The Iraqi government's refusal to do so is the reason the bombing went on so long. Do you really think a man who'd let that happen would have cared if the whole country eventually starved to death?"

Alireza's eyes wavered slightly. "What of the inno-cents the bombs killed?" she said through gritted teeth.

Bolan nodded. "There were some, and it's one of the most regrettable things I've ever lived through. But every effort was made to keep civilian casualties at a minimum."

"You talk of human lives as if they were no more than statistics."

"It might sound that way, and that's regrettable, too. If there were better words to express the reasoning that finally resulted in war, I'd use them. All I can tell you is that the Coalition felt it was the only way to end the matter, and that everything possible was done to prevent unnecessary casualties."

"That doesn't help the innocents who did die," Alireza snapped.

"No, it doesn't—the innocents in Iraq *and* Kuwait. But it helped a lot of Iraqis who'd have starved to death, and a lot of Kuwaitis who'd have been mur-dered."

The confusion on Alireza's face deepened. "What of the ones you've killed since then, Striker?"

"I've killed only those who tried to kill me or other allied troops," Bolan replied. "Russian Spetznaz sol-diers, Iraqi troops allied with the UAR. Terrorists."

"How nice," Alireza said sarcastically. "And what of your man Eldridge? Are you any less guilty be-cause Eldridge does your dirty—"

"Let's get something perfectly clear," Bolan interrupted. "Eldridge is not *my* man. He deserted. He's no longer under my command."

"Really? What about the nuclear weapons stolen from Israel? Does Eldridge have them?"

"I don't know, but I'll find out. I'm going after him as soon as my men can rearm."

Alireza jumped to her feet. "How am I to know that?"

Bolan stood up and walked across the room. He looked the woman in the eye. "You have my word."

Alireza opened her mouth to speak, then closed it and turned away.

A long, uneasy silence filled the room. Then Amilah Alireza turned to her daughter. "Talia?"

Alireza looked up.

"You're being naive."

The younger woman frowned.

"Do you really think Jaluwi is here to help us?" her mother asked. "Do you really think he'll be any better than Shawiyya and Saddam Hussein?" The old woman threw back her head and laughed. "The United Arab Republic! One country united, and we'll all live happily ever after!" The old woman lowered her eyes and her expression became serious. "It's been tried before, Talia. You're too young to remember. Nasser tried it before you were born in 1958. He even called his union of Egypt and Syria the United Arab Republic." She stopped. Kindness and wisdom seemed to flow from her eyes, mixed with a sadness that came from what the old woman would like to see happen, and what she knew would. "We haven't lived peacefully with one another since Abraham left Ur, Talia. Under this new United Arab Republic we'll be divided into providences. And the providences will consist of Syrians, Iraqis, Kuwaitis and Jordanians. The providences will begin to war on one another." She took a sip of her tea, then said, "I'm not saying we'll never live in peace. I'm saying we'll never live in peace under a Hitlerlike dictator such as Hamoud Jaluwi."

For several minutes the room remained silent. Alireza stared at her mother. Bolan watched the young woman's determination seep away even more.

Finally Alireza looked up into her mother's eyes, then back to the floor. Slowly she stood and left the room, returning a moment later with a suitcase.

Looking Bolan squarely in the eyes, she said bitterly, "I'll get you and your men out of Iraq. But if we meet again, and you find yourself with a knife to my throat, don't make the mistake of handing it back to me."

Bolan opened the door, then turned back to Alireza's mother. "Thank you."

Amilah Alireza smiled. She embraced her daughter, then held her at arm's length. "My dream, Talia," she said. "I now understand it."

The mercenary stared at her mother. Bolan watched, wondering what the old woman meant.

"This man is the bear who saved you, Talia."

THE FULL MIDNIGHT MOON illuminated the men seated on the parade ground and cast a weird radiance over the camp. The wind whipping across the river sent a cold chill through the air. At the desert's edge in the distance tiny, whirling tempests of sand blew toward them, dying suddenly when the miniature tornadoes hit the grassy areas closer to the water.

Colonel Joshua Eldridge halted his sermon abruptly as the trucks came rolling down the path that paralleled the river. His face remained passive, but deep within his soul he shouted praise. Turning back to the men seated below, he gripped the edge of his makeshift pulpit with both hands. "In a few moments, gentlemen," he said, "all will be revealed unto you."

The trucks came to a halt. Several of Eldridge's Twelve dropped down from the cabs and begin preparing the Multiple Launch Rocket System as the colonel's voice boomed through the night. "Let us return to the text. In Revelation 12," he shouted, "we learn that a red Dragon will appear. He'll have seven heads and ten horns." The colonel paused and looked down at the troops.

The ranks had thinned considerably since he'd begun weeding out the doubters, and there was more weeding to do. It was obvious by their reactions to tonight's sermon that many of the men still questioned his authority. Not as a colonel, but as—

Sergeant Jerry Peck suddenly caught Eldridge's eye. He frowned at the man near the rear of the huddled mass. Peck. Yes, Peck was a good example. Peck's questionnaire had been so-so, but the sergeant had agreed with Eldridge on every question the colonel had asked during his interview.

Eldridge's mood turned suddenly cold. He couldn't be fooled. Peck had simply figured out what was happening to those who didn't pass the interview. Selfish self-preservation rather than true conviction had been the motive behind the sergeant's answers.

The colonel raised his eyes, returning to the men in general. "Who can tell me what the Dragon's seven heads represent?" he asked.

Silence came from the men. Finally one of his Twelve near the front raised a hand. "Iraq, of course," he said. "Syria, Lebanon, Jordan and—"

"Iran!" another of Eldridge's disciples shouted. "Yemen and Oman!"

"And Saudi Arabia!" another yelled.

Eldridge nodded. "And the ten horns?"

Lieutenant Ferguson, the colonel's most trusted of the twelve, stood in the center of the crowd. "The same seven!" he shouted. "The countries who have joined the United Arab Republic! And the three who are leaning toward it. Libya, and the United Arab Emirates!"

Eldridge frowned. All of the answers were coming from his Twelve Disciples. The rest of the men were shifting uneasily, like Peck. His eyes darted again to the sergeant, who stared out into the desert.

Eldridge went on. "The woman of whom I spoke earlier will bear a child!" he shouted into the wind. "The Dragon will prepare to eat the child, but the woman will flee into the wilderness." He paused for effect. "And who is this Dragon?"

"Satan!" half a dozen voices shouted. "The Serpent!"

"The boy will grow into a great ruler of nations," Eldridge went on. "Who is the boy?"

"The Antichrist!" his Twelve chorused.

Eldridge's voice softened for effect, the way he'd heard his father lower his speech so many times at the tent meetings. "Then, in the thirteenth chapter," he said, "we learn that some of God's own people are destined for death during these times. Who are God's people?"

"We are!"

"Are you afraid?"

Again there was no response from the men in general. But in one robotlike voice the Twelve shouted, "No!"

Eldridge's frown deepened. His disciples were doing fine, but the rest of the men still weren't joining in. He realized sadly that only the Twelve he'd chosen originally were true believers.

Eldridge felt a sob threaten to burst from his chest. He sighed, too low to be heard. The Lord had always said there would be more nonbelievers than believers. "Woe to you people of the world," he said, hoping the scripture might fall on at least one ear and convert it, "for the devil has come to you in great anger, knowing that he has little time!"

He got no response.

"Lightning and thunder will issue forth from the throne of God!" Eldridge shouted. He turned toward the rocket launchers and held his breath. Perhaps when they saw the rockets the damned would repent. If they didn't, they'd join the other Sons of the Serpent in shallow graves in the desert.

Letting out his breath, Eldridge cried, "Turn! Turn and see the fire that will rain down from the heavens!" As the men's heads turned to the trucks, Eldridge heard the gears of the MLRS grate.

The launchers began to raise the nuclear rockets.

"See the glory of God!" Eldridge screamed into the stillness of the night. "See the fire that we will rain down on the heathen of the earth to start the New World!"

The launchers ground to a halt. Pointed toward the heavens, the massive nuclear warheads on the nose cones gleamed under the stars.

INSIDE THE TENT the lantern light flickered over the frightened faces of three men. Sergeant Jerry Peck listened to the wind whistle outside the tent, the horror of what he'd seen just ten minutes earlier still etched in his mind. He watched the canvas tent flap flutter back and forth. The irregular vacillation reminded him of his brain.

Should he try to escape this madness before it was too late? If he tried, and was caught, he'd be executed.

Peck turned back to the two men seated across from him. Both were Green Berets, damn it, just like him. The best of the best.

But also, like him, they were scared.

"What are we going to do, Jerry?" Wimpy Harrison whispered. The dull lights in the tent formed deep shadows around the huge hump in the bridge of Harrison's nose. Wimpy had been the top contender, scheduled to fight Reno McCarty for the Army's heavyweight crown before the war had broken out.

Wimpy Harrison wasn't afraid of anything. Except this.

Peck shook his head. "I don't know," he said flatly. "We're in a fix."

To Wimpy's side Don Franklin snorted. "Begging your pardon, Jerry, but that's the understatement of the year. The century. Or maybe, under the circumstances, I should say the millennium."

Peck studied the man. He was small, wiry. A different kind of warrior than Wimpy, Franklin had barely passed the rigorous physical tests that qualified him for Special Forces. He was a thinker, though, and his insight into human nature more than made up for any physical mediocrity.

But so far the "brain" of the unit hadn't solved the problem, either.

"What are we going to do?" Wimpy repeated.

"The answer's simple," Franklin answered. "We've got to get out of here. It's the practical application of that knowledge that's hard."

"I don't understand all that stuff Eldridge keeps saying," Wimpy said, shaking his head. "I mean, I know it's from the Bible. I went to Sunday school when I was a kid. But—"

"Oh, it's from the Bible, all right," Franklin interrupted. "But it's a sick, twisted version of Scriptures." He smiled at the larger man like a kindly grandfather. "What Eldridge has done, Wimpy, is take isolated verses from the Book of Revelation and make them fit into his paranoid delusions."

Peck nodded. "The Bible doesn't tell you to try to blow up the world, Wimpy," he whispered. "Whatever that is that Eldridge is spouting, it's *not* Christianity."

"It certainly isn't," Franklin agreed. "All three of the legitimate religions that began in this region of the world—Judaism, Christianity and Islam—they all have prophecies about the end of the world as we know it now. But none of them tell their followers to go get the end started. That's left up to God." Franklin stared into the glow of the lantern. "Eldridge isn't a Christian. He's a madman."

Peck shook his head and leaned over his side, resting his elbow on the ground and cupping his head with his hand. "What I don't understand is how he's gotten so many men to go along with him."

Franklin shook his head. "I don't think he has," he said. "I imagine most of the men—besides Eldridge's staff—are wondering how to get out of here, just like us. And what's happened to his Twelve Disciples is fairly easy to figure out."

Peck listened. Wimpy frowned, confused.

"Some of those men never believed in anything before," Franklin went on. "For the first time in their lives they've got answers to their questions about God, the universe... all the things mankind has struggled with since time began. However warped and errone- ous Eldridge's philosophy might be, the men who had nothing... at least now they've got something."

Wimpy shook his head in frustration. "So what are we going to do?"

Before either Peck or Franklin could answer, a dark shadow suddenly stepped through the tent flap into the light. Peck, Franklin and Harrison jerked toward the intruder like little boys caught raiding the icebox af- ter bedtime.

"Sergeant Peck," Lieutenant Ferguson said, "Colonel Eldridge needs to see you. Be in his tent in thirty minutes."

Peck nodded. "Yes, sir, Lieutenant."

Ferguson disappeared once more.

Peck crawled to the flap and looked through to make sure the man had really left. Returning to the lantern, he glanced from Harrison to Franklin. "That settles it. I thought I'd pulled the wool over his eyes, but it looks like I was wrong. And we all know what happens on those one-way trips into the desert." He took a deep breath. "It's cut and run for this GI."

Wimpy's mouth fell open. "You're going to de- sert?" he whispered.

"It's not desertion. Not under these circum- stances," Franklin said. "Besides, I've got a feeling we're already deserters—all of us."

"What do you mean?" Peck asked.

Franklin shrugged. "Think about it. Everybody knew that Eldridge and Colonel Pollock were having problems. Then Pollock got called back to Washington, or wherever he went. As soon as he was gone, Eldridge passed out the questionnaire, and the next thing you know he's got a new staff, people are disappearing and we're running guerrilla strikes through southern Iraq. Eldridge left the compound virtually defenseless. Does that sound like a man who intended ever to go back?" He didn't wait for an answer. "And these search-and-destroys of the villages. Women, children, harmless old men. Have you ever been ordered to kill them before?"

"I didn't do it," Peck said.

"Me, neither," Wimpy agreed. "I couldn't."

"I didn't, either," Franklin said. "I don't think anybody did—except the Twelve. And what about the missiles? Israeli nukes? Give me a break. If all this was U.S.-sanctioned, we've got plenty of nukes of our own. Why steal from the Israelis?"

"It doesn't make sense," Peck agreed. "Unless you're right. Eldridge is the one who deserted. And he took us with him." He stared down at his watch. "I've got to get going. My only chance is to get a head start. Get somewhere and hide."

Wimpy Harrison stood. "I'm going with you, Sarge."

Franklin nodded. "It's only a matter of time before the colonel gets around to us."

Without further discussion the three men gathered their gear and moved to the tent flap.

Lanterns glowed inside the other tents encircling the parade ground. Soft, worried whispers drifted through the flaps. Silently Peck led the other two men away from the rocket launchers and toward the river.

A beam of light suddenly hit Peck in the face as they reached the perimeter of the camp. Lieutenant Ferguson stepped out of the shadows. "Halt!" he ordered, raising a flashlight in one hand, an M-16 in the other.

Peck stopped in his tracks. "Just heading to the latrine before I go see the colonel, Lieutenant."

"The latrine's over there," Ferguson growled, indicating the other side of the camp with his head.

Harrison stepped forward. "Hey, guy?" he whispered.

Ferguson turned toward him.

The ex-boxer's left fist hooked through the air, cracking against the lieutenant's jaw like a pistol shot. The flashlight and M-16 fell to the ground, followed by Ferguson.

"Let's go!" Franklin whispered urgently.

The three men took off toward the riverbank. Behind them they heard excited voices.

A rifle shot pierced the night air, and the big heavyweight went down as if he'd been hit by George Foreman.

Peck flew forward, struggling to the cover of the bulrushes at the river's edge. A volley of rounds blew past him, slapping wetly into the mud. Behind him he heard a scream. He looked over his shoulder to see Franklin fall facedown.

The sergeant's lungs threatened to burst as he slid through the mud along the bank. He slipped, fell and struggled back to his feet. He heard boots pounding after him in pursuit.

Peck continued to slosh through the mud, frantically trying to distance himself from his pursuers. His heart pounded like a jackhammer inside his chest, and he wondered briefly if it were from the exertion, the fear of being caught or the horror he knew still remained at the Special Forces camp.

For the first time in years Peck called upon the God he'd been introduced to as a child. "Lord, please!" he mumbled as he slipped and fell facedown in the mud again. "Please help me! Get me out so I can warn somebody!"

And God heard him.

IN ONE SMOOTH MOVEMENT Lyons drew the suppressed .45 from his shoulder holster and squeezed the trigger twice, firing from the hip.

The first 230-grain hardball caught a UAR fighter between the breastbones. The man grunted, dropping his AK-47 and clutching his chest with both hands as he fell to the floor of the motel hall.

Lyons's second round smashed into the side of the other man, spinning him around and into the wall. Blood splattered across the white Sheetrock as the terrorist struggled to turn back. A third .45 round hammered through the man's spine into his heart.

The ex-cop hurried down the stairs, Blancanales at his heels. A bearded man appeared in the hall, looking down at the man on the floor as the Able Team warriors neared the open door to the room. "Abdul," he said, *"Ashshane eh . . . ?"* He glanced up in time to catch Lyons's fourth round in the nose.

Lyons let the .45 lead the way into the room. He checked the bathroom and closet—both empty—while Blancanales dragged the men inside and closed the door.

"Wherever the strike is supposed to be," Politician whispered, "they're getting ready to go now."

Lyons nodded. "Any other movement in the hall?"

Blancanales shook his head.

"Good. That means they haven't heard us yet . . . maybe." He ejected the partially spent magazine from the Colt and rammed a full load into the grip. "We'll do a door-to-door, Pol. Let's get by on the spitter as long as we can. But you stay ready with the noisemaker just in case."

Blancanales grinned. "Who knows? Maybe we'll get lucky for once." They moved back to the hall door. "You know the old saying—God watches over drunks and Stony Man fools."

"Yeah," Lyons said as he grasped the doorknob. "Just don't forget Murphy's Law."

"Is Murphy a burned-out old cop like you?" Blancanales asked as Lyons opened the door.

"A *realist* like me." Lyons led his partner silently along the carpet to the next room, knocked on the door, then stepped out of view of the peephole.

Blancanales stood almost against the door, shielding his weapons and other combat gear from the occupant.

"Who is it?" a voice asked from inside.

"Manager," Blancanales replied, smiling.

A chain lock slid back and the door opened. Lyons bent around the frame and shoved the suppressor into the chest of a man in khaki pants and a white dress shirt. He pulled the trigger twice, then pushed the terrorist back into the room and fired twice more.

Another pair of terrorists in the process of changing from "musician" clothing to combat gear fell to the floor.

"Our luck's holding," Blancanales whispered as they moved to the next room.

"Or running out." Lyons knocked again.

This time the gray-haired man who had handled the check-in answered the door. The ex-cop pumped two .45s into him point-blank.

As he shoved the UAR man back into the room, a figure suddenly lunged from the bathroom just to the right of the door. Fingers wrapped around Lyons's wrist, trying to twist the .45 from his grip. A voice screamed, *"Ezzedine! Yisa'id!"*

Lyons saw two men next to the beds lunge for AK-47s against the wall. As he struggled to free the .45, he felt Blancanales drive a shoulder into his back. He sprawled to the floor on top of the terrorist as a blast of gunfire ripped over his head. Hot, empty brass showered down onto his back. He sent a fist pummeling down into the screaming face beneath him, then rolled off the man and looked up in time to see the other two terrorists fall under Politician's barrage.

A door opened in the hall behind the Able warriors.

Lyons sprang to his feet and raced back to the hallway. Risking a glance around the corner, he saw more half-dressed terrorists racing through doors. He jumped back as one of the men spotted him and cut loose with a steady stream of 7.62 mm stingers from his AK-47.

Lyons heard more automatic fire—smaller caliber—burst from the end of the hall. He counted down from three, then swung the Atchisson 12-gauge into the hall and cut loose with a 3-round burst of triple-aught buck. At the top of the stairs leading to the back exit he saw Schwarz put the finishing touches on his rear assault.

Blancanales pushed past him and raced to a door on the other side of the hall, Lyons moving to the room adjacent to the one they'd just left. He lifted his leg, kicked and heard Blancanales do the same behind him.

The ex-cop's foot sent the metal trim flying from the frame. As the door swung open, he dropped to one knee, saturating the room with 12-gauge shot. Two more UAR gunners fell to the carpet in bloody shreds.

Politician's assault rifle burped steadily across the hall as Lyons hurried to check the bathroom and closet, then raced to the next room on his side. As he prepared to kick, a door opened at the end of the hall and a terrorist in desert cammies leaped into the hall, firing.

Lyons dived to the floor beneath the assault, rolled to his side and tapped the trigger. Three loads of shot erupted from the Atchisson's barrel, nearly cutting the

UAR man in two. Rising quickly to all fours, the Able leader drove his shoulder through the door, rolling to a halt next to the bathroom. Autofire again sailed over his head. Another triple-tap from the Atchisson left two more half-dressed terrorists staining the light blue motel room carpet a deep, wet purple.

Blancanales was kicking in another door by the time Lyons returned to the hall. The ex-cop hurdled the bodies and assault rifles that littered the ground as he raced on along the corridor. Driving his foot into the wood just below the lock, he crouched low, the 12-gauge ready.

The room was empty. But it hadn't been. The curtains around the open window blew lazily in the breeze.

Lyons turned to Schwarz at the top of the stairs. "Gadgets!" he shouted, pointing into the room. "The parking lot!"

Schwarz turned on his heel and raced out of the building.

The Able Team leader kicked in the final door on his side of the hall. A swarm of 7.62 mm "bees" flew out of the room, one round ripping through the sleeve of Lyons's coveralls. He jumped to the side of the door, his back against the wall, as the barrage continued.

Taking a deep breath, the ex-cop hooked his thumb inside the trigger guard and stuck the Atchisson into the doorway. Moving the weapon back and forth, he fired blindly, spraying the room. The gunfire inside the room stopped abruptly.

Lyons leaned around the edge of the doorway. Two men lay sprawled on the floor.

Blancanales had just entered the last room on his side of the building when Lyons got back to the hallway. The Able Team leader started after him, then heard a door opening at the other end of the hall.

A man wearing cammie pants and a white undershirt scampered from the room and headed toward the stairs leading to the lobby. Lyons turned toward the fleeing man, kicking himself mentally. They'd started their door-to-door assault at the room from which the first men had emerged, forgetting there was another room just below the stairs. Lifting the Atchisson, he tapped the trigger.

The terrorist disappeared up the steps, the 12-gauge round gouging a hole in the wallboard next to the stairs. Lyons raced after the man. He took the steps three at a time, leaping into the lobby just as the UAR man reached for the glass door held firm by the Toyota. He squeezed the trigger again, and the shotgun roared in the small room. Twelve-gauge buckshot tore through the back of the terrorist's white shirt. Several of the pellets sailed wide, shattered the door and sent a thunderstorm of glass down over the man as he slumped to the floor of the lobby.

Suddenly the motel was as quiet as the graveyard it had become.

Lyons descended the steps and walked back down the hall to where his teammates stood waiting. He started to speak, then the loud wail of sirens approaching from a distance stopped him.

The Able Team leader turned to his two men. "Either one of you in the mood to explain all this to the locals?"

Schwarz grinned. "Not us."

"Then let's get out of here."

They hurried up the back steps to the Bronco.

CHAPTER NINE

Late night became early morning. The moisture in the air vanished as the station wagon cruised down the barren, bombed-out road, moving deeper into the desert.

Even with the air-conditioning in the station wagon a thin coat of sweat covered Talia Alireza's body. The little 410 shotgun-derringer in the garter holster had begun to chafe the tender skin between her thighs. Gingerly she shifted her legs.

The woman watched a cloud drift across the moon as she guided the vehicle west toward Jordan. Here and there the road was still blocked by rubble, and she'd be forced to leave the road, relying on the men in the back seat to push the station wagon through the sand until they could return once more to the pitted blacktop.

The woman glanced into the rearview mirror and saw the warriors in the two back seats. In some ways the tough road had been a blessing in disguise. It gave her a reason to bring six strong men with her, and lent some small credence to the story that she was transporting top-secret UAR documents to Amman.

Outside the tightly rolled windows the desert wind howled. A sudden gust blew sand across the windshield. Alireza slowed the station wagon, steering blindly through the storm until visibility cleared again. As she picked up speed, her eyes drifted to her side where the man she knew as Striker sat, his eyes closed.

Alireza felt an immediate surge of desire flow through her. Her jaw clamped shut in anger, she forced herself to turn back to the highway.

Another checkpoint appeared in the distance. Alireza glanced again at the man at her side. His eyes were still closed. She slowed the station wagon, rolling down the window as the Iraqi-UAR soldier stepped down from the guard shack onto the shoulder of the highway.

Alireza picked up the stack of forged passports and the orders she'd gotten from an old Mossad acquaintance still in Baghdad. It had been a rush job, and a favor to boot, and she wondered again just how realistic the documents would appear to the trained eye.

Beneath the barrier of the station wagon door Alireza's hand moved between her legs to the grips of the American derringer. The soldier walked forward, carrying a clipboard and an AK-47. Alireza waited, forcing herself to look calm. The papers had passed muster at the checkpoint at the outskirts of Baghdad but the nearer they got to the border, the more closely they'd be scrutinized.

The solder leaned down, resting a forearm through the open window. Behind him Alireza saw two dozen other men watching the station wagon, their hands on the pistol grips of their assault weapons.

"State your business," the guard ordered in Arabic, his eyes darting from Bolan to the men in the back seat.

Alireza shoved her orders into his hand. "Transportation of documents," she said briskly.

The man studied the letter. "Let me see the documents."

Alireza shook her head. "Impossible. Read closer. They're classified, and you don't have clearance."

The soldier stiffened. Alireza repressed a smile. While Iraq hadn't hesitated to use all of its human resources, male and female, during the Gulf War, women were new in the combat zones. The soldier's resentment exemplified that of many who weren't accustomed to taking orders from a female.

"Who are these men?" he asked gruffly.

Alireza let the smile show through. "You don't think our government would entrust classified material to a woman without protection, do you?" She saw the man relax slightly. "Besides," she said coyly, "I'm hardly strong enough to dig the car out of the sand when we're forced to leave the road."

Her helplessness seemed to appeal to the soldier's manliness. He laughed. Stepping back, he waved them through.

Bolan's eyes opened as soon as they were out of sight of the guard shack. "You handled that well."

The woman didn't answer.

Thirty miles from the Jordanian border Alireza saw the narrow road leading south. She pulled the station wagon to a halt on the shoulder, turned and rested her arm on the back seat. "From here on our orders will do us no good if we're stopped. They state that we're going to Jordan, and only a fool would leave the highway and accidentally take this side road. Certainly not someone who has been entrusted with important papers.

"We should be in Saudi Arabia in two hours," she went on, "unless we encounter a border patrol. They aren't known for either patience or leniency. I suggest you try to get in the first shot."

Bolan's words cut through her like a razor. "We need to know something. If that happens, will you be shooting with us or at us?"

Alireza turned to stare him in the eye. "I don't know," she said honestly. She threw the station wagon into drive, crossed the road and started down the sandy path.

The sun had risen high in the sky by the time they crossed the rickety bridge and doubled back across the winding Wadi Hawrun. Alireza saw Bolan look down at the map in his lap. "Should be less than ten miles now," he said.

The station wagon slowed, topped a hill, and suddenly they saw the Iraqi tanks and jeeps parked on both sides of the road.

Bolan leaned forward. "Floor it!" he yelled. His boot shot across the front seat onto hers, smashing her foot down on the accelerator. The station wagon coughed, sputtered, then fishtailed forward through the camp.

As she regained control of the wheel, Alireza looked up into the mirror. A half-dozen men jumped into three jeeps behind her.

"Get ready," Bolan commanded his men as Alireza guided the vehicle through a precarious series of twists in the road.

Katz rolled down the rear window of the station wagon. He and James extended their rifle barrels through the opening. McCarter and Manning leaned out of the vehicle, their AK-47s primed and ready.

The gunfire from the jeeps began as they topped another hill. Streams of 12.7 mm machine gun rounds flew from the weapon mounted in the lead vehicle. Alireza trod harder on the accelerator as she saw Bolan lean out his window to return fire.

Suddenly Alireza heard a loud pop, then her world began to spin like a carnival ride out of control. She felt her arms leave the steering wheel. Her mind whirled as images of Bolan and the others flashed past.

Then all went black.

The next thing she knew, Bolan was tugging her arm, dragging her out of the overturned station wagon as the firing continued around her. The big Stony Man warrior lifted her in his arms and ran, dropping her on the other side of the car.

Still dazed, Alireza saw Bolan rise over the chassis, heard the chatter of his AK-47. Struggling to her knees, she pulled the Bernadelli 9 mm pistol from her belt and stared down the road.

Bolan continued to fire. The jeep with the machine gun fishtailed off the pathway, and then it, too, overturned.

Forty yards back up the road the men of Phoenix Force rose suddenly from the sand. They fired from both sides of the road into the two jeeps following. The Iraqis jerked and gyrated in the vehicles as they were shredded by the combined firepower of the Phoenix team.

The Executioner reached down to take Alireza's arm, but she shook him off. For a moment their eyes met.

Bolan hurried to the jeeps where his men were already throwing the bodies to the side of the road. "Get in!" he ordered. "There'll be others coming any minute."

Alireza's legs were unsteady as she rose to her feet. She watched Bolan slide behind the wheel as the others climbed in. Slowly she raised the Bernadelli.

Their eyes met again.

The merc felt as if she'd been poked with a stun gun as the electricity coursed through her. She lowered the weapon.

"Come with us," Bolan urged.

Alireza stared at him. She felt the warmth, the compassion that exuded from the man. However erroneous the American's ideals might be, *he* was good, and she fought the voice in her heart that screamed to her, told her to jump into the jeep, race across the border into Saudi Arabia and change sides once again.

"Come with us, Talia."

"No."

Bolan threw the jeep into gear. Alireza stepped to the side of the road. Sand flew from the tires as the jeep raced past, Bolan's gaze still locked onto hers.

BARBARA PRICE WATCHED Kurtzman through the glass divider between the comm center and intel room. Seated atop his work platform, the computer genius let his fingers fly across the keyboard. Since the attack on Stony Man that had rendered his legs useless so long ago, the computer had taken over even more of Kurtzman's world than it had previously.

Price smiled faintly, continuing to watch Kurtzman as she moved through the door in the glass. Bear's hair was soaked in sweat, his eyes pasted to the screen.

Mounting the wheelchair ramp, Price came to a halt behind Kurtzman. Over his shoulder she saw the words ACCESS DENIED flash onto the screen.

With a sigh he hit the Enter button and the screen cleared. He began to type again.

Price placed her hands on his shoulders, feeling the tense muscles at the base of his neck. "Good *night,* Aaron," she said. "Your shoulders feel like petrified rope." She began a gentle massage.

Kurtzman's fingers never wavered as he pounded the keyboard. "I'll give you exactly three and a half days to stop doing that."

Price chuckled. "You look as if you've been through the wringer. Broken into Jordan yet?"

"Can't say that I— Whoa...wait a minute...." He cleared the screen again. "I know what's wrong...."

The computer wizard's fingers flew too fast for Price to follow. But whatever he entered, it worked.

SECURITY STAGE ONE: CLEARANCE ACCEPTED appeared on the screen.

"What's that mean?" she asked.

"It means we sit here and wait for about five minutes while they try to backtrack through the line to make sure it's a friendly country that's come calling."

"What'll they find?"

Kurtzman twisted in his chair and grinned up at her. "Iran," he said. "Let's get some more coffee while we wait. He wheeled his chair around Price, rolled down the ramp into her office and stopped in front of the coffee maker. He was pouring into her cup when Price heard the teletype click on.

The Stony Man controller took the cup and hurried to the machine as the computer paper began rolling out. Leaning forward, she said, "Terrorist strike. Cowboy Hall of Fame, Oklahoma City."

The machine didn't stop.

Price waited as more lines crept from under the roller. "The *Mississippi Belle*. A riverboat. My God, they're machine-gunning tourists and throwing them into the river."

"Where's Able Team?" Kurtzman said. "Still in Colorado?"

Price nodded. The machine halted, and she tore off the teletype and set it on her desk. One of Kurtzman's assistants would pick it up later and add it to the disk files. "Able ran into more UARs than they'd been led to expect," she said. "A motel. They—" She halted in midsentence as the teletype began to click again.

Machine-gunning—Busch Gardens, Tampa, FL.

Bomb explosion—Boot Hill, Dodge City, KS.

Machine-gunning—Pacific Science Center, Seattle, WA.

Beneath each of the three notifications were the words "UAR suspected."

"They're at it again," Price said as the reports continued to roll in. "The strikes are synchronized to the second." She turned to Kurtzman, her hands on her hips. "Where's their communications center, Aaron?"

Kurtzman shook his head. "I don't know. I'll get back on it as soon as I'm done with the Jordan files." He ran a hand through his hair. "Any chance of getting Able to any of those sites in time?"

Price shook her head. "From Pueblo? Even Dodge City's at least an hour, figuring takeoff, landing. We'll just have to hope the Feds and locals..." She let her voice trail off, then said, "What the hell. We might as well *try* Dodge." She hurried to the radio.

Price keyed the mike. "Stony Man to Able One," she said. "Stony Man to Able One. You copy, Able One?" She let up on the button.

A moment later Carl Lyons's voice came on the air. "Able One, Stony. Go ahead."

Behind his voice Price heard the roar of a moving engine. "Ten-twenty, One?" she asked.

"Highway 50. About eight miles east of Pueblo— we're almost back to the airport. What have you got?"

"All hell's broken loose again. Simultaneous strikes are going on all over the country. I'll ten-five Mott, have him get ready to lift off. The only strike you're close enough to is—" Price halted in midsentence as the teletype clicked on once more. "Stand by, Able," she said, and hurried back to the machine.

Houston, TX—Sam Houston Coliseum.

Louisville, KY—Churchill Downs.

Colorado Springs, CO—Broadmoor Hotel.

The Stony Man controller ripped the paper from the machine and lunged back to the microphone. "You're on your way to Colorado Springs, Able. The Broadmoor. I'll get the exact ten-twenty and pass it on to Mott and handle air clearance. Further advice when you're in the air."

"Affirmative, Stony Man. Able One out."

"Stony Man clear."

Kurtzman had already wheeled into place in front of Price's computer. A page from the Colorado Springs phone book appeared on the screen. "The Broadmoor," he said. "One Lake Circle." He pressed more buttons, and a map of the city replaced the page. "South part of town. Just north of the zoo. Tell Mott to follow I-20 north, northwest, and stay low. He should be able to spot it from the air." Killing the screen, he wheeled back through the doorway into his office.

Price keyed the mike, got Mott on the air and relayed the information.

"Ten-four, Stony Man," the ace flyer said. "I can see Able Team pulling off the highway right now."

Releasing the mike, Price sat back and took a deep breath. For the next fifteen minutes or so, until Lyons, Schwarz and Blancanales reached Colorado Springs, she'd have nothing to do—the part of her job that drove her crazy. Jumping to her feet, she hurried into the intel room.

The muscles in Kurtzman's shoulders had relaxed when she placed her hands on them again. She looked up at the computer. ACCESS AUTHORIZED now flashed on and off at the bottom of the screen. A moment later a file appeared in tiny letters.

Moving to the side, Price saw Kurtzman frown as his eyes scanned the lines. "Jaluwi *did* spend some time in Jordan," he mumbled. "Right after the fake assassination. But then he left, and it doesn't say anything about where he went. Let's try..." He tapped more keys, cleared the screen, then tapped again.

"Any info on how they faked the assassination?"

Kurtzman shook his head as more letters appeared. He continued to type. "No, but there are any number of ways it could have been done. A good sniper. Dummy explosion mounted in his cheek. It doesn't matter. What does matter is that it reeks of KGB assistance."

"We knew that."

Kurtzman nodded. "Yep." He paused, smiling as the screen lit up once more. "South America. Rio. Guess Jaluwi wanted to get a suntan during his recovery period. But we're at another dead end, damn it."

"What can you do?"

Kurtzman shrugged. "Tap into Brazilian networks. Immigration, tourism, the like. It won't be as hard as the intelligence systems, but once I'm in it'll be like looking for the proverbial needle in the haystack."

Price nodded. Patting her friend on the shoulder, she turned back to the door.

As she entered her office, the teletype kicked on again.

THE LIGHTS OF THE CITY and the bright three-quarter moon cast a spectacular radiance over the area surrounding Colorado Springs. As Able Team floated through the air, Lyons saw the purple-hued Rocky Mountains set against a royal blue, star-filled sky. The crisp air gradually warmed as he continued toward the ground. Directly below the descending warriors lay the Broadmoor Hotel.

"Able One to Stony Man," Lyons said into his headset mike. "Got an update for us?"

"Affirmative," Price's words came back. "Several SWAT teams have already converged. They've driven most of the UAR force inside the main building. A few terrorists are holed up in the pro shop on the south golf course."

"Got a total number of the enemy?"

"Approximately fifty to sixty, by most counts. Six confirmed kills."

"Ten-four." Lyons looked down at the grounds around the huge, sprawling hotel at the foothills of the mountain. Tennis courts, golf courses and a riding stable became discernible as he continued to drop through the air. In the center of the oval drive in front of the main entrance stood a well-lit lawn and garden, and as they neared, Lyons saw the scattered specks of bodies—cops and civilians—who had already fallen to the guns of the United Arab Republic.

"Able Two and Three," Lyons said into the mike.

"Go ahead," both men replied.

"Gadgets, steer toward the south golf course," Lyons directed. "Check out the pro shop, then make your way toward the hotel. Pol, land as close to the front entrance as you can, but not so close that you take any bullets."

"I'll keep that uppermost in my mind."

"I'm going to land on the roof and make my way down through the floors. We'll meet and regroup in thirty minutes in the Golden Bee."

"Where and what's a Golden Bee?" Schwarz asked.

"An English pub-type place downstairs."

"How do we find it?"

"Read the signs in the halls," Lyons said dryly.

As his chute neared the Broadmoor's roof, the sporadic sounds of rifle and machine gun fire drifted up into the sky. Lyons pulled down on the canopy toggle, steering toward one of the flat areas of the multi-tiered hotel. A sudden gust of wind shot him over the edge, away from the building. He reversed his pull, but the chute dropped past the roof and he started down along the edge of the wall.

Lyons tugged harder, crabbing the chute at a forty-five-degree angle to the wind. Sailing back over a balcony that jutted from the fourth floor, he reached up and released the suspension lines.

The chute sailed back up into the air, the black nylon disappearing against the sky as Lyons dropped to the balcony floor. Swinging the Atchisson into assault mode, the ex-cop slid open the sliding glass door from the balcony. A stifled shriek met him as he burst into the living room of an elaborately decorated suite. An elderly man stood in the center of the room with one arm around his wife's shoulders, his hand clasped over her mouth.

Lyons smiled. "Relax. I'm one of the good guys."

The man dropped his arms. "Thank God," he whispered as the woman began to sniffle.

"Any activity this high up yet?" Lyons asked as he crossed the room to the hall door.

The man shook his head. "I don't think so. Some running in the halls, but I think it was just people trying to get back inside their rooms."

Lyons nodded. Slowly he opened the door and looked out into the hall. Clear. Turning back, he said, "Lock the door behind me and stay put." Not waiting for an answer, he moved cautiously into the hall, the Atchisson leading the way. "Able One to Two and Three," he whispered into the headset as he moved toward an elevator sign that pointed down an adjoining hallway. "You copy?"

"Affirmative," Schwarz replied. "I'm about a hundred yards east of the pro shop. Gathering up my chute now. Some firing at and around the building.

More on the other side of the lake at the riding stable. SWAT has it under control.''

"Then let it be. Start making your way toward the hotel." Lyons cleared his throat. "Pol, you on the ground yet?"

Static ground through the headset into his ears as Lyons relased the mike. Then the noise cleared and the Able Team leader heard the sounds of automatic fire over the waves.

"I've landed," Pol said. "But I'm pinned down—" Lyons heard the sound of his M-16 chattering on full-auto "—just outside the main entrance. It might take a little while to get to you."

Lyons stopped at the corner, hearing approaching footsteps. Instinctively he stuck out a foot as a flash of desert camouflage rounded the corner. A man holding a submachine gun stumbled, the weapon flying from his fists to the floor as he rolled.

Cop or terrorist? Lyons made the decision in a heartbeat. Dark features, beard, brown *desert* cammies rather than blue SWAT or gray urban camouflage fatigues. But the real giveaway was the subgun itself.

Lyons didn't know many American police departments who issued their officers Chinese Type 64 silenced submachine guns.

The ex-cop pulled the shotgun's trigger as the terrorist lunged for the fallen 64. A lone shell of buckshot caught the UAR gunner in the side of the face, ending his participation in the assault.

The Able Team leader looked around the corner and down the hall. The man had been alone. Moving back down the corridor to the body, he ripped the desert camou fatigue blouse from the man's chest and draped it around his shoulders. He was taking a chance, he knew, of being shot by the "good guys." But the garment could come off at a second's notice, and the cops were more likely to take time to ID their targets than a bunch of half-crazed terrorists.

Passing the elevator, Lyons opened the door to the stairs. On the landing below he heard voices. Schwarz's story about the Mexican boy at the Pueblo school came back to him. The Able Team leader didn't know what language the men on the stairs were speaking, but it sure wasn't Spanish.

Peering over the railing, he saw two men, the same brown-and-tan cammies. One faced up the stairs, the other down.

Lyons pulled the camouflage blouse tighter around his shoulders and started down the steps, making no effort to conceal his footsteps. The terrorists looked up. Seeing the desert cammies, they smiled.

The smiles had already started to fade as Lyons squeezed the trigger. A 12-gauge blast struck the nearest man square in the chest, blowing him across the landing and into his partner. Both men hit the concrete wall, then collapsed to the floor.

The Able Team leader aimed down at the mass of arms and legs flopping in front of him. Squeezing the trigger again, he sent another load from the shotgun through the bloody remains of the first man and into the second.

Lyons hurried down the steps, jumping over the bodies. Reaching the mezzanine floor, he pressed his face against the window in the steel fire door, seeing a wide staircase that led from the second floor into the main lobby. Gunshots echoed dully from the other side of the door.

He reloaded his weapon, then eased open the door. A sign overhead pointed the way to conference rooms, suites and a ballroom. For all he could see, the intricately decorated floor was deserted. As the gunfire continued below, he slipped through the opening and moved toward the stairs.

At the top of the steps Lyons dropped to one knee and peered through the mahogany rails. A small liquor store was across the hall at the foot of the steps. On the other side of the glass, visible between a shelf of liqueurs, several UAR men crouched behind the counter. A man wearing a smock that bore the Broadmoor logo lay in a pool of blood at their feet.

SWAT cops, in front of a newsstand down the hall, had the terrorists in the liquor store pinned down. But from the angle at which they fired—an angle they had to maintain or leave themselves wide open—kill shots were impossible.

Lyons slung the Atchisson and drew the .45. Sticking the barrel through the rail, he sighted on the window and gently pulled back the trigger.

It was very much like shooting ducks in a shooting gallery. The difference was, *these* ducks deserved what they got.

A round hole appeared in the liquor store window. The .45 slug crashed through a bottle of brandy and sent fragments of glass and liquor flying from the shelf.

The terrorist on the other side of the bottle rolled to his side on the floor. Lyons got off rounds in rapid fire, each suppressed slug that streaked from the Colt leaving another UAR man dead.

Dropping the empty magazine onto the floor, Lyons rammed a full one home, rose to his feet and threw the camouflage blouse from his shoulders. "Police!" he yelled as he descended the stairs. He saw the SWAT team take aim, then raise their weapons.

Lyons burst through the lobby. He passed the registration desk, ducked under a sign that pointed the way toward the Golden Bee and raced down the hall.

Four terrorists burst from the entrance to a restaurant as Lyons drew abreast with the door. Using the Atchisson as a truncheon, the ex-cop drove the barrel into the sternum of a UAR man with a thin, wispy beard. The man gasped as the air rushed from his lungs. The barrel of the shotgun still embedded in the gunner's chest, Lyons pulled the trigger. A muffled roar erupted as blood and bone blew out the terrorist's back.

A loud crack sounded above the gunfire farther down the hall. Lyons stepped back from the remaining trio of terrorists. Holding the trigger back against the guard, he cut a figure eight of auto shotgun fire back and forth through the men. He was already halfway to the corner of another hall when the last terrorist hit the floor.

Making the turn, he raced to a swinging door that bore the smiling cartoon face of a black-and-gold bee. Automatic fire spattered the frame around the door as Lyons neared, black dots marring the bee's smiling face. The ex-cop turned and fired off a quick triburst, then dived through the opening.

Suddenly his feet pedaled air.

Lyons's shoulder struck the sharp edge of a step as he tumbled down a staircase, rolling to a halt on the carpet of the eighteenth-century-style English pub. He sprang to his feet—and felt the hot steel muzzle of a recently fired assault rifle press against his left cheek.

BOLAN DUG DEEPER into the sand, shoveling the granules over his body until only his nose extended aboveground. On the other side of the dune he heard the Spetznaz patrol continue to pass. He was in no immediate danger, of that he was certain. He'd spotted the slow-moving column from the air, landing and gathering his sky-camou parachute with plenty of time to conceal it and himself. Besides, if the Iraqi-disguised Soviets had seen him, they'd have already taken action.

After leaving Alireza on the Saudi border and eluding the Iraqi patrol, the Executioner had led Phoenix Force into Saudi Arabia without further incident. They'd hitched a ride aboard a British supply plane from Al-Jalamid to Kuwait City with plans to re-equip immediately and set out for Eldridge's camp.

Those plans had changed.

Terrorist hits had taken place all over Kuwait City while the team had been in Baghdad. The UAR had simultaneously hit the airbase and the palace and were currently attacking a recently rebuilt saltwater distillation plant. Bolan had decided to return to Iraq alone. He could recon the camp and make the necessary strategical decisions while Phoenix Force battled the terrorists.

When the time came to put the Executioner's plans into action, the rest of the Stony Man warriors were less than an hour away by air.

On the other side of the dune the sound of slow-moving tanks faded away. Bolan rose from the sand, brushed the residue from his fatigues and broke into double time. The 120-degree heat was enervating. He ripped a bandanna from his pocket, twirling it into a sweatband and tying it around his forehead as he ran.

From three hundred yards out he spotted the figure sprawled on its back. Limp and lifeless, the man was immediately identifiable because of the green beret atop his head. Bolan increased his pace, his hand ripping the canteen from his web belt as he neared the fallen man. Kneeling next to the soldier, he stared down at the name on the fatigue blouse as he twisted the cap off the water.

Peck.

The sergeant's sand-encrusted eyelids barely lifted as the Executioner pushed the canteen to his lips. Water ran from the corners of his mouth. He coughed, trying to speak.

"Don't try to talk," Bolan said. "Drink."

Peck shook his head. "Got to...talk... Eldridge is mad." His eyes fluttered under the lids. "In...*sane.* Thinks God..." His eyes closed.

Bolan pushed more water between the open lips, and Peck came around again.

"The Bible..." the sergeant said. "Twisting it... changing it...crazy...thinks God wants him to... end the world."

The warrior watched the man's eyes close again. He held his fingers against the soldier's carotid artery. The pulse was barely perceptible.

The Executioner leaned close, his lips almost touching the dying man's ear. "Peck," he whispered, "does Eldridge have the nukes?"

Peck's eyes struggled to open again, failing. Slowly, his face a grimace of pain, he nodded. Then, after a quick series of short, raspy breaths, his breathing stopped altogether. The pulse beneath the Executioner's fingers halted, as well.

Bolan dug a shallow grave in the sand. After offering a heartfelt prayer to the Universe, he made his way toward the river, wondering at the sergeant's words. The hallucinations and ravings of a man near death? Maybe.

Maybe not.

Maybe Eldridge *did* think he was on a mission from God. And so far the nukes hadn't shown up anywhere else.

Who else could have stolen them?

At the river Bolan turned north. An hour after he buried Peck he reached the slight rise next to the Euphrates just before the camp. As he neared the crest, he fell onto his stomach and crawled to the top.

The Executioner looked over the ridge in time to see the last of Eldridge's tanks pull away and join the other vehicles headed into the desert. The column continued toward the horizon until it became nothing more than a tiny snake slithering across the sand.

Bolan sat up, his gaze still locked onto the vanishing forces. What had happened was all too evident. Peck had escaped, and the deranged colonel was taking no chances.

He was moving his base to parts unknown. And on foot the Executioner had no way of following and learning where the new camp might be.

Bolan pulled out the radio from a pocket, slipped the headset around his ears and switched it on. As he started to speak, he heard Katz say, "Stony Man One. Phoenix One to Stony Man One. Talk to me, Striker."

"Stony Man One," the Executioner said.

"Got some pretty scary info from home," Katz told him. "We need you back right away."

"Affirmative. Tell Grimaldi to meet me at the arranged site." Bolan rose, turned and jogged back through the sand. He thought of Peck, Eldridge and the Israeli nukes, and wondered briefly whose news would be worse—Katz's, or his?

CHAPTER TEN

Hamoud Jaluwi pivoted as the white streak raced toward him. Bringing the racket low behind his hip, he sent the blurring object back over the net with a vicious backhand.

The tennis ball skidded across the concrete, then smashed into Iraj's groin. Jaluwi's opponent fell moaning to the court.

The UAR president burst into laughter as he walked to the net and jerked his towel off the post. Wiping the sweat from his neck, he said, "One must always protect what is dear to one, Iraj."

The man nodded painfully as he got up.

A large, corpulent form entered the tennis area as Jaluwi toweled his hair. Medals covered the barrel chest beneath the man's tunic; gold braid fell over the epaulets on the shoulders. Heaving and puffing, General Kaganovich took a seat on the bench at midcourt, clasping his hands over his rotund belly.

Jaluwi studied the general as he folded the towel and dropped it back over the net. Had he ever seen the man in less than full dress uniform? He didn't think so. Bloated as he was, a streak of vanity still ran through the United Arab Republic's Soviet adviser. The bulky uniform served two purposes. First, it reminded one and all of Kaganovich's rank. And second, it helped conceal the layers of tallow that lay beneath it.

"Good morning, General," Jaluwi called out as he walked across the court.

The Russian nodded.

"In the mood for a game?" The UAR leader suppressed a smile as he asked the question, a mental picture of the man waddling round the court entering his mind.

Kaganovich snorted, shaking his head. "First things first. We have things to discuss."

Jaluwi held out his hand, indicating a door to the side of the court. "Then let us begin. I was about to have breakfast. Won't you join me?"

"I have already eaten," the Russian said as he struggled to his feet.

Yes, he would have, Jaluwi thought. First things first. He turned, concealing the contempt he suspected showed on his face as he led the way to the elevator.

The elevator descended to the third floor below the ground, where the steel door opened onto a small dining room. The UAR leader's eyes drifted briefly around the room, taking in the random paintings on the walls, the gaudy furniture.

Saddam Hussein had built this underground fortress years before the Gulf War. Later he'd furnished it with works of art taken from Kuwait. Individually each piece was brilliant, priceless. Jaluwi sighed. But

Saddam was Saddam, and his vulgarity was reflected in the lack of theme within the decor.

Jaluwi ushered his guest to a white cast-iron table. Kaganovich plopped down into the chair across from him, folding his hands once more round his immense girth.

A man wearing an Iraqi army uniform appeared from the kitchen. The yellow UAR patches on the sleeves brought a smile to Jaluwi's face. "Coffee, Khalid," he said. Then, turning to the general, he asked, "What will you have, Gennady?"

Kaganovich shook his head, looking impatiently at the waiter, then back at Jaluwi. "We have problems to discuss, Mr. President."

Jaluwi waved Khalid away. "What's on your mind, my comrade?"

"We have received more intelligence reports. The nuclear weapons stolen from the Israelis—"

"Has it been determined beyond doubt that they *were* stolen?" Jaluwi asked. "The Jewish dogs are a treacherous lot. They could be planning—"

Kaganovich shook his head. "The warheads and missiles were stolen. I have it on the best authority. And now we know who stole them."

Jaluwi waited.

"Colonel Eldridge sent men into Israel the day before he deserted the American Army."

"*If* he deserted, General. The Americans can be as treacherous as their Jewish puppets."

Kaganovich waved the thought away. "Mr. President, my sources are the best. Eldridge did desert, and he had become what the Americans call a 'walking time bomb.'"

Khalid appeared again, carrying a silver tray. He set a small steaming glass of coffee in front of his president.

Jaluwi turned back to the general as the man moved away. "So where's Eldridge now? Why hasn't he been eliminated?"

Kaganovich blew air from his nostrils. "That's easier said than done. He's somewhere in the desert, but we can't locate him without employing air surveillance. And as you are well aware, the Allies still rule the skies, shooting down any aircraft they see."

"Yes, yes," Jaluwi said impatiently. "The great Yankee protectors of the universe. That will end soon enough. In the meantime there must be other ways to pinpoint Eldridge's position."

"We had him located on the Euphrates, but when our troops arrived, he'd abandoned the site. I have the Spetznaz searching the desert again." A tinge of mockery crept into his voice. "But as you've noticed, I'm sure, the desert is quite large."

The sarcasm irriated Jaluwi, but he forced a smile. "Perhaps your troops could use some assistance. The Republican Guard is now completely under UAR command."

Kaganovich snorted. "The Spetznaz is the finest special forces group in the world. They'll find him."

The president's smile hardened. "Yes, so you've told me. Let's hope the world's finest soldiers are more successful than they were in their bungled attempt to eliminate Colonel Pollock and his men.''

Kaganovich's face reddened.

Jaluwi took a sip of his coffee. It was time to change the subject—he'd pushed the Russian as far as he dared. In spite of his contempt for the fat, egotistical soldier, the UAR still needed its Soviet ally.

Setting his coffee glass on the table, Jaluwi said, ''I can see a dangerous chain of events unfolding.''

Kaganovich nodded. ''The U.S. would never use nuclear weapons first. They fear public opinion too much. But Eldridge is another story.''

''You believe he'll bomb Baghdad?''

Kaganovich shrugged. ''He'll bomb something. If not, why steal the missiles? And Baghdad is the logical site. He might very well aim at Jerusalem or Tel Aviv, as well, in the hope that *you* will be blamed.'' The Russian shifted in his chair. ''The American-Israeli alliance may be strained for the moment, but if push becomes shove, they'll protect their Jewish friends. And there's more. India has threatened to use her own nuclear arsenal if the war escalates.''

Jaluwi nodded. ''And, of course, Mother Russia couldn't stay out of the fray.''

Kaganovich turned up the palms of his hands in a dramatic gesture. ''We'd try, of course, but it's unlikely we could remain neutral.''

Jaluwi saw the truth in the statement. The Soviet Union's primary interest in the UAR stemmed from a desire to obtain warm-water ports in the Gulf. When the war was over and the UAR ruled the entire Arab world, they believed they'd achieve that end from a grateful ally. But a Middle East devastated by nuclear war would be almost as good—in some ways, even better. The Russians could simply march in and take over not only the ports, but the oil wells, too. Like they'd done in Afghanistan, they'd claim they'd been invited to create order out of the chaos. And with the Gulf region in total shambles, they wouldn't even meet the resistance from freedom fighters that had eventually defeated them in Afghanistan.

"Yes, a dangerous scenario indeed," Jaluwi said. "A potential World War III." A quick flash of fear swept through his chest. He didn't care if millions of his fellow Arabs died in his quest for power. They were expendable. The fools would die believing they had fallen in a jihad and were on a fast train to paradise.

But what if *everything* was destroyed?

What would Hamoud Jaluwi rule then?

The servant appeared and refilled Jaluwi's coffee glass. "There's an obvious answer to the problem," Kaganovich said when the man left.

"Yes?"

"Back off. Call a halt to all hostilities here and abroad. Strike a bargain with the Americans. Agree to end the UAR movement. You could then install temporary vassal rulers in the Arab countries." He covered his mouth with a fat fist and coughed. "After a period of time, the Americans will claim victory and go home. They always do. When they're gone, we will begin again."

Jaluwi stared down at his coffee, watching the steam rise from the glass. The idea had merit. He could still rule the entire Middle East behind the scenes. But it meant an indefinite delay in his plans to create a new Arab superpower that would rival the U.S. and the Soviet Union.

Jaluwi looked at Kaganovich, who stared at him, waiting. He could tell the general didn't care one way or the other—the Soviets had no down side in the problem. They'd get what they wanted regardless.

"The potential for—" Kaganovich began.

Jaluwi held up a hand. "Please give me another moment to think."

If worse came to worst, and nuclear weapons *did* obliterate the Gulf, he was safe here. And he had more money hidden away in Switzerland and the Cayman Islands than a man could spend in a lifetime. He could relocate anywhere in the world and live a life of luxury.

In a heartbeat Hamoud Jaluwi made up his mind.

No. He'd never live in exile, and there would be no compromise.

What good was money if power didn't accompany it?

The fear in his heart lifted as soon as the decision had been made. He'd take his chances. And if nuclear war did come, he'd emerge from this bunker to rule whatever was left.

The UAR leader smiled in false sincerity. "We won't give up, General. I'll create a unified Arab world, and the Soviet Union will be my friend and share in the wealth."

The general returned the smile. "We'll stand by you," he promised.

Yes, Jaluwi thought, until he got what he wanted.

The servant returned, carrying a cellular phone. "You have a call, Mr. President. Security."

Jaluwi flipped the switch and held the instrument to his ear. "Yes?" he said. "Has she been searched thoroughly?" There was another pause, then he said, "Escort her down. I'll interview her here." He hung up.

Kaganovich looked at him curiously.

"The woman I spoke to you about yesterday, the half-Jew who has volunteered her services."

"The one who was aligned with the Americans? The one who was with the Mossad? I can't believe you would even—"

"Yes," Jaluwi interrupted, "the problems are obvious. But may I remind you that many of my people have been assassinated by Pollock and his men?" He laughed. "True, we set them up because they were political opponents who *had* to die. But they still held positions that must now be filled. I can use a woman of her skills... if she's sincere."

"I would be very, *very* careful, Mr. President. Even if she isn't a spy, her sudden 'Arab awareness' is still highly suspicious. It might be short-lived."

Jaluwi sipped his coffee as a hum began to emanate from the elevator shaft. "Yes, which is why I've taken out an insurance policy against that possibility."

The doors rolled back and three UAR Republican Guards armed with Czech Skorpion machine pistols stepped out of the car. A tall raven-haired woman, her hands cuffed behind her back, followed them out. Three more guardsmen carrying AK-74s brought up the rear.

Jaluwi watched the woman walk forward with a catlike grace. Even in her restraints her face reflected confidence, power. Her bound hands had drawn her khaki shirt tightly across her chest, forcing her generous breasts up and out. The buttons of the shirt stretched against the placket, threatening to burst from the garment at any moment.

Blood rushed to the UAR leader's groin. Yes, the woman's very soul bespoke confidence and power.

"So," Jaluwi said, "you are Talia Alireza. I welcome you."

Alireza nodded.

The UAR leader looked up into the dark, sultry eyes. "Tell me, Alireza. Why should I trust one who was raised a Jew, worked for Jewish intelligence and *is* a Jew."

"I'm half-Jewish," the woman replied, her head held high. "My mother is Iraqi."

Jaluwi couldn't suppress the chuckle that emerged from his lips. "Yes, so I'm told. Perhaps I can half trust you, then."

The soldiers broke out in polite, controlled laughter.

"You may trust me implicitly," Alireza said. "I've seen through the lies of the West. They posture themselves as the world's peacekeepers, but in keeping that peace they murder thousands daily."

Jaluwi nodded. His gaze dropped back to her breasts, then rose again. "We can discuss the problem without end," he said. "The bottom line is that your credentials speak for themselves. Your abilities could be put to great use by the Arab people. But, for the present, I can't be certain about your loyalty." He lifted the phone from the desk and said, "Bring my other guest down."

Replacing the phone on the table, Jaluwi looked up once more. "You'll be temporarily assigned here. In time you'll have an opportunity to prove your loyalty. Prove to me that you can be trusted, Alireza, and your responsibilities will be increased."

The woman nodded.

Jaluwi waved one of the soldiers toward her. "Remove the handcuffs. We'll need them no more."

As the guardsmen moved in, the elevator began to descend. As soon as the cuffs were off, Alireza rubbed her wrists and said, "May I ask a question, Mr. President?"

"Of course."

"I'll be near you here. If you don't trust me, how do you know I won't attempt to—"

"I've taken another precaution just in case your mind changes again," Jaluwi interrupted. "I've employed a time-honored custom that has been used since the days of ancient Mesopotamia."

Alireza watched him curiously, continuing to rub her wrists. The elevator door opened, and two more Republican Guards stepped out, escorting a prisoner.

"In the days of ancient Babylon," Jaluwi said, smiling, "Nebuchadnezzer took hostages to ensure the loyalty of his vassal rulers. I've done the same." He turned to the guard holding the handcuffs. "Put the restraints on *her.*" He pointed at the old woman huddled between the soldiers.

Then, looking back at Alireza, he saw the horror that replaced the confidence in the woman's eyes. Jaluwi chuckled. "Don't worry. You need only follow orders, my fickle little mercenary, and your mother will be safe."

THE GRINDING GEARS of heavy machinery screeched over the noise of the rotors as Jack Grimaldi set down the chopper inside the demolished compound. American and Kuwaiti soldiers, most carrying sledgehammers, picks and cement trowels rather than rifles, crowded the area inside the recently reerected perimeter fence. Demolitions men worked at various areas throughout the grounds, carefully setting light charges of C-4 plastique and reducing the huge slabs of concrete rubble to transportable scrap.

Bolan dropped down from the helicopter and hurried toward the metal temporary building in the middle of the complex. His eyes flickered over a dozen shirtless men huddled around a crane as it hoisted a steel girder into the air.

The compound was being rebuilt. The Spetznaz and the United Arab Republic might have slowed down the Allied movement in the north of Kuwait, but they hadn't stopped it.

The interior of the metal building felt like an oven as the Executioner strode through the door. A box fan, plugged into a small portable generator, sat in the corner. Its whirling blades did little to alleviate the heat, succeeding only in redistributing the hot, dry air that filled the room.

Bolan stopped just inside the door. He saw Katz, James, Encizo, McCarter and Manning seated around the conference table. Wet fatigue blouses hung limply from the shoulders of the Phoenix Force warriors, and the strain of the seemingly never-ending mission had begun to show.

Still, behind the weary expressions the Executioner saw the strength that made each man what he was—a well-trained, well-conditioned fighting machine, with the mental toughness to transcend the boundaries of physical endurance and move into the realm of spiritual strength that comes only through total dedication to a cause.

The Executioner took a seat at the head of the table. A black field telephone, also linked to the generator, sat in front of him. A portable speakerphone had been attached to the instrument.

Through the open door Bolan heard a power saw start up across the grounds. The steady hum had a soothing, calming effect that made him want to close his eyes, drift off to sleep. Instead, he looked at Katz, seated just to his right. "What happened at the salt-water distillation plant?" he asked.

The Phoenix Force leader shrugged. "Minor damage. We got it stopped. Repairs won't take long."

Bolan nodded. "So why was I called back?"

Katz stared down at the table in front of him. "I've only got a sketchy idea. Brognola wanted to talk to us all at the same time." He pointed at the speaker-phone. "The base is getting us a direct line to Stony Man right now."

The words had barely left the Israeli's mouth when the phone rang shrilly. Bolan lifted the receiver. "Yes?"

"Ready with the call to America," a voice on the other end informed him.

Bolan covered the mouthpiece and held the phone away from him. He looked back to Katz. "This line secure?"

Katz nodded. "I saw to it."

The power saw continued to drone in the distance as Bolan flipped the switch to the speaker. "Hello, Striker?"

"Me, Hal."

"We've got problems, guy, *big* problems. Rather than lose anything in the translation, I'm going to have Barb and Aaron fill you in."

A moment later Bolan heard Kurtzman say, "Striker?"

"What have you got, Bear?"

"I finally broke through on the computer," Kurtzman reported, "and once I got on Jaluwi's trail, more side info came out. But first things first. Jaluwi hid out in Rio right after the phony assassination. From there he went to Baghdad.''

"He's in Baghdad now?"

"No," Kurtzman said, "he's moved again. It took some doing, but with the intel I gathered through Syria and Jordan I was able to gain limited access to Iraqi files. Saddam Hussein was still in the process of rebuilding Babylon when he disappeared. He's already redone a couple of the palaces. We think Jaluwi's there.''

"Underground bunker?" Bolan asked.

"Right. Saddam was a charter member of AA— that's a twelve-step program called Anxiety Anonymous.''

"He had good reason to be," Bolan said. "He was considerably less than twelve steps ahead of a bullet when he vanished.''

"Right again. But that's the good news. Ready for the bad?"

Bolan scanned the faces of the five men around the table. All sat listening solemnly. "Shoot.''

"The only thing that'll take out the bunker is a direct, large-scale air strike.''

"So let's mount a direct large-scale air strike," Bolan said. He watched one of the demolitions men walk past the open door, carrying an insulated box of blasting caps. The man began to apply a charge beneath a large block of concrete.

Brognola's voice came back on the line. "That's where it gets tricky. Bear's also uncovered several sites in Iraq that have Soviet nukes ready to go. We're not talking just shorts and middies, Striker. The Russians have brought in long-range missiles, too."

Barbara Price finally entered the conversation. "We suspect Jaluwi will use them the moment he feels threatened, and an air strike would give him plenty of time..." Her voice trailed off.

Bolan remained silent for a moment, then finished Price's sentence for her. "Enough time to launch the nukes. The Soviets could have Jaluwi aim his missiles anywhere they want, including Washington."

"Right," Brognola said, "not to mention New York, London, Paris..."

"Under the circumstances," the warrior said, "the UAR would take the blame. The Russians could claim they didn't have anything to do with it."

"Exactly," Brognola came back. "Unfortunately there's more."

"Eldridge has the nukes stolen from Israel," Bolan said.

There was a long pause. Then Brognola said, "Right. How'd you know?"

A cold feeling of dread ripped through the Executioner as he recalled the words of the soldier he'd found in the desert.

Eldridge...mad...thinks God wants him to...end the world.

"Striker? You still there?"

"Yeah," Bolan said, returning his attention to the speakerphone. Briefly he filled in the Stony Man crew on what Sergeant Peck had said.

A sudden thought chilled the Executioner. "Does Israel know about the Soviet nukes in Iraq?"

Price let out a breath. "The Mossad gave *us* the information."

Bolan gripped the edge of the conference table. "Then we're already on borrowed time. We've got a three-way standoff. Eldridge, Jaluwi and the Israelis. Five-way when you consider that the chances of the U.S. and Soviet Union staying out of this thing when it erupts are practically nil. Then—" The Executioner stopped speaking as one of the C-4 charges exploded dully across the compound. "What we're looking at here is the beginning of World War III. The first player who pushes the button sets the whole thing in motion."

The explosion of plastique outside the building drifted away. Except for the twirling blade of the box fan in the corner, the room fell into silence.

A dull, lifeless static echoed over the international line.

The Executioner broke the silence. "Okay," he said. "We'll take them in order of priority. Eldridge is the loosest cannon we've got. Who knows what hallucinations are going through his mind? He might decide it's time to start Armageddon at any moment." He paused, his mind racing as he considered the situation. "Jaluwi comes next. He's not likely to strike until he sees an immediate threat. We'll just have to try to persuade Israel to hang tight for the time being, then show them proof that the threat's been neutralized as soon as this is over."

Katz leaned toward the speakerphone. "And we'd better do that *fast,*" he said. "My people aren't famous for sitting back and letting their enemies gain advantage."

Bolan nodded. "Barbara," he said, "I need some uniforms. Republican Guard—make sure they've got the new UAR shoulder patches—for Yakov and Rafael. Soviet for me, David and Gary." He glanced down the table to where Calvin James listened intently. "And Libyan army in Calvin's size. Give us some rank, but not enough to draw undue attention. How fast can you get them here?"

"Bear," Price said, "would you see what the Company has on hand in Riyadh." As the computer keys began to click in the background, the Stony Man controller asked, "Where do you want them delivered, Striker?"

Bolan hesitated. They shouldn't need the disguises on the first leg of the mission. But as soon as they finished with Eldridge, the uniforms would be critical to infiltrating Jaluwi's armed underground fortress. "Just deliver them to the base here."

Kurtzman spoke up. "Between the Company and Navy Intelligence we've got everything you need right there in Saudi Arabia. I've already got them on their way—take an hour or so by plane."

"Good," Bolan said. "We'll be about that getting ready." He disconnected the line.

The Executioner stared into the determined eyes of the men of Phoenix Force. Get Eldridge, then get Jaluwi—the remainder of the mission had finally come into focus, splitting into two distinct divisions. Simple, if you looked at it on the surface. Nearly impossible when you read between the lines.

Katzenelenbogen, Encizo, James, McCarter and Manning. If anyone could pull it off, it would be them. He couldn't have asked for finer troops to lead on what might very well be a suicide mission—not just for Phoenix Force, but for the entire world.

Bolan stood. "What are we waiting for?"

Then, as if in answer to the Executioner's question, a loud explosion sounded outside the building.

Concrete chips and sand rained to the earth as the Stony Man warriors stared through the open door. As the dust cleared, a demolitions man moved to a new site and began placing another charge of C-4. Soldiers with wheelbarrows and shovels moved in to clean up the mess.

In the rubble that remained of what had once been a tall concrete building, Bolan and the members of Phoenix Force saw firsthand the destruction that even a small charge of explosives could cause. It was hardly the first such sight the battle-hardened warriors had witnessed.

But this time it took on a whole new meaning.

LYONS FELT the sharp front sight at the end of the barrel of the assault rifle bite into the skin of his face. He turned slowly toward the man holding the weapon.

"Not the friendliest greeting I've ever gotten, Gadgets," the ex-cop growled.

Schwarz shrugged as he lowered the M-16. "Sorry, Ironman. Didn't recognize you tumbling down the steps—your good side and all."

Automatic fire continued to sound dully outside the Golden Bee as Lyons looked past Schwarz and saw a brawny man with a handlebar mustache. The man wore a Powerhouse Gym "rag" sweatshirt and clutched a Colt All-American 2000 9 mm pistol in one of his beefy hands.

Schwarz hooked a thumb over his shoulder, indicating the man. "Meet Lieutenant Garbo," he said. "Off duty-CSPD, Narcotics. Garbo came in here thinking he'd grab a quick beer after his shift. He gave me pretty much the same greeting I gave you when I came in the door."

Lyons nodded, and Garbo returned the greeting.

The Able Team leader took in the rest of the Golden Bee with a quick glance. Schwarz and Garbo had secured the room as best they could under the circumstances. Legs—both male and female—extended from under the tables. Several women huddled on the floor next to a beer keg near the bar.

"You talked to Pol since we hit ground?" Schwarz asked.

Lyons nodded. "He's pinned down outside." He keyed the two-way and spoke into the mike in front of his face. "Able One to Two. You there, Pol?"

The roar of gunfire sounded over the air behind Blancanales's voice. "I'm here—" the Able warrior paused, and Lyons heard the chatter of his M-16 "—at least for the moment."

"Give us a ten-twenty," Lyons said. "We'll see if we can give you a little backup."

The automatic fire continued in the background as Blancanales spoke again. "Just to the left of the main entrance there's a hallway leading toward the courtyard." He stopped and Lyons heard the M-16 again. "Third door on the right from the front. I'll be the guy trying to hide behind the ice maker and a pop machine." The assault rifle rattled again.

"We're on our way." Lyons turned to Garbo. "You got anything besides the Colt on you?"

"Just this," the off-duty cop said. He lifted his left foot, rested it on a chair and jerked the cuff of his jeans over a powerful calf. Tapping the S&W Chief's Special in the ankle rig, he added, "I didn't realize I was heading back to Nam when I got off work this evening."

Schwarz stepped forward, drawing his Beretta and handing it butt first to Garbo. "Add this to your arsenal and hold down the fort here."

Lyons led his partner back up the steps. "Ready?"

"Let's do it."

The Able Team leader opened the door, and they emerged cautiously into the hall.

Stepping over the bodies of terrorists and policemen alike, the two men made their way cautiously back to the lobby. A strange silence had descended over the area. Except for the dead men littering the floor, the shops and open areas appeared deserted.

Sporadic firing continued, but it had moved outside the building.

Lyons and Schwarz slipped out the door and turned to the left. They were halfway to the hall leading back to the courtyard when autofire erupted from the trees across the drive. The big ex-cop turned to confront a terrorist who was wearing a red bandanna around his forehead and leaning over a concrete bench.

Schwarz beat his companion to the punch by a millisecond. Dust flew from the top of the bench as autofire raked its surface. The deformed bullets ricocheted up, riddling the man's chest. The gunner screamed and straightened up.

Lyon's double-tap of triple-aught buck followed, drilling into the man's chest and obliterating the smaller rifle holes. The terrorist's screams were cut off as he collapsed to the grass on top of his weapon.

A sudden burst of gunfire echoed behind them. "Cover our rear," Lyons whispered to Schwarz. He stuck his head down the hall. A half-dozen bodies lay in a pile in front of a door marked Ice and Vending. At least a dozen more men in brown cammies were lined up along the wall, ready to make a concerted assault into the room.

Lyons jerked back. The terrorists were about to rush the room and overpower Blancanales in a suicide mission. Leaning around the corner, the Able Team leader pulled the Atchisson's trigger, and the shotgun jumped in his hands. Flesh-shredding shot saturated the hallway like giant grounds of pepper caught in a stiff wind. Screams echoed over the booming 12-gauge blasts as the automatic shotgun pounded back against the ex-cop's shoulder again and again.

Only one UAR gunman escaped the Atchisson's wrath. As the shotgun ran dry, he turned and sprinted down the hallway.

Lyons slung the shotgun and drew the Python. Dropping the front ramp sight to the middle of the terrorist's back, he double-actioned two raging 125-grain hollowpoints between the man's shoulder blades. The terrorist dropped to the floor like a sack of dry cement.

The big ex-cop hurdled the fallen bodies as he sprinted down the hall, Schwarz at his heels. He stopped at the side of the door. "It's us Pol," he barked. "Hold your fire." Waiting two seconds, he stuck his head around the corner and saw Blancanales seated just where he'd said he'd be.

Schwarz pushed past Lyons into the room. The electronics wizard extended a hand and pulled Blancanales to his feet. "Can't let you out of my sight for a minute, can I?" He grinned at his partner.

Lyons stepped inside the room and unslung his autoshotgun. The battle continued to rage across the grounds as he reloaded the Atchisson. He heard another gunfight break out inside the hotel proper. Sticking his head through the doorway, he scouted the hallway right and left, then turned back to his team. "Let's get back to the war."

The Stony Man warriors were halfway down the hall when the headset buzzed suddenly in Lyons's ear.

Barbara Price's usually calm voice held a thread of fear. "Stony Man to Able One. Come in, One. *Now.*"

"Able here," Lyons replied.

"Be advised. Word just received from the White House. President's daughter, son-in-law and grand-daughter are registered as guests at the Broadmoor. Repeat—the Man's family is there, Able One."

Lyons stopped in his tracks and turned to Blancanales and Schwarz. Both men stood motionless behind him. The expressions on their faces told him they were as stunned by the news as he was. "You got a room number, Stony?"

"Negative, One."

Lyons raced down the hall and into the lobby, coming to an abrupt stop at the registration desk. The ex-cop didn't need to ask Price for a name. The President's daughter had married a martial arts expert turned Hollywood action-adventure hero during the Man's first term in office.

Two terrorists manned the desk. One held a Broadmoor registration card in his hand; the other spoke Arabic into a hand-held walkie-talkie.

The Able Team leader didn't hesitate. Leveling the Atchisson at the man with the radio, he pulled the trigger and sent him jerking to the floor in a squall of 12-gauge shot.

The second man tried to raise his AK-47, but Schwarz and Blancanales dropped him with a duet from their M-16s.

Lyons vaulted the counter and tore the card from the dead terrorist's hand. "Room 304. Let's go!"

Racing down the hall, Lyons ignored the deathtrap elevators and tore open the door to the stairs. The

Able Team warriors vaulted the steps three at a time, stopping when they reached the door to the third floor.

Machine-gun fire sounded from the other side of the door as Lyons cracked it open. Down the hall he saw four UAR gunmen lying on the carpet. Five more stood with their backs against the wall, trying to edge toward the open door of what he presumed was room 304.

The ex-cop swung the door open and dived to the floor as Schwarz and Blancanales lunged in after him, their M-16s firing as one, the Atchisson's slower booms roaring loudly above the autofire.

One by one the terrorists against the wall slid slowly to the floor. Suddenly the hallway fell silent.

Lyons sprang to his feet and led his men forward. When he reached the edge of the door, he spoke calmly. "Montgomery?"

The room beyond the doorway remained silent.

"Montgomery, we're friendlies...."

There was a long pause. Then a familiar voice said, "I damn sure hope so. But just for the fun of it, guy, let's make sure. Flip some ID inside." The movie star paused. "Otherwise, I'm going to shoot the next thing I see."

Lyons felt a grin spread his face. Jim Montgomery hadn't always been an actor. As well as a master of karate and aikido, he'd been a SEAL in Vietnam. The man was far more than just a celluloid superstar.

Pulling the Justice credential case from the breast pocket of his coveralls, Lyons tossed it around the corner.

A moment later the voice said, "Come on in. Slow."

Lyons swung the Atchisson over his back and led Able Team into the room. They stepped over the body of a fatigue-clad terrorist whose neck jutted from his shoulders at an odd angle. A chalky white shard of neckbone pierced the man's skin as his eyes stared vacantly into space.

Montgomery stood just in front of the bed, the AK-47 he'd taken from the terrorist after breaking the man's neck aimed at the doorway. Faded blue jeans, a pale blue western shirt and orange ostrich boots covered the movie star's sinewy body as his suspicious eyes bore into Lyons's.

Against the far wall his wife's head emerged from behind the bed, her three-year-old daughter clutched tightly to her breast.

Montgomery lowered the rifle. Lyons hurried past him to the window. Outside on the grounds he heard the gunfire dying down. Only sporadic shots now echoed up to the third floor, and SWAT-clad officers as well as regular patrolmen had begun a mop-up search of the grounds.

The siege was over. Lyons wiped sweat from his forehead with the back of his hand, staring up into the blackened sky.

Suddenly an "almost-there" solution to the secret of the UAR command post floated into his mind. And then it clicked, the answer suddenly hitting the ex-cop squarely between the eyes.

Lyons stared in awestruck disbelief as the flashing neon lights of the Sinor zeppelin turned away from Colorado Springs and started over the mountaintops to the west.

The answer had been there all along, too obvious to be noticed.

The Able Team leader turned back to the room. Blancanales, Schwarz and Jim Montgomery stared at him curiously.

"Good Lord, Ironman," Blancanales said, "you look like you've just seen a ghost."

Lyons hurried toward the telephone next to the bed. "I just got wise," he replied as he snatched up the receiver.

CHAPTER ELEVEN

"It's the only possible answer," Lyons said excitedly into the phone. "It was at the synagogue, here and at half a dozen other strike sites." He turned toward the door as four Colorado Springs PD SWAT team members entered the Montgomerys' room.

"The UAR has hit all over the nation, Ironman," Barbara Price reminded him on the other end of the line. "The zeppelin couldn't have been at all of the sites."

Lyons pressed the phone into his ear as he turned back to the window. "No, but it wouldn't have to be. It could be at the big one—like it has been—and link up the smaller hits by cellular phone or radio. And with a satellite hookup the zep would have contact with Baghdad." He paused as the zeppelin's lights continued to fade over the mountains. "They've got worldwide communication—we've known that all along. The zep even explains the Olympic strike in Barcelona, and some of the other European ops Phoenix Force worked." He stopped and waited for Price's comment. When the mission controller didn't speak, he went on. "It's the perfect setup, Barbara. They're trying to set a new world air record. They want publicity, so they go where the action is. It fits the old undercover axiom to a T—the zep's got a story, and a reason to be where it is.''

Price drew in a breath. "Let me get Kurtzman on the other line."

Lyons heard the intercom click. A moment later Bear came on.

The Able Team leader repeated his suspicions, finishing with, "Tap into whatever system you have to, Bear. Get me the skinny on Sinor."

The rapping of Kurtzman's keyboard keys echoed over the line. A moment later the Stony Man computer ace said, "Here it is—Sinor International, advertising and public relations firm. Stock dividends in the form of—"

"Skip that part, Bear. Who's at the top?"

The keyboard clicked again. "It's part of a big conglomerate known as the Pan-Am Corporation. Worldwide holdings in—"

"Get me some *names*, Bear, human beings. Something that a simple burned-out ex-cop can understand."

More clicks. "Board of directors—president, Lars Gustaffson, Stockholm, Sweden. VP, Roger M. Hendly, New York—"

"I hate to sound like a racist, Bear," Lyons said impatiently, "but are there any Arab names on the board?"

Kurtzman paused. A moment later he said, "Affirmative, Ironman. Ali Mahmoud. Naturalized citizen born in Baghdad. But he's been here over twenty years."

"Get him on the screen. Go NCIC first," Lyons instructed. "Anybody on the board of directors could pull a few strings and take over the company's operation." He turned back to the room while he waited.

Blancanales remained on guard at the door. Schwarz and the SWAT team members were helping the Montgomerys to throw their luggage together. The President's granddaughter sat in the middle of the bed, giggling and chattering as she dressed a doll.

A cop wearing sergeants' stripes entered the room. "Is the fighting about over downstairs?" Schwarz asked him.

The sergeant nodded. "We're doing the mop-up now."

Kurtzman came back on the line as two men in gray suits walked in the door. "Mahmoud's as clean as your mama's laundry with NCIC," the computer wizard said. "Let me try Interpol and the CIA."

Lyons turned to the suits as they flashed Secret Service credentials. "Where are you taking them?" he asked, indicating the Montgomerys with his head.

"For right now, to another room," an agent with a flattop haircut said. "We'll get them out of here to another hotel as soon as we're sure there's no UAR stragglers still hiding."

Lyons nodded as Kurtzman came back on. "Negative at Interpol."

The big ex-cop blew air between his clenched teeth. "Go ahead and try the spooks," he said into the mouthpiece, "but I'll be surprised if you find anything there, either. My guess is that Mahmoud's a deep-cover mole who's been in place for years just waiting to be useful. He'll have kept his nose clean.''

As the keys clicked once more, Lyons watched Jim Montgomery lift his daughter into his arms. The Secret Service agents and SWAT team escorted the Montgomerys out of the room.

Schwarz moved next to him in front of the window, staring through the glass toward the vanishing lights of the zeppelin. ''Anything?'' the electronics man asked.

Lyons shook his head.

Kurtzman came back on. ''You're right. Mahmoud doesn't even rate a Company dossier. Not even a note about sympathies toward radical Arab causes.''

''He's our man, Bear. I can feel it.''

Kurtzman paused at the other end. ''My computer chips say no, Ironman, but I've seen your crazy cop intuition pan out too often to ignore it. What do you need from me?''

''Barbara, you are still with us?'' Lyons asked.

''Affirmative.''

Lyons's fingers tightened around the receiver. ''The zep's headed west. Get some surveillance planes off their butts and into the air. But tell them to keep their distance. We've got to assume the zeppelin's wired to self-destruct if they're discovered.'' The ex-cop paused, clearing his throat. ''Bear, as soon as the planes get a fix, see if you can project a flight course with your magic machines. Barbara, tell Charlie Mott we're on our way to the airport. ETA is fifteen minutes.''

Lyons replaced the receiver and stood up. "Let's go."

Blancanales looked up from the doorway. "Where we heading?"

The team leader took a final glance over his shoulder. "West."

A STRANGE CYCLE of emotions streamed through Colonel Joshua Eldridge's soul as he toured the new camp. One minute he'd feel an almost uncontrollable desire to shout, praise God and sing hosannas to the heavens, and a second later his spirits would drop and a slow, cold anger would darken his spirit. Without warning the anger would disappear and be replaced by the blackest depression he'd ever experienced. Then the joy would fill his heart again, and the whole progression of conflicting passions would repeat itself.

Eldridge strolled past the site where the stage and podium were being erected. He came to a trio of men pounding the stakes into the ground that would soon support his command tent. The sight of his servants—no, *God's* servants—working elated him.

One of the men, wearing a floppy camouflage boonie hat, dropped his sledgehammer and saluted. "Almost ready, Colonel," he said nervously. "Have you all set up in five minutes."

Eldridge started to say, "Good work, soldier," then changed his mind. The days when the U.S. Army was his god were over. Oh, he still served an army, all right. But now it was a higher legion, manned by angels and commanded by the Supreme General Himself.

"Bless you," Eldridge said, placing a hand on the soldier's head. He saw confusion fill the young man's eyes as he turned and walked on.

His mood swung suddenly to anguish. In his mind's eye he saw his father the day before the charlatan preacher had hung himself, and the memory led Eldridge back into the anger portion of his emotional roller coaster.

Joshua Eldridge, Senior had laughed, cried and shouted in hatred during his final sermon. As always, he'd collected what few valuables the poor farmers could provide and buried them in his pit. But an hour after the sermon, when the pickup trucks carried the men in overalls and the women wearing bonnets back home, Eldridge had found his father's body swinging from a rope looped over the cross behind the pulpit.

Eldridge ground his teeth together as a brief flash of fear invaded the joy-anger-depression cycle. Then his temperament became suddenly cheerful once more. No. He wasn't like his father. The rogue pastor's lightning-fast mood swings had come from guilt-induced insanity, the awareness that his soul was damned for all eternity. His own shifting disposition could be explained. Yes, easily explained. The joy came from the knowledge that he'd been anointed by God to carry out the Lord's Plan. The anger was directed at Sergeant Jerry Peck. Peck's escape had forced Eldridge to move the campsite in case the sergeant reached Kuwait and alerted the Allies.

And the sorrow that blackened the colonel's heart?

It was for the lost souls, many in his own camp, who wouldn't see the Light before Darkness came.

Eldridge stopped next to the mobile rocket launchers. One of his Chosen Twelve stared through the windshield of the closest vehicle. The colonel nodded and saw the man reach forward to the lift control. Gears ground grittily, and the rockets rose toward the sky once more.

Another of his Twelve walked forward. "We'll have everything in working order by midday, sir," he said, bowing his head slightly. "Two aimed at Baghdad and one at Babylon. The other at Tel Aviv." A grin covered his face. "As you ordered."

Eldridge nodded again. He turned and stared back to where the men had finished erecting his tent. Bending at the waist, he entered the flap and saw the new camel hair tunic on his bunk.

Colonel Joshua Eldridge had discarded the vocabulary of the Army. Now the time had come to abandon the clothing, as well.

Removing his uniform, Eldridge dropped it onto the floor and pulled the hair shirt over his head. He leaned down, removed the leather pistol belt from his trousers and slipped it around his waist. He looked up into the small shaving mirror fastened over the wager basin on his table. "'John did baptize in the wilderness,'" he quoted into the mirror, then frowned, wondering if he looked anything like John the Baptist had looked nearly two thousand years earlier. "'And John was clothed with camel's hair, and with a girdle of a skin about his loins.'"

Eldridge strode determinedly out of the tent and up the stage steps to the podium. He watched as more of his Twelve hooked up the microphone, then called the troops to the parade ground. Scanning the soldiers as soon as they'd assembled, he saw the shocked expressions the camel hair produced on their faces.

Yes, there were still many doubters among the ranks. Men who couldn't, or refused to, understand. What was he to do with them?

Suddenly Eldridge's vision blurred. Then lights flashed in his brain. The Voice called to him.

Well done, my good and faithful servant. Send the unbelievers away and continue only with those devoted to My Will.

As quickly as it had blurred, Eldridge's vision cleared. He leaned forward to speak into the microphone, and his voice boomed across the desert. "Prepare ye the way of the Lord and make his paths straight." He stared down at the faces below.

His Twelve Disciples were enthralled. The rest of the men looked astounded.

"The world is about to end," Eldridge said calmly. "In a few short hours we'll launch a chain of events to prepare the way for the Lord to return to earth." He paused, then went on. "Those of you who wish to leave camp and return to Kuwait may do so. Take what vehicles and provisions you need. We won't need them." His eyes passed over the frozen men. "Those of you who would stay and help me continue the work of the Lord may remain." He waited.

No one moved.

"Go, I say!" Eldridge screamed.

The troops stood as if made of stone.

Eldridge looked down and saw a private named Reynolds at the front of the assembly. The short, thin man stared fearfully up at the pulpit as sweat streamed down his face. "Go!" Eldridge screamed at him.

Reynolds continued to stand, frozen in fear.

Eldridge turned to Lieutenant Ferguson, who stood at the edge of the makeshift stage. "Seize him!" he screamed, pointing at Reynolds.

Ferguson and three more of the Twelve grabbed Reynolds's arms as Eldridge dropped from the stage into the sand. The troops parted like the waters of the Red Sea as the colonel and his men dragged the shocked private to the center of the parade ground.

Eldridge picked up a rock the size of his fist. He turned to Reynolds, who was still held tightly by Ferguson and the others. "Who will cast the first stone?" he screamed at the top of his lungs.

No one answered.

"I will!" Eldridge shouted and hurled the rock.

The stone struck Reynolds between the eyes. Blood spurted from his forehead as he crumpled to the sand.

The colonel remounted the stage as the rest of his Twelve picked up rocks. Behind him he heard dull, wet plunking sounds as the missiles hit their target. By the time he stepped back behind his pulpit, Private Reynolds was unrecognizable.

Eldridge spoke softly this time, his voice barely audible over the loudspeaker. "Go" was all he said.

At the rear of the assembly a tall, lanky corporal glanced anxiously toward the motor pool. Slowly he took an uncertain step toward the vehicles.

A sergeant near the front moved cautiously after him. Both men glanced fearfully over their shoulders toward the rostrum.

More men moved hesitantly after them. Then, as if on cue, the entire company began to run.

"Yes! Run!" the man in the camel-hair shirt screamed from his pulpit. "Run! But you shall not escape my judgment!" He felt suddenly hot, then cold. A sudden, fuzzy confusion rushed through his brain as if one of the white clouds in the heavens above had entered his head. "The *Lord's* judgment," he said, amending the statement.

Eldridge stood frozen as the vehicles pulled away from the camp and roared south toward Kuwait. He looked down at the parade ground. Except for the lifeless body of Private Reynolds, only his Twelve Disciples remained.

A THOUSAND FEET below the helicopter, the Euphrates River twisted and turned as it made its way north toward Baghdad. Bolan pulled the binoculars from their case on his web belt and leaned forward, aiming the lenses down through the nose of the HueyCobra. "There, Jack," he said, pointing through the windshield. "That's where the camp was."

The Executioner turned over his shoulder. Grimaldi sat behind and slightly above him in the pilot's seat. "Take her down to see if we can spot the tracks."

Grimaldi nodded and the aircraft began to descend. As they neared the deserted site, Bolan refocused the powerful lenses of the binoculars, and the telltale signs of recent occupancy appeared. Charred remnants of camp fires spotted the terrain. The tall grass along the river had been beaten down where Eldridge's vehicles had stood the day before.

The tire treads of heavy trucks as well as tank tracks led through the sand to the northwest. Grimaldi dropped the chopper to five hundred feet and began following the trail. Fifteen minutes later the Stony Man pilot spoke into the headset. "We're getting close to Karbala, Striker. You don't suppose—"

Bolan shook his head as he answered. "No way, Jack. Eldridge needs his privacy for this deal. Drop down a little farther. The tracks should turn pretty quick."

No sooner had the Huey descended than the trail angled farther west. "My guess is they'll be somewhere along the Ubayyid River," Bolan said. "Take her back up high. We don't want them to spot us."

The chopper rose once more, soaring toward the clouds. As they neared the sparkling waters of the Wadi al-Ubiyyad, the Executioner looked down to see the tiny spots in the sand. Twisting the rings of the binoculars, he made out the line of tents set at one end of the camp. At the other end some sort of platform had been erected.

A lone M-1 Abrams and a pair of Hummers stood just to the west of the tents. Four huge trucks had been parked on the other side. Bolan frowned as he zeroed the lenses. The trucks were mobile rocket launchers, and even at this distance the warheads on the rockets were unmistakable.

Katz spoke up, voicing Bolan's own thoughts. "Something's happened, Striker," the Phoenix Force leader said from the rear of the Huey. "Other than the nuke trucks there are hardly any vehicles left. Certainly not enough for that number of tents."

"Affirmative," the Executioner agreed. He twisted in his seat again. "Turn her around, Jack. Get us back out of sight."

Grimaldi nodded, and the chopper U-turned through the clouds. Two minutes later six figures dived from the HueyCobra, the canopies of their pale blue parachutes obscured against the azure sky.

As soon as the chutes were buried in the sand, Bolan led the men toward a tall dune in the distance. Dropping to his chest halfway up, he crawled to the crest and peered over as Katz moved in to his side.

The camp sat four hundred yards in the distance. Pressing the binoculars against his forehead again, the Executioner sighted in on a strangely garbed man. Dressed in some type of animal skin, the man walked from the rocket launchers toward one of the tents. Other men, all wearing the skins, busied themselves at tasks about the camp.

The Executioner handed the binoculars to Katz. "What do you make of it?"

The Israeli shook his head behind the lenses. "God only knows. Peck was right. The bastard has gone completely off his rocker."

Bolan rolled onto his side as the rest of the team crawled through the sand around them. "Whatever it is, it doesn't matter. The bottom line is that Eldridge has taken the final plunge off the deep end, and he's gotten a few basket cases to dive in with him." He took a deep breath. "Which means he might set off the firecrackers any time."

Katz nodded. "The man's a nuclear time bomb. We've got to get in there quick."

Manning's head rose slightly over the dune. Sand fell from his face as he squinted toward the tents. "No way we're going to cover that open terrain without being spotted."

"How about an air strike?" Encizo suggested. "Grimaldi could—"

A shaking head from the Executioner halted the Cuban in midsentence. "Too risky." He pointed across the open desert. "Look at the rockets. They're set up, ready to blow. All it'll take is a finger on the button."

"We'll have to wait until dark, then," James said. "Like Manning said, there's no way to cross without being seen."

"We don't have until dark," the Executioner told him. He frowned down into the sand as a plan began to take shape in his mind.

The rest of the men quieted, waiting.

A few moments later Bolan lifted his eyes. Staring at Katz, he said, "This is going to be risky, to say the least, but I don't see any other way that has a thread of a chance." The Executioner watched the men's

faces change from optimistic to skeptical and finally
to resolved determination as he outlined what he had
in mind.

When he finished, Bolan said, "I don't have to tell
you what's riding on this. If we fail, we lose everything. So if anybody thinks they've got a better idea,
I'm willing to listen."

He waited. One by one the men of Phoenix Force
shook their heads.

"Then let's get at it," the Executioner said. Moving back out of sight down the sand dune, he unzipped his pack and began to unbutton his shirt.

AARON KURTZMAN WHEELED back from the computer and rubbed his bloodshot eyes with his fists. He
laced the fingers of both hands together. Finally he
had answers to the two burning questions that had
plagued the warriors of Stony Man Farm throughout
the whole mission. He'd located both Jaluwi and the
UAR communications post.

But those two answers had opened a can of worms
that led to a thousand more questions.

Kurtzman rubbed his eyes again, then turned toward the comm room. Barbara Price sat facing the
other way, the phone pressed into her ear, her hand
scribbling frantically on a notepad next to the radio.
In order to bypass the intercom Price had pressed the
button beneath her control console and rolled the glass
wall separating them back up into the ceiling. The
mission control and intel rooms were now one huge
open area, and information could be relayed to the

operatives in the field as soon as it came over the screens. The process saved only seconds, but seconds saved lives.

Kurtzman stared at the teletype to Price's right. Since the outbreak of the UAR attacks that had coincided with the Broadmoor, the machine had remained threateningly silent, and he almost wished the news of more violent outbreaks would suddenly appear on the roller.

Twisting in his wheelchair, the Stony Man computer wizard looked down the ramp to the work pit where Akira Tokaido, Carmen Delahut and Huntington Wethers sat keying data into their own computers. "Akira," he called softly, "do you have the flight plan projected yet?"

"Not yet," he replied without looking up. "It's still too soon. There are numerous possibilities. But the FAA has finally got the zeppelin zeroed in on radar." He pointed to the screen. "Take a look."

Kurtzman rolled back to his computer, hit the keys and a multicolored map of the southwestern portion of the U.S. appeared. Tapping into the FAA radar system, he saw a tiny dot flashing near the town of Cortez, in the far southwestern corner of Colorado.

Sensing movement to his side, Kurtzman turned back toward Price. He watched her stand up, her gaze glued to the silent teletype as his had been a moment before. Then, suddenly turning away, she strode purposefully across the open room and up the ramp to his console.

"Three Starfighters just hit the air from Lowry AFB in Denver," she said. "They should intercept the zep within minutes." She squinted at Kurtzman's screen. "Any idea where they're headed yet?"

"If you draw a straight line from Colorado Springs, you end up in Oceanside, California. But that doesn't mean that's where they're going." He ran a hand through his damp hair. "They'll be coming up on the Grand Canyon before long. A short jog south, and they could hit Flagstaff or Phoenix. Las Vegas wouldn't be far off course the other way." He looked up.

Price frowned. "Vegas is a definite maybe. What better example of 'Western decadence'?" The frown deepened. "We're still working on the worse-case scenario that the zep is wired with explosives." She glanced over her shoulder toward the radio. "Mott just got Able Team off the ground a minute ago. I'm tempted to have them take the damn thing out over Grand Canyon."

Kurtzman looked her in the eye. "Not a real good plan. You have any idea how many campers and hikers are down there this time of the year?"

Price pulled a chair out from the console and sat next to him. "I'm not sure there *is* a real good plan. At least not at this point." Her face hardened, and Kurtzman saw the strength of character that made Barbara Price the exceptional mission controller that she was. "I don't want to do it, Bear," she said, "but if it comes down to a 'few' or 'many'..." Her voice trailed off. "We'll have to wait and watch."

Kurtzman let a sardonic smile creep over his lips. "Look on the bright side. If Striker and Phoenix Force don't neutralize the other threat, this will seem like small potatoes. You heard from them?"

"Grimaldi dropped them near Eldridge's new camp. They'll be ten-three until they neutralize the threat."

Kurtzman nodded. He stared back across the room, his eyes falling again on the teletype. "It's been quiet." In his peripheral vision he saw Price follow his line of sight.

She put what Kurtzman was thinking into words. "The quiet before the storm, Bear. The quiet before the storm."

THE WOOL SOVIET dress uniform burned like fire in the heat, scouring the Executioner's skin like a wire brush. Eyes down, the visor of his major's cap pulled low to hide his face, he glanced to his side as he trudged silently through the sand.

David McCarter and Gary Manning, in Soviet captain and lieutenant uniforms respectively, walked on his left. To his right, in UAR Republican Guard attire, were Yakov Katzenelenbogen and Rafael Encizo.

The men's assault weapons had been necessarily abandoned on the other side of the sand dune, and their only arms were the pistols hidden under their tunics. Calvin James, the only member of the team still in American battle gear, walked behind the "prisoners," prodding them along with his M-16.

The tents were four hundred yards ahead. To the left was parked what remained of Eldridge's motor pool. Bolan counted the tiny forms in the bizarre camel skins as they hurried about various tasks around the camp. All had assault rifles looped over their shoulders.

Eldridge was down to a dozen or so men. Under normal conditions that would have made for an easy strike. But these were hardly normal conditions, the Executioner thought as his boots plodded through the sand.

It only took one finger to push a button.

Katz broke the silence. "They should spot us soon, Striker."

Bolan nodded. "But they won't recognize us. Not for a while, anyway. When they do, it's full speed ahead. We'll just have to hope we get close enough to take them out before anybody reaches the launchers."

One of the figures at the camp suddenly stopped in his tracks, turning in the direction of the oncoming procession. A moment later the rest of the skin-clad men dropped what they were doing and hurried to his side, staring across the desert.

"Hit them on the two-way, James," Bolan ordered. "Use some kind of phony call name. Quick."

Behind him the Executioner heard Calvin James key the mike at his walkie-talkie. "Dolphin Four to U.S. Special Forces camp. Dolphin Four to camp."

The heads of the men watching them turned in unison toward the motor pool. One of the men, wearing a camouflage boonie hat above his skins, started toward the trucks.

"They're monitoring a vehicle radio," Bolan said. "Keep them busy, James. Don't give them time to think this out, or they'll realize it's fishy. Let's speed it up."

The men of Phoenix Force increased their pace.

The man in the boonie hat opened the door to a Hummer and slid inside. Bolan watched one of the other men hurry toward a tent and disappear inside.

A moment later the squelch of James's radio wailed behind them. The hot desert sun continued to burn the back of Bolan's neck as a voice said, "U.S. Special Forces camp. Unit calling, identify and go ahead."

"Dolphin Four," James said. "Navy SEAL Team Four. Encountered enemy fire a few hours ago and got separated from my unit. Ran into a few unfriendlies. I'm bringing them in."

Silence came from the other end of the airwaves.

"It's thin, man," James whispered as they kept on toward the camp. "It won't take long for them to figure out—"

"Keep stalling," Bolan said. His eyes flickered from the multitide of tents to the scant number of vehicles left in the motor pool. Something had happened. Either Eldridge had let most of the men go, killed them, or there'd been a mutiny. Whatever the case, they could use it to their advantage.

The man who'd disappeared into the tent suddenly stepped back out and pointed across the desert. Another figure wearing skins and a pistol belt emerged behind him. The man's silver hair shone in the sunlight.

"Speak of the devil," McCarter said under his breath.

Bolan nodded, focusing on Eldridge. The colonel walked toward the Hummer. A hand stretched the curly cord of a microphone through the open window. Eldridge took it.

Behind him, Bolan heard the insane man's voice come over the air. "Colonel Eldridge here. State your business, soldier."

"Tell them you ran into some of the men heading back to Kuwait. Tell them you're a believer, James. You've come to join the effort."

"Dolphin Four to camp," James said. "And begging the colonel's pardon, it's *sailor*, not soldier. Colonel Eldridge, you're just the man I'm looking for. Bumped into some of your deserters a few hours ago, and they told me what's going down. They don't believe in you, Colonel." He paused dramatically, then said, "But *I* do, sir. I want to join with you in these last hours."

For a minute that lasted an eternity, as Bolan and Phoenix Force continued to plod through the sand toward the camp, the Executioner watched Eldridge stare across the desert. Silently the Executioner prayed that Eldridge's insanity would work against him. He *had* to buy James's story, as thin as it was. At least long enough for them to get close enough to stop World War III.

Finally Eldridge's voice boomed again. "Welcome, my son," he said over the airwaves. Then the radio clicked off.

The Hummer backed away from the motor pool, turned toward them and sped across the desert.

"Oh-oh," James said.

Bolan squinted against the sun. They were less than two hundred yards from the camp now. Luckily none of the men had thought to use binoculars, or they might have already been recognized.

But before long they'd be within eyesight. And depending on who was in the Hummer...

"Okay, slow down," Bolan ordered. He slipped the suppressed Beretta from under his tunic, thumbed the safety to semiauto and held it out of sight under his armpit. Pulling the cap lower over his forehead, he watched the Hummer as it neared. The driver was the only occupant.

"We'll have to play it by ear," the Executioner said. "If the driver recognizes us, I'll try to take him out before he can hit Eldridge on the radio. We'll grab the vehicle and—"

Bolan never got a chance to finish.

Sand flew from the wheels as the Hummer turned broadside and skidded to a halt ten feet in front of them. A wild, crazy grin covered the driver's face as the Executioner moved behind the vehicle, letting it shield him from the camp.

Bolan looked up into the man's eyes. The grin turned to a snarl of savage hatred as the driver saw the face of Colonel Rance Pollock.

The Executioner raised the 93-R as the driver lunged for the radio. A lone 9 mm round sputtered from the suppressed weapon and into the temple of the man in animal skins.

The driver's foot fell from the brake, and the Hummer started to roll forward. Bolan ripped open the door, reached in and shoved the pedal to the floor with his hand.

McCarter and Manning opened the rear door, reached over the seat and jerked the body into the back with them and Encizo. Katz vaulted up into the shotgun seat in front as Bolan slid behind the wheel.

His heart pounding in his chest, the Executioner turned the vehicle toward the camp and started forward. Forcing himself to drive at a moderate pace, he said, "I'm going to head toward the motor pool. At the last second I'll cut toward the launchers. When I hit the brakes, get out and cut those crazies off from the nukes. David, you and Rafael lay down cover fire. Gary, get to the launchers and get them disarmed."

Bolan saw Katz turn toward him in the shotgun seat. "And me?" the Israeli asked.

The Executioner felt his jaw tighten as the man with the snow-white hair grew larger in the distance. "You come with me, Katz," he said. "We're going after Eldridge."

CHAPTER TWELVE

A river of sweat ran from Carl Lyons's face down his neck, soaking the collar of his coveralls. He looked down at the microphone clutched in his fist and saw that the knuckles of his hand had turned white. Loosening his grip, he watched the blood rush back into the joints.

The ex-cop twisted in his seat. Charlie Mott sat behind the controls of Stony Man modified OH-58 Scout. Beneath the California A's baseball cap Mott's eyes were hidden behind mirrored sunglasses. But the wrinkles that shot out from the sides of the lenses, and Mott's jaw chomping up and down on the wad of gum in his mouth, told Lyons that the pilot's usual "cool" was being severely tested.

Lyons glanced over his shoulder. The strain showed on the faces of Blancanales and Schwarz, as well. Politician stared thoughtfully down at his hands, as if the master of mental warfare had drawn his own mind inward to ponder the situation. Gadgets was just as quiet, his eyes flickering from the Scout's windshield to the side windows, then back to the windshield.

Lyons turned back in his seat as the radio scratched. Barbara Price's voice came over the private Stony Man frequency. "Base to Able. Stony Man to Able..."

"Go," Lyons said.

"Location?"

Lyons glanced at the screen in the chopper's control panel and gave the coordinates. He leaned over, looking down to see the winding river that separated Arizona from California. "Just crossing the state line now."

"Roger," Price came back. "Bear's still got the zep routed toward Oceanside. Any visual change?"

"Negative, Stony. Destination still unknown. I was hoping *you* might have something." Lyons paused. "I've got a feeling we'll find out soon, though. We're going to run out of land before long, and I doubt that the Pacific Ocean is their target."

The red lights of the radio scanner suddenly locked onto the USAF frequency. A voice Lyons had been in contact with for the past two hours came over the airwaves—Air Force Captain Jackie Graham. "Raven One to Justice One."

Graham led the squad of four F-117A Stealth fighters that were flying high above the clouds, ready to be called into action at a second's notice. The fighters were unequipped with the secret Stony Man frequency, and there had been no time to install it in the planes. The odds that the zep was equipped to scan the AF airwaves were remote, but not impossible. Therefore, Graham and Lyons had spoken cryptically.

"Come in, Raven," Lyons said.

"How's our 'test plane' holding up?" Graham asked.

"Still maintaining course. We're waiting for—" Ahead in the sky the zeppelin suddenly veered to the north. "Stand by, Raven," Lyons said, switching back to the Stony Man frequency. "Able to Stony Man. Our bird is turning its wings. Repeat, turning north at..." He glanced back to the screen and gave the reading.

"Hang on," Price instructed. In the background Lyons heard her repeat his words to Kurtzman. A moment later she said, "If they hold that course, it'll take them over the San Gabriel Valley, then north-central L.A., Griffith Park and Hollywood. But the whole of Los Angeles is a possible."

Lyons felt pain shoot up his arm. He looked down to see that his fingers had tightened around the mike again. "Roger. Again we've got a multitude of targets. But I'd look for something big."

"Bear's running it through the computer right now."

Lyons forced his hand to relax again. "They've been hitting sites that are symbolic of America," he said. "Look for something like that in the path." He switched back to the AF frequency. "Raven, you still have visual on the test plane?"

"Affirmative, Justice."

The Stony Man crew flew on in silence as they waited for Kurtzman to come up with possible strike sites. Then, suddenly, a new voice broke in over the Air Force frequency. "Raven, Justice...are you there?" it said in accented English. "This is your *test plane.*"

Lyons froze, his fingers wrapped around the mike as the crackle of static replaced the voice. As the Scout continued through the air, he heard Price's voice on the Air Force frequency. "Party speaking, identify," the controller said crisply.

"I believe you know who we are," the voice came back. "But I'm at a disadvantage. Raven? Justice? Colorful names. Very American. But what departments are they?" The voice didn't wait for an answer. "It doesn't matter. But since we'll be talking for a few minutes, I'll address you as such." The voice chuckled. "And you may call me...why not call me Storm? As in Desert Storm. It's a word you Americans seem so fond of."

Lyons, Schwarz and Blancanales and even Charlie Mott continued to sit, stunned into silence. The UAR being able to monitor the frequency had been a long shot.

But the long shot had come through.

"I'm surprised it took you so long to discover our little zeppelin joke," the man calling himself Storm said. "But now that you have it'll do you no good. You've suspected that we're wired to explode if attacked. Otherwise you'd have already done so."

Lyons thumbed the mike button. "That's affirmative. But that doesn't mean we're going to hold back forever. Suggest you land immediately, Storm—unless you'd like to go up in smoke. Look down at the ground. Nothing but wide open space. This would be the perfect place to take you out." The ex-cop held his breath, then said, "Raven, prepare to engage the enemy."

"Affirmative," Graham replied.

Hysterical laughter cackled over the airwaves. "We're all prepared to become martyrs in the service of the United Arab Republic."

"Good," Lyons said. "Because that's just what you're going to be."

"Wait!" Storm said.

Lyons heard a scream in the background aboard the zep.

"Perhaps I misstated myself," Storm went on. "There are some on board who don't care to die." He paused, then said, "Say hello to your fellow Americans, Miss Catlin."

Dianne Catlin was the missing reporter for the *Viewpoint* television news show.

The familiar TV voice quavered as it spoke. "Please don't do anything that will make them—"

Storm cut her off. When he returned, his voice had lost the ironic ring. "We have Miss Catlin and four other hostages aboard," he snarled. "And we'll kill them all if your planes attack."

Plans and counterplans raced through Lyons's brain. Should he try a bluff? Maybe. But not yet. Not until he knew more. "So what do you have planned, Storm?" he asked.

The black humor returned to the voice. "It'll do no harm to tell you now. As you said, we've picked targets that represent our decadent American life-style. And what's more American than baseball? We're all going to a baseball game, Justice. I've always wanted to see Dodger Stadium.''

Lyons felt his heart pound in his chest. He switched back to the Stony Man frequency. "Able One to Stony," he said into the mike. "Bear, check the schedule and find out if there's a game—"

"Just did," Kurtzman said. "It's the top of the third inning. Los Angeles leads by one." The Stony Man computer wizard paused and cleared his throat. "The gate was forty-nine thousand, seven hundred forty-four."

The scanner locked onto the Air Force airwaves again. As if to confirm what Kurtzman had just told Lyons on the other frequency, Storm said, "You're about to witness the UAR's greatest triumph to date, Justice. We're about to sacrifice fifty thousand people in the name of the United Arab Republic."

Lyons looked down and saw the edge of the greater Los Angeles area appear on the horizon. "Thanks, Storm," he said. "You've just made up my mind for me. We're talking five lives versus fifty thousand." He reached up and wiped the sweat from his brow with the back of his hand. "Raven," he said into the mike, "prepare to blow these creeps right out of the sky."

This time the maniacal laughter sounded positively inhuman, sending cold chills down the ex-cop's spine. "No," Storm said when he regained control of himself, "we aren't talking five and fifty thousand. We're talking fifty thousand and *twelve million*." He clicked off, and static echoed over the airwaves again.

Lyons frowned, then keyed his mike again. "Okay, Storm, explain."

When the terrorist's voice returned, it was low, gravelly, and Lyons could almost see the face that spoke. "There are twelve million people in the Los Angeles area," Storm said, "and if you interfere with our plans at the stadium, they'll all die." He continued to chortle dementedly. "We're wired to explode as you guessed." He paused dramatically. "But what you didn't guess, Justice, is that the explosion will be biological. We're loaded down with the nerve gas you call VX."

The cackling laughter ended suddenly as Storm clicked off the radio.

THE HOT MIDDAY SUN beat down on the Hummer as Bolan drove through the desert, angling casually toward the motor pool. Eldridge and the other men in the bizarre camel-skin costumes stood motionless at the edge of the camp, watching. As the tiny figures grew larger, the Executioner glanced toward the stolen Israeli nukes on the other side of the camp.

The four mobile rocket launchers were parked in a line, roughly eighty yards away. The trucks appeared unattended. If he could get within fifty yards of the camp before anyone ID'd them, then twist the Hummer's wheel and floor the accelerator, there was still a chance to angle past the colonel and his crew and cut them off from the nukes.

Suddenly another man in skins stepped out of one of the tents. He hurried to join the group, a small camouflage case clutched in both hands.

"Oh-oh," Katz said.

Eldridge took the case and removed a pair of binoculars. Bolan felt his heart leap into his throat. His face would be partially blocked by the Soviet cap and the Hummer's sun visor. There was still a chance that Eldridge wouldn't recognize him. But the colonel was bound to wonder why his own man wasn't driving the Hummer.

Eldridge raised the binoculars to his forehead. For a brief second he remained motionless. Then Bolan saw him drop the glasses to the sand, his mouth falling open in shock.

The colonel turned to his men, his arms flailing. Eight of the soldiers raised their M-16s. Eldridge and three others turned and sprinted toward the rocket launchers.

Bolan twisted the wheel, flooring the accelerator. "He's spotted us!" he shouted as the Hummer fishtailed through the sand toward the launchers. "Open fire. Same plan. Just do it faster!"

The Special Forces opened fire, sharp cracks sounding across the desert. Empty brass floated through the air as 5.56 mm stingers slammed into the grille and peppered the windshield of the Hummer.

From both sides of the vehicle Bolan heard the return fire of James's M-16 and the rest of Phoenix Force's handguns. Three of the renegade soldiers fell

as the Hummer's tires found traction in the sand and
raced to cut Eldridge off from the nukes.

Bolan let out a breath as the Hummer neared the
mobile launchers. They were less than thirty yards
away now, and Eldridge and his three men were still a
good fifty, and on foot. It would give the Executioner
plenty of time to skid to a halt between the men and
rockets. Manning could begin disarming the nukes
while he and Phoenix Force held them—

Suddenly, from the corner of his eye, the Executioner saw one of the colonel's downed men rise un-
steadily to his feet. Blood streamed through the camel-
hair shirt as the man lifted an M-72 hand-held rocket
launcher and took aim at the Hummer.

Bolan yelled over his shoulder. "James! Four
o'clock!"

Automatic fire sounded from the back seat. More
rounds struck the would-be rocketeer's chest, sending
new blood spurting from the camel hair. The dispos-
able launcher tube fell forward slightly. Then the
weapon exploded in a torrent of fire.

Bolan felt the concussion as the antitank round hit
the ground ten feet short of its mark. Suddenly the
Hummer spun like a top through the sand. The steering wheel was ripped from the Executioner's grip as a
windstorm of sharp, stinging sand blew through the
windows, blinding him and the members of Phoenix
Force.

Thick, acrid smoke filled their nostrils as the Hummer ground to a halt twenty yards from the nuclear

rockets. Wiping the grit from their eyes, Bolan and the Phoenix Force warriors stumbled from the vehicle.

Manning, James, Encizo and McCarter laid down cover fire, dropping two more of Eldridge's guard as Bolan and Katz sprinted toward the line of mobile launchers. But the loss of the Hummer had given Eldridge the edge he needed, and as the Stony team plodded through the ankle-deep sand, they saw the colonel and his men split and head toward the individual trucks.

Bolan drew the Desert Eagle, took aim and dropped the nearest man with a duo of roaring .44 Magnums. At his side he heard the boom of Katz's Beretta and saw another of the skin-clad men fall.

The Executioner pivoted, turning the big .44 toward Eldridge. Before he could level the sights the crazed colonel had ripped open the door of the last truck in line and disappeared into the cab.

The warrior twisted, firing again. The third man heading for the launchers dropped as a Magnum round severed his spine.

Bolan raced toward the front of Eldridge's truck, Katz at his heels. Behind him he heard the shooting suddenly stop as the last of Eldridge's men fell beneath the gunfire of Phoenix Force. Through the windshield he saw the colonel working furiously beneath the dashboard, his face a mask of intensity.

Ten feet from the mobile launcher Bolan cut to the side of the truck and raised the Desert Eagle, aiming through the open window on the passenger side. He saw the colonel's expression soften.

Eldridge looked up, slowly raised a hand and beckoned the Executioner forward. His lips twisted into a mirthless grin, and Bolan saw him mouth the words "Go ahead. Shoot."

Bolan stopped in his tracks. Eldridge had done something out of sight beneath the dashboard. What, he didn't know. He walked cautiously forward.

"Go ahead and shoot me, Pollock," Eldridge taunted as the Executioner reached the window. "If that's part of the plan, then so be it."

The colonel giggled like a little boy as Bolan stopped next to the window and looked down at the launch control panel beneath the dash.

Multicolored lights blinked in the panel. The words BYPASS ACHIEVED: READY TO FIRE flashed in red on the screen. And Eldridge's fingers were coiled around a metal lever, ready to jerk down and send the nuclear rocket streaking through the sky to begin Armageddon.

Bolan focused on the colonel's fingers.

Eldridge had wrapped them securely around the lever with white adhesive tape.

"No!" STORM SCREAMED over the radio. "Don't speak! *You* don't speak when I'm speaking! Do you understand?"

Lyons bit down hard on his lip, the anger swelling like fire in his chest, threatening to make him rip the microphone out of the Scout's radio. He'd formed a mental picture of the man calling himself Storm during the fifteen minutes since their first communiqué, and while he knew such images were rarely accurate, the ex-cop still focused his silent wrath on a short, stocky man with deep bronze skin, heavy eyebrows and short black hair with a receding hairline.

"I asked you if you understood!" Storm screamed again into the radio.

"I understand," Lyons said through clenched teeth.

"Then you'll listen, and you'll listen closely. We have enough VX on board to totally destroy your precious decadent southern California. Do you need details on how nerve gas works, Justice?"

"No," Lyons said. He knew. A single drop of VX on exposed skin would cause death within minutes. The ex-cop looked down as they passed over Orange County. Below, he saw both Disneyland and Knott's Berry Farm, and wondered how many innocent men, women and children were at the two amusement parks alone. Not that it mattered exactly where *anybody* was. With the shifting breezes in the L.A. area the nerve gas would eventually blanket the whole metropolitan area.

"If you don't follow my orders to the letter, we'll release the gas. Item one—you'll dismiss the fighter squadron immediately. They have exactly two minutes. If they don't, I'll release the gas."

Lyons thumbed the mike. "You hear him, Graham?"

"Affirmative. Waiting orders."

"Take off," Lyons said.

Storm came back on. "Item two—even as I speak, UAR ground forces are moving toward the stadium.

You, Justice, will give orders to the police and security personnel in the area that they will be allowed to enter the stadium without being detained."

"I can't do that," Lyons said. "I don't have any authority over—"

"Liar!" Storm screamed. "You're a *liar!* If you don't have the authority, then get it. If you don't, everyone below will die!"

Lyons gripped the microphone in both hands and heard the plastic crack under the pressure. He let up, then keyed the mike again. "What are your ground troops going to do?"

"Kill the people in the Stadium," Storm said simply.

Lyons shook his head in wonder. "And you think we can just stand by and let you massacre fifty thousand people?"

"If you don't, we'll massacre millions."

Lyons hesitated, then said, "Okay, Storm, I'll try to get clearance to let them pass. But like I said, I don't currently have the authority. And getting through channels will take time."

"You have ten minutes," Storm said.

Lyons laughed into the mike. "You seem familiar with all the 'decadence' we have in this country, Storm. Haven't you ever heard the term 'faceless bureaucrat'? Ten minutes won't cut it. I need more—"

"You now have nine minutes!"

"Then you'd better let me get started," Lyons said. "There'll be about twenty yards of red tape to cut through before we can pull this off." He switched back to the Stony Man frequency. A plan had been forming in his mind for the past few minutes. In some respects it seemed as insane as what the UAR were planning. But the whole situation was insane, and sometimes, fire could only be squelched with more fire. "Able to Base," he said. "You copy Storm's last transmission, Barbara?"

"Affirmative, Ironman. Report from LAPD and stadium security just came in. Close to two hundred UAR vehicles just converged on the parking lot. There's a Mexican standoff for the moment. But the cops figure they're outnumbered five to one."

"Get on the horn and get more blue suits moving that way," Lyons said. "Call in CHIPS. The governor got the Cal National Guard on alert."

"Affirmative, One."

"Get them there, too."

The airwaves went silent for a moment, then Price said, "We can't just let them go in and mow down fifty thousand people, Ironman. But what about the nerve gas?"

Lyons didn't answer. "What special units are in the area right now?"

"LAPD SWAT, a couple of FBI Rescue units, Sheriffs—"

"Uh-uh," Lyons broke in. "I'm talking military. Airborne."

"Just a second," Price said. A moment later Kurtzman came on the line. "There's a Delta Force squadron that's been working out of the naval base in San Diego."

"Get them in the air," Lyons said. "But tell them to stay high, and I mean high. Away from the zep. Find another radio frequency we can communicate on that the zep can't possibly have. And while you're at it, see if you can get me a physical description of Ali Mahmoud—I've got a hunch he's in the zep right now going by Storm."

"Affirmative, One." Price left the air.

Lyons switched back to the Air Force frequency. "Justice to Storm," he said. "I've started the snowball rolling. But I can't promise it'll be done in ten minutes."

The voice that came back was cold, emotionless. "Then you can erase Los Angeles from your map, Justice."

Lyons glanced down again as the chopper passed over Watts. Then, taking a deep breath, he turned in his seat to face Schwarz and Blancanales. Both men stared back at him, their faces blank. "Let me tell you what we're going to do..."

He did.

Two minutes later the expressions on the faces of the other Able Team members had changed to masks of incredulity.

Charlie Mott whistled through his teeth as he continued to guide the chopper through the sky. "Thank God I'm just a fly-boy," he muttered.

HAMOUD JALUWI watched General Kaganovich waddle past the four guards posted just inside his office door and enter the room. "Mr. President," the Russian announced, "I have excellent news. Our satellites have finally located Eldridge's camp. He's near Ar-Ramadi."

Jaluwi stood up, the skin of his face feeling suddenly tight. "And?"

"According to the photos, the camp is nearly deserted." The general stopped, shaking his head in wonder. "And those who remain seem to be, well, dressed strangely."

Jaluwi slammed his fist on the desk. "I don't care how they dress!" he exploded. "What of the nuclear weapons?"

"They're there," Kaganovich said, nodding. "They were photographed, as well, and the angle settings of the mobile launchers were run through the computers in Moscow." He stared the UAR leader in the eye. "Two are aimed at Baghdad, as we feared."

"And the other two?"

"Tel Aviv, and here," the Russian said without hesitation.

Jaluwi dropped back into his seat and lifted the phone. "Prepare to launch nuclear missiles on Tel Aviv, Haifa and Jerusalem."

One of the guards turned from the door to face them. "But, Mr. President," he said hesitantly, "Jerusalem is a holy city for Muslims as well as Jews. We can't—"

"Silence! You're a guard, not an adviser!" Waving a hand through the air, he said, "Get out! All of you." Then he turned back to Kaganovich as the men left the room. "What's Moscow doing?"

The Russian stood erect. "We're ready with both long- and short-range weapons. Western Europe and the U.S. But we won't strike first."

"You won't have to," Jaluwi said. "Eldridge's weapons will destroy both Baghdad and Babylon." He looked up at the ceiling. "But we're safe here." He thought back to the guard's statement about Jerusalem.

And besides, Jaluwi thought. The only holy city is the one I'm presently in.

IN HIS OFFICE at the Israeli Ministry of Defense Moshe Netanyahu leaned forward, rested his elbows on the desk, closed his eyes and pressed the phone tighter to his ear. "Yes, sir...yes, sir..." he said into the receiver. Forcing his eyes open, he glanced up at the wall. Tiny colored lights sparkled like eyes in the electronic world map in front of him. He picked out Baghdad, Damascus and Tehran. "Sir," he said, "are you sure?"

"Yes," the voice on the other end of the line replied.

The receiver slipped in Netanyahu's sweaty palm as he nodded. "Then God help us all," he whispered into the receiver.

"Yes," the voice repeated, then the line clicked dead.

With trembling fingers Moshe punched a button on the phone dial. A moment later he heard the line picked up in the control room on the other side of Tel

Aviv. "Prepare to launch on Baghdad, Damascus and Tehran."

The answer he got back sounded like an echo of his own words of a moment before. "Sir, are you sure?"

Feeling as if he'd traded roles with his superior from the last call, Netanyahu said simply, "Yes."

The man in the launch control room said, "God help us all," so Netanyahu just agreed and hung up.

GENERAL HAROLD "Hack" Addington stared through the window on the third floor of the Pentagon and dialed the emergency White House number. As he waited for the line to connect, he stared out his office window at the building across the street and wondered how many times during the past twenty-two years he'd told himself he'd never have to make this call.

"It" would never really happen.

The politicians of the world could be stupid, sure, but not *that* stupid. No one was really going to start a war that might end the world.

A woman's voice answered on the first ring. "Yes, General. He's been waiting for your call. One moment."

A second later the President of the United States asked, "Hack? Is it true?"

Addington hesitated. He knew it was true. It had been confirmed by four sources, and it only took three to pass officially from the nebulous realm of rumor into hard fact. But his mind rebelled, almost forcing him to stick his head in the sand and refuse to believe that *it* was finally happening.

"Hack? Did you hear me?"

"It's true, Mr. President. It's been confirmed by satellite, Army and Navy intelligence and the CIA. It's true, all right. The Soviets are ready. They're one button away."

On the other end of the line Addington heard the President gasp. Then the Man regained his composure. "For God's sake, Hack, the cold war is supposed to be over."

"Yes, sir," Addington said. "Uh, I don't know the details, and I know it's classified, but I understand you have some independent operation under way. Something that might stop all this madness?"

"Yes, I do."

Addington cleared his throat, almost choking on the air that came out. "Can we count on it being successful, sir?"

The Man sighed. "We can't count on anything anymore. Get our response ready. I'll bring the keys."

AT STONY MAN FARM Barbara Price swiveled in her chair and watched Aaron Kurtzman wheel down from his ramp and cross the room. She opened her mouth to speak, then closed it again. Kurtzman did the same.

At this point there was nothing else to do or say.

Price had already linked Able Team with the Delta Force squadron stationed at San Diego, and she'd arranged for the equipment Lyons had ordered to be airlifted to a site near Dodger Stadium.

Kurtzman's computers were no longer needed to locate the UAR strike site—the man calling himself Storm had arrogantly provided them with that information himself. Jaluwi and Eldridge had both been located, and like Price, the computer genius had entered another maddening period of "hurry up and wait."

Price turned her eyes to the stainless-steel table mike, then let them flicker to the speaker in the radio itself. From that screened box they'd learn whether Lyons's half-crazy plan to neutralize the zeppelin was successful. Or if fifty-thousand people had been killed at Dodger Stadium, or millions were about to die from nerve gas. And it was from that same instrument that they'd find out that Bolan, Katz and the rest of Phoenix Force had stopped Eldridge, or that the deranged colonel had launched his nukes.

Carmen Delahunt crossed the room to the coffee maker. A quarter inch of cold, stale brown liquid stood at the bottom of the glass pitcher. The woman opened the cabinet above the machine, pulled out a coffee can and box of filters, then stopped. She put them back in the cabinet and reached for a jar. Turning around to face the Stony Man crew, Price saw the near-hysterical half smile on her lips as she spoke.

"I'd better make instant. Just in case. Anybody else want some?"

"I do," Tokaido said.

Five heads turned as one to stare at him. In the entire time he'd been at Stony Man Farm none of them had ever seen the young Oriental drink anything but water and fruit juices.

Price forced a smile. "You're always telling us what caffeine does to a person's heart rate, Akira."

Tokaido glanced at the radio. He shrugged indifferently.

The Stony Man mission controller's smile faded as the magnitude of the simple gesture struck home.

CHAPTER THIRTEEN

The Executioner stared through the open window at the hand taped to the nuclear control lever.

"Why don't you pull the trigger, Pollock?"

Bolan looked up at the dementedly laughing mouth. The colonel's lips were corkscrewed in a crooked smile, but the mirth ended there. Heavy bags of dark, flaccid skin hung beneath his eye sockets, and the eyes themselves seemed to have fallen backward into his skull, as if trying to retreat somewhere into the maddened brain.

"Go on," Eldridge breathed, "do it. It won't stop the will of God."

Bolan moved slowly toward the truck. "This isn't God's will, Eldridge. It's yours."

Katz appeared on the other side of the launch vehicle. The one-armed Israeli stuck the Beretta through the window and leveled it on Eldridge's head.

The colonel turned slowly, staring at the open bore. "Ah, the Jew," he said. "Maybe you'd like to be the one to do it."

Katz looked down at the control lever, then up at Bolan. Slowly he lowered his weapon.

"Nobody wants to shoot you, Eldridge," the Executioner said softly.

The colonel's head swiveled and he glared at Bolan, his dark, empty eyes now overflowing with hatred. "No?" he said. "You've been trying to get rid of me ever since you were assigned to this command, Pollock." The thin lips curled up again into a snarl. "And don't think I don't know why. Don't think for a minute that I don't know who sent you here. I know who your master is."

"Who?" Katz asked. "Who is our master?"

Eldridge jerked back to the other window. "Satan!" he screamed.

Bolan glanced down at the control board. A sharp tug down was all it would take to begin World War III, and it didn't matter if Eldridge did it on purpose, or if his body weight pulled the lever after he had a bullet in his head. No matter how the Executioner shot him, Eldridge would fall forward.

The hand, and with it the lever, would go down.

Behind him Bolan heard the rest of Phoenix Force approach. He held his hand up, stopping them. "Talk to us, Eldridge. Explain all this. We want to understand."

"Liar!" Eldridge screamed. "You serve Satan!"

Katz shook his head. "If we've been serving the wrong master, it's been through ignorance rather than choice. Give us a chance, Eldridge. I'm beginning to think you're right. The Master of Deceit has fooled us."

A flicker of hesitation entered Eldridge's eyes. Bolan could see what Katz was trying to do, and it just might work. Katz knew the Bible, both Old and New

Testaments. If anybody could reason with Eldridge, it would be Katz. And even if all he did was distract Eldridge, then maybe, just maybe, the Executioner would be able to reach through and grasp the colonel's wrist.

From there it was anybody's guess as to what went down.

Bolan saw the back of the colonel's head again as Eldridge spoke to Katz. "This will be your last chance to repent," he said in a low, gravelly voice. "You realize that, don't you?"

Katz nodded. "Tell us. We want to understand."

Bolan leaned forward slightly into the window.

Eldridge twirled to face him. "What are you doing?" he screamed.

Bolan shook his head. "Nothing. I just want to be able to hear you."

Eldridge frowned, uncertain. "Drop your weapons."

Bolan let the Desert Eagle fall into the sand. He heard Katz's Beretta hit the ground on the other side of the truck.

Eldridge nodded to the Executioner's 93-R in the shoulder rig. "Two fingers."

Slowly the Executioner gripped the butt of the pistol between his thumb and index finger, pulled it from the holster and let it fall next to the big .44. He placed his empty hands on the truck door and leaned forward. "Talk to us. We can't hurt you now."

Eldridge threw back his head and cackled like a hyena. "Hurt me?" he cried, tears streaming down his cheeks. "Hurt me? You could never have hurt me, Pollock! The entire army of Heavenly Hosts has protected me for this moment."

"Tell us about it," Katz urged. "Please."

Eldridge turned back to the other window. "You're Jewish?"

Katz nodded. "Yes, but I was raised in France. I was Catholic."

"Then you should understand," Eldridge said. "Can't you see what has happened? The prophecies have been fulfilled."

"What prophecies?" Katz asked calmly. "Tell me about them."

Bolan leaned farther into the truck. This time Eldridge didn't notice.

The colonel turned toward the control panel and shook his head in disgust. "Oh, ye of little faith," he muttered under his breath. "Jaluwi. Haven't you seen what has happened?" His voice began to rise with the zeal of a tent revivalist. "I saw a creature rising up out of the sea.... He had seven heads and ten horns...and the Dragon gave him his own power and throne and great authority." He glanced over his shoulder at Bolan, then went on. "I saw that one of the heads was wounded beyond recovery—but the fatal wound was healed!" Lifting his eyes, Eldridge stared up at the heavens through the windshield. "Tell me, who does that sound like to you?" he asked.

Bolan thought back to the phony assassination attempt that Jaluwi had staged. There had been several days in which the world had thought the UAR leader *had* died. Of a head wound. "I think I understand," the Executioner said.

"Yes!" Eldridge screamed, nodding excitedly and turning toward him. "Hamoud Jaluwi is the Antichrist!" He leaned forward and started to pull the lever.

"Wait!" Bolan shouted.

Eldridge turned back. His eyes narrowed now into tiny fishlike slits. "What?"

"I don't understand why God would need us," the Executioner said. "*Any* of us. If He's ready to destroy the world, surely He could do it without our help."

"I'm confused, too," Katz said quickly. "You said all the prophecies had been fulfilled. But I don't think they have."

Eldridge's head jerked toward the Jew. "What are you talking about?"

Bolan took advantage of the opportunity, leaning still farther into the truck.

Katz's eyes flickered from the Executioner back to Eldridge. "Jaluwi's head wound was a fake. He was never really injured. Okay, he organized the ten Arab countries into one. I can see how that could represent the ten heads of the Creature. But I've read Revelations, Colonel, and the Old Testament prophets, too. There are dozens, no hundreds more prophecies that have to be fulfilled before all this comes to pass. And that just hasn't happened."

Eldridge's voice rose an octave. "They *have* been fulfilled!" he shouted in self-righteous furor. "They have!"

Katz held up his hands, palms out. "Okay," he said softly, "but please wait just long enough to explain one of them to me, the one I have the most trouble with. Then we'll both help you pull the lever—if that's what you still want."

"What?" Eldridge asked impatiently. "What else don't you understand?"

"The Temple in Jerusalem," Katz said. "Christ predicted it would be destroyed."

"And it was."

"Right. But in Revelation 11:1-2," Katz went on, "it's prophesied that the Temple will be rebuilt *before* the end of the world." He paused. "That hasn't happened, Eldridge. In fact, there's a Muslim mosque sitting on the site where the Temple used to be. And that's only one of many unfulfilled prophecies." The Israeli stared deeply into Eldridge's eyes. "God's not ready to end things yet, Colonel," he said. "You're not doing the Lord's will here. You're doing your own."

Another flash of indecision suddenly covered Eldridge's face. He looked fearfully from Katz to Bolan, then back to the Israeli. "No," he whispered, "you're trying to confuse me. You speak the words of the Creature."

Katz shook his head. "I speak the words of truth, Colonel. If you believe in the prophecies, you have to believe in all of them. You can't just pick and choose from the Bible and make it fit your own ends.''

Eldridge shook his head violently.

Katz glanced up at Bolan, then went on. "You're the one who's been misled, Colonel. This isn't the time to end the world, and you're not the man.''

"No,'' Eldridge said quietly. Then his voice rose steadily from a whisper to a scream. "No, no, no!''

He lunged forward, wrapped his free hand around the one taped to the lever and jerked down.

As THE SCOUT HOVERED, Carl Lyons caught sight of an AH-IS HueyCobra approaching from the rear. Schwarz and Blancanales slid open the back cargo door.

Wind rushed into the chopper as the Huey stopped, floating fifteen feet away. A U.S. Army Delta Force sergeant wearing an OD green fatigue blouse and khaki pants raised what looked like a small shotgun, aimed at the Scout and pulled the trigger. A three-pronged grappling hook shot across the space separating the two aircraft and hooked around the doorway of the Scout.

The sergeant turned and said something to the pilot. The Huey inched away, taking up the slack in the nylon line. Turning back, the Delta man attached a heavy coil of rubber cable and a small metal supply box to the line, then motioned over his shoulder. The Huey rose slightly, and the cable and box slid down the line to the Scout.

Schwarz and Blancanales pulled the items in and closed the door as Lyons picked up the microphone. Programming the radio for the new frequency Stony Man had provided for communication with Delta Force, he thumbed the button. He had to be sure the enemy couldn't monitor the new frequency, and now was as good a time as any to find out. Since Storm had already established a line of communication, all he'd have to do was ask.

"Justice to Storm," Lyons said, "Justice to Storm. Come in, Storm." He waited as the static returned to the air.

Fifteen seconds later he tried again. Nothing.

Lyons switched to the Air Force frequency they'd used earlier. "Justice to Storm."

"Come in, Justice," the accented voice said. "Have the orders been given?"

"We're encountering some bureaucratic problems just like I told you we would. It'll be a few minutes."

"Your time is up," Storm yelled into the radio. "I'll release the gas in two minutes if my demands aren't met."

Lyons grasped the mike. They'd never make it in that length of time. "Storm, listen. The way things stand, you can wipe out Dodger Stadium and live to tell about it. But if you release the gas, I promise you we're going to blow you out of the sky five seconds later. What I'm saying is that you're going to be able to have your cake and eat it, too—if you just don't get impatient." He paused for effect. "Don't blow it now. What difference can a few more minutes make?"

There was a long silence from the zeppelin, then Storm's voice came back. "I'll give you five more minutes," he growled. "No more."

"Fair enough," Lyons replied. "I'll get back to you as soon as you've been cleared." He let up on the mike and turned to Mott. "You heard the man, Charlie. We don't have much time. Take her up." As the chopper rose high into the air, Lyons switched back to the Delta frequency. "Justice to Delta."

The radio crackled, then a voice said, "Captain Becker here, Justice. We're high in the sky overhead, awaiting orders."

"Your first order is to stay high, Captain. Way above the clouds for now. If they spot you from the zep, we're all dead." He glanced down again. "And so are the folks below."

"Affirmative, Justice. Your HQ—whoever they are—briefed us in-flight. How do we know when to move?"

Lyons hesitated. That could be a problem. Keying the mike, he asked, "Have you got visual on the zep?"

"That's affirmative. They're over the stadium now."

"Then you'll be able to see us go down. Don't do anything. Repeat—do nothing until you see us enter the cabin. After that, it won't make any difference if you're seen."

Becker sighed. "That's cutting it damn close, friend."

"There's no other way. How many men have you got up there?"

"Whole troop's ready to go," Becker replied. "How many do you need?"

Lyons frowned. Delta had been formed in the tradition of the British SAS. Four men made an operational squad, and four squads formed a troop. That meant a total of sixteen men he could count on. "If it turns out we need you, send them all," he said. "It'll give us a little more room for error."

Becker snorted. "Right. The good Lord and the Army both know you've got precious little room for error anywhere else."

"Ten-four on that," the ex-cop came back. "But remember, Captain—you guys are backup. Plan B, so to speak. With any luck we can neutralize the threat before they get to the controls, land the zep ourselves and all go home."

Lyons switched back to Stony Man's private frequency. "Barbara, you got Mahmoud's description yet?"

"Better than that," the mission controller said. "Does Gadgets have the portable fax handy?"

Lyons glanced into the back of the chopper where Schwarz was already unzipping a padded bag. The electronics expert extended the cord over the seat, and the Able Team leader plugged it into the dash.

A moment later a copy of a passport photo rolled out of the machine. Lyons grinned as he took it from Schwarz. For once his preconceived mental picture had been close.

Ali Mahmoud *was* bald.

"He's five-seven, a hundred and fifty-five," Price informed him. "Dark complexion, brown and brown. Large round scar on his right cheek."

"Ten four." Lyons broke off contact as the Scout reached high altitude. They'd moved gradually farther west across L.A. as they rose through the air, and now the ex-cop could see the Sinor zeppelin several hundred feet below as it hovered over Dodger Stadium. He felt vaguely light-headed, and knew they were pushing the boundaries of how high they could get without oxygen. "Take her directly over, Charlie," he instructed, "then start down."

Lyons crawled over the seat into the back, and Schwarz handed him a chute. He shook his head. "I won't have room for it. Not going down the way I am." He saw a brief spark of concern in both men's eyes. Then Schwarz shrugged. "Your funeral."

Gadgets and Pol bolted the rubber bungee cord to the machine gun mount next to the door and secured themselves in the retaining harnesses. Lyons reached down, lifted his own harness over his shoulders and buckled it around his waist. "Let's go."

Schwarz slid the door open, and Lyons looked down. Far below he saw the zeppelin. The stadium, even farther away, looked like a tiny, oval-shaped amoeba. For a brief moment Lyons thought back to their drop over the synagogue in Washington. It had been relatively the same as what they were about to do now, but there was one major difference—if they'd fallen from the end of the cords over the synagogue, they'd have landed on the roof ten feet away. If this cable didn't hold up, they'd fall close to a mile, burrowing into the playing field somewhere around second base.

Able Team would give a whole new significance to the term "dugout."

The three men looked at one another, then jumped.

HALF IN, HALF OUT of the mobile launch vehicle's cab, Bolan caught Eldridge's wrists with his right hand. The lever stopped halfway down the slot. A yellow light flashed on and off in the panel.

"No!" Eldridge screamed. "You cannot stop the will of the Lord!" He yanked down again with both hands.

Bolan felt the pressure against his wrist as the lever dropped another inch. He struggled to keep it up as the yellow light continued to flash tauntingly.

"No!" Eldridge yelled again, leaning farther forward and throwing his body weight down on the lever.

The Executioner's feet pedaled air, vainly searching for purchase against the slippery outside of the truck door so that he could propel himself the rest of the way into the cab. From his present clumsy angle he was unable to get his strength beneath him where he needed it.

From the corner of his eye he saw Katz raise his prosthetic arm. A dull, distant click echoed through the cab as the Israeli cocked the .22 pistol hidden beneath the synthetic flesh.

Eldridge turned toward the man, releasing the lever with his free hand and balling his fingers into a fist.

Bolan got both hands around Eldridge's and jerked up. The ignition handle returned to an upright position with a hollow click. The flashing yellow light became a steady beam of green.

An animal-like howl issued forth from Eldridge's mouth. His fist shot forward, catching Katz squarely in the jaw. The Israeli dropped to the ground, unconscious.

Before Eldridge could turn back, Bolan released one hand from the lever, lunged past him and grabbed the steering wheel. Eldridge twisted back toward the panel as the Executioner pulled himself the rest of the way into the cab. Bolan got his hand back under the level a split second before Eldridge jerked down again.

Through the windshield the Executioner saw the rest of Phoenix Force fanning out, trying to get a clear shot at the deranged colonel through the windshield.

With a demented shriek Eldridge raised an elbow, striking the Executioner under the chin. Bolan's teeth clamped together, a salty, iron taste filling his mouth as blood rushed from his tongue. His ears rang as if a thousand bells had just gone off inside his head. His vision blurred a fuzzy, indistinct gray.

Another elbow strike caught him in the jaw, and he felt his grip loosen on the lever. Eldridge yanked down again. The lever returned to the halfway position, and the flashing yellow caution light returned.

"Shoot!" Bolan roared to Phoenix Force at the top of his voice. "Shoot him!"

Encizo's voice came back. "Can't get an angle, Striker!"

Bolan wormed another two inches into the cab. "Shoot him!" he yelled again.

"We can't!" McCarter yelled back. "We'll hit you!"

The Executioner twisted, driving his own elbow back. It glanced off Eldridge's ribs, doing no damage. The men of Phoenix Force were real pros. They knew that if Mack Bolan had to die to stop World War III, then Mack Bolan had to die. But they also knew that the stray round that killed the Executioner would also free Eldridge to pull the lever down the rest of the way. And if they riddled the cab with bullets, killing both men beneath an indiscriminate barrage of fire, the combined weight would engage the lever as Bolan and Eldridge toppled forward.

The flashing caution light sent radiant yellow shafts bouncing through the cab as the two men continued to grapple for control. His chest now resting on Eldridge's thighs, Bolan twisted away, dropping lower, struggling to get farther under the lever.

Eldridge leaned suddenly forward and drove the point of his chin savagely into the Executioner's spine. Bolan felt needles of pain shoot through his body, head to toe.

"You are damned!" Eldridge screamed.

Dropping still farther, Bolan pushed up with both hands. The lever returned to the upright position, and the steady green light came back on. Eldridge shrieked in fury and brought his chin down again into the Executioner's back.

Bolan pushed up with all his strength, holding the lever at the top of the slot. Both his shoulders and arms were below the leverage point now, and he was pushing up at a forty-five-degree angle. He could hold Eldridge off indefinitely now, unless . . .

Eldridge's head shot down into the warrior's spinal cord again. The shock vibrated through the Executioner's body, stinging like the fires of hell and threatening to paralyze his limbs.

His fingers tingled around the lever, loosening. The flashing yellow light filled the cab once more.

Bolan shifted his weight, getting both shoulders behind his left arm. He knew what he had to do. If he blew it, or was too slow, there wouldn't be another chance.

Thumbing the safety strap away from the handle of the Pentagon dagger, Bolan drew the weapon. His tingling fingers encircled the rubber handle in a hatchet grip. Mentally he willed strength into his near-paralyzed hand.

The Executioner waited until he sensed Eldridge's head descending again. Then, with all the strength left in his arm, he brought the five-inch blade up and back behind him. The needle-tipped point struck bone, and Eldridge screamed in pain.

Bolan pushed harder. The blade slid off the bone into something soft.

Eldridge's screams suddenly stopped. His weight fell limply forward onto the Executioner's back. Slowly, cautiously, Bolan shoved the lever back to the top of the panel. The green light returned.

The warrior lay quiet, exhausted. He used what remained of his strength to hold Eldridge and the lever up. Then the doors opened on both sides of him, and an arm moved past the Executioner. A flashing stainless-steel blade cut the tape from Eldridge's hand. James and Encizo lifted the colonel off Bolan's back.

The Executioner sat up and turned in the seat. Sitting next to him, supported by James and Encizo, was Colonel Joshua Eldridge, who stared through the windshield toward the heavens above, one of his wild eyes frozen forever in death.

The other eye had disappeared somewhere behind the Pentagon dagger embedded through the socket into his brain.

LYONS FELT AS THOUGH he'd bought a ticket on the wildest roller coaster in Disneyland. The Able Team leader hit the end of the bungee cord again, his fall slowing as the rubber stretched—farther than the ex-cop would have ever guessed possible. Reaching the end, he jerked suddenly up again, bouncing back through the sky toward the Scout. Above him he spotted Schwarz and Blancanales.

The men of Able Team fell again, bounced, rose, bounced, rose. Each new rebound slowed their momentum until they dangled in the air like worms beneath some giant, flying fisherman's float.

Lyons looked down as his stomach settled. Mott had done well estimating their fall. The top of the zeppelin floated less than thirty feet below. Farther down he saw the oval coliseum of Dodger Stadium. The game was still going on.

Glancing overhead again, he saw Schwarz hanging ten feet above. Still higher, Blancanales jiggled from the rubber line, swaying gently back and forth in the wind. Speaking into the face mike in front of his lips, he said, "Good job, Charlie. Now take her down, slow."

The chopper engine revved, and the line began to drop through the air. Lyons's boots hit the top of the zeppelin's envelope. He reached overhead, unhooking the D-clasp that held him to the line. Just as his fingers released the catch, a sudden gust of wind jerked the chopper up and to the side.

Schwarz and Blancanales sailed back into the air as Lyons stumbled, desperately trying to get his footing on the slippery canvas balloon. He fell forward on his side, sliding feet first toward the edge. Reaching out, he got an elbow around one of the struts encircling the envelope just as his legs slid off into the air.

Lyons dangled helplessly for a moment. Then another sudden gust lifted him up, propelling his body away from the zeppelin at a ninety-degree angle. He reached out with the other hand, grasped the strut and swung himself back in.

The ex-cop wrapped both arms around the strut and sat, catching his breath as the wind died down. He glanced to the west as Mott guided the Scout back over the zeppelin. Dark clouds were forming over the ocean.

A storm was coming, which meant the wind could pick up again any second. Another reason to get inside the zeppelin as quickly as possible.

Lyons looked at his watch as Schwarz and Blancanales landed on top of the zeppelin. Able Team had synchronized watches before leaping from the chopper, but by anybody's time they had less than two minutes remaining before Storm released the gas. The ex-cop pulled the winder from his belt and flipped it open with the thumb stud. He turned to Schwarz and Blancanales. "Go ahead," he said. "Give me—" he glanced again at his watch "—a minute-fifteen. Then go in, whether you see me or not."

Pol nodded. "That's cutting it close, Ironman."

Lyons rose to a kneeling position on the canvas. "So what else is new?"

As Schwarz and Blancanales attached their rappeling gear to struts on opposite sides of the balloon, Lyons jabbed the tip of the winder through the canvas and sliced it open.

A sudden hiss shot from the envelope, then quieted. In the wind the sound would go unnoticed inside the cabin. Lyons dropped through the opening as the other two Able Team warriors disappeared over the sides of the balloon.

The ex-cop began the climb down through the zeppelin's honeycombed frame. No, he thought as he navigated the narrow passages, he'd never have been able to squeeze through with a chute on his back.

Reaching the bottom, Lyons sliced through the canvas again. A moment later he stood on the roof at the rear of the zeppelin's aluminum cabin. He looped an arm around one of the cables holding the cabin to the envelope and jammed the winder back into the nylon pouch on his belt. Pulling a small metal box from his coveralls, he flipped open the lid.

Somewhere over the ocean thunder roared. Wind whistled between the envelope and cabin as Lyons twisted the cap off the bottle of hydrochloric acid. He glanced again at his watch.

Thirty-three seconds remained before Storm released the gas.

Kneeling, Lyons positioned himself upwind and tipped the bottle, pouring the acid onto the aluminum in the pattern of a three-by-three-foot square. Tiny wisps of smoke rose from the roof, disappearing into the wind as he drew an X within the square with the remaining liquid.

The ex-cop stood and drew the Colt Python, staring at his watch as the acid burned away. Giving it twenty seconds, he took a deep breath, leaped up and released the cable.

Two-hundred-plus pounds hit the juncture in the middle of the X. Lyons felt the roof give way beneath his boots. The metal snapped up on the sides as he shot down through the opening. A sharp corner sliced through the leg of his coveralls and into the back of the Able Team leader's thigh as he fell.

Glass crashed on both sides of the zeppelin as Lyons hit the floor of the cabin. He looked up to see Schwarz and Blancanales swinging through the windows at the ends of their rappeling lines.

Hitting the floor on one knee, the Able Team leader rolled, coming to a halt next to a small table. He turned to see the frightened face of a tall blond woman with pale blue eyes.

Dianne Catlin.

Lyons turned toward the front of the craft. A half-dozen terrorists in desert cammies were scattered around the cabin. They looked up in shock, the AK-47s in their hands momentarily useless. A bald man dressed in a blue business suit had risen from his seat and now stared at the three Able Team warriors in amazement. A circular scar covered the man's right cheek, looking as if someone, or something, had at one time taken a bite from his face.

Ali Mahmoud. Lyons had been right. The Pan-Am board member *was* Storm.

Mahmoud drew a Walter PPK from under his jacket and snap-fired a shot across the room, the bullet flying past Lyons and lodging harmlessly in a couch at the end of the cabin. Then the man raced toward the zeppelin's controls.

CHAPTER FOURTEEN

Less than a thousand feet below, the swampy land paralleling the Euphrates rushed up to meet him. The Executioner jerked the rip cord. The parachute flew out over his head, billowed in the wind and jerked him back up through the air.

Slowly he began to fall again. Grasping the toggles at the rear of the risers, Bolan steered toward a break in the bulrushes. Feet and knees pressed tightly together, he rolled through a classic landing, spreading the force of the drop over his body like a well-trained judo man hitting the mat.

The Executioner gathered in the canopy as he watched the men of Phoenix Force hit the muggy earth around him. He glanced quickly overhead. Somewhere above the clouds Jack Grimaldi was already on his way back to Saudi Arabia. The Stony Man warriors' HALO free-fall had meant the Allied plane would have shown up for only a split second on Iraqi-UAR radar.

Katz, James and the rest of the men gathered around Bolan and began stripping off their jumpsuits, replacing them with the counterfeit uniforms that had been provided earlier in the mission. Bolan watched Encizo don his UAR desert camou blouse.

Again the uniforms would be a thin disguise, hardly solving the infiltration problem for them. The best the Executioner could hope for was that they'd slow the reactions of the UAR and give the men from the Stony Man team a split second of "hesitation time" in which to react to whatever happened.

Bolan buttoned the hot wool tunic to his throat and turned toward the ancient city of Babylon in the distance. Squinting, he could see the Lion Monument at the Northern Palace. Beyond the statue of the great beast stood the recently rebuilt Southern Palace of Nebuchadnezzar. Just to the west was an artificial hill, and peeking over the top of the grass was the building once known as the Saddam Hussein Guest House where the megalomaniac had entertained dignitaries from around the world.

The Executioner's eyes turned back to the Northern Palace. According to Kurtzman's intel, it was below this structure that Jaluwi's multilevel underground headquarters bunker lay.

When the men were dressed, Bolan led them along the river toward the city. Again they made no effort to conceal themselves. Their uniforms were "friendly" this time, and Bolan not only didn't fear being stopped by a curious UAR patrol, he hoped for it.

Sweat beaded his forehead by the time they heard the jeep's engine behind them on the river road. All six men turned as the vehicle rounded a curve. Katz broke from the group, waving his arms to get their attention, and the vehicle skidded to a halt.

The two UAR soldiers in the jeep stared in confusion at Bolan, McCarter and Manning's Soviet garb. "You're with General Kaganovich's party?" one of them asked. "Why are you . . . ?"

Katz broke from the group, walking forward in his UAR lieutenant's uniform. He threw his hands in the air and laughed. "Our jeep overheated," he said in Arabic, his hand falling slowly to the flap holster on his hip. The smile never left his face as he drew the sound-suppressed Beretta and pumped a 9 mm round into each of the men.

"Get them out of sight—quick," Bolan ordered. He took a seat in the back of the jeep as Encizo and James dragged the bodies into the weeds along the river.

"They hidden?" Manning asked as the two returned and Encizo slid behind the wheel.

"Just like Moses in the bulrushes," James said, grinning beneath the visor of his Libyan officer's cap.

Encizo drove at a moderate pace as they neared the half-size reproduction of the ancient Ishtar Gate. Intricately carved bulls and fanciful dragons glowered at the men from Stony Man as they pulled to a halt in front of the blue-glazed stones. A small rectangular guard shack stood just outside the gate. Through the windows Bolan saw four UAR men with Kalashnikovs. A sergeant stepped forward, his eyebrows lowering in puzzlement as he approached the jeep.

The Executioner's eyes quickly swept the immediate vicinity. Other than the guards, the area was deserted. The warrior would never know what gave them away. The sergeant dropped to the ground, drawing his side arm.

Bolan whipped out the 93-R from beneath his tunic and drilled a 3-round burst into the sergeant's throat.

Katz, James and McCarter rose to their feet in the jeep. The three fired as one, their suppressed Berettas spitting 9 mm death as the rounds tore through the glass of the guard shack and punched into the heads and hearts of the three remaining guards.

"Let's go," Bolan said, ramming a fresh magazine into the Beretta. "From here on we're on borrowed time."

Encizo threw the jeep into gear, and they drove through the gate. A right-hand turn put them on Procession Street, where only a few months earlier statesmen from around the world had watched soldiers dressed in the livery of ancient Mesopotamia parade as part of Saddam Hussein's International Babylon Festival. They drove past the side wall of the Northern Palace and turned left.

A small temporary building sat just outside the iron gate. A young lieutenant exited the metal door and walked forward as Encizo pulled the jeep to a halt.

Bolan turned to Katz. "Tell him I'm Major Yetsnikov. I have with me a representative from our ally Libya, and we must speak to President Jaluwi and General Kaganovich immediately." He turned back, glowering at the young lieutenant with intimidating eyes.

Katz spoke in Arabic. The lieutenant frowned, shrugged and answered. The Israeli turned to Bolan, his lips barely moving as he whispered, "He says he's received no notice that you were coming."

Bolan puffed out his chest and made his voice angry and impatient as he said, "Tell him I can't be responsible for the UAR's communication incompetence, and that if he ever hopes to rise above his present rank, he'll let us pass without further detainment."

Katz nodded, turned back to the young officer and barked the message with an equally irritated voice. The lieutenant's bewilderment became fear. He mumbled something and saluted stiffly.

Katz turned quickly to Bolan. "He'll have to call into the compound and okay it. He says he hopes you'll understand—he can't do any more."

Bolan stared at the frightened young man. "Tell him we'll come with him to make sure it gets done right." As Katz repeated the message, he opened the door and exited the vehicle with the exasperated pageantry of an offended ranking officer.

The Executioner and Katz followed the lieutenant inside the building. Six more soldiers sat at desks scattered throughout the room. They shot to their feet when they saw Bolan's uniform.

The lieutenant walked to his desk and lifted the phone. Bolan nodded to Katz, then drew the Beretta from under his tunic, stepped forward and brought it down on the top of the lieutenant's head. Next to him the Israeli's suppressed 92 coughed twice. A man at the desk just to his right fell forward onto a stack of printed forms. Blood poured from the wounds in his chest, soaking the papers.

Bolan turned the 93-R toward a desk along the wall where a corporal was fumbling with the Makarov on his belt. A 3-round burst of Parabellum hollowpoints pierced the man's sternum as Katz took out an Iraqi pencil pusher seated at a desk in the middle of the room.

Two sergeants at the rear of the building had drawn Soviet-made TT-33 automatics by the time the Executioner dropped his sights their way. Squeezing the trigger four times, the Executioner cut a figure eight back and forth between them. The smell of cordite filled the room as the near-silent weapon coughed again and again before locking open. As Bolan dropped the empty mag and shoved in a fresh load, the final UAR man fell to a double-tap from Katz's pistol.

The Executioner bent over the young lieutenant. The man lay on his side, moaning. Blood trickled from the top of his scalp and down his face. Rolling him onto his back, Bolan pressed the Beretta's suppressor against the man's quivering upper lip. "English?" he asked.

The young man nodded.

The Executioner jerked the man to his feet and turned to Katz. "Show him your toy."

Katz shoved the index finger of his prosthetic arm a few inches in front of the man's eyes.

"You see the hole?" Bolan asked.

The young man moaned again and nodded.

"It's .22 caliber," Katz said. *"Magnum."* He grabbed the lieutenant by the shoulders, twirled him around and jabbed the finger into his back. "If you don't do exactly as you're told, it'll sever your spine." With his good arm the Israeli replaced the Beretta beneath his tunic. A hard smile curled the corners of his mouth. "I'll be walking right behind you, my young friend. Do you understand?"

Another nod.

"Then what are we waiting for? Like they say in the movies, 'Take us to your leader.'"

IN THE BATHROOM on the third floor of the Northern Palace Talia Alireza felt the sharp, stinging spray of the shower caress her body. She closed her eyes, letting the sensual pleasure work like a drug and drive away reality for a few moments.

Alireza opened her eyes. The spray hit her breasts, dripping off the tips like a waterfall. She leaned forward and pressed her forehead against the shower stall.

This time she'd been certain that her allegiance to the UAR was sound. Instead, once again, she found herself in moral turmoil.

Turning off the shower, Alireza opened the door and reached for a towel. As she blotted the moisture from her skin, the vision of her mother being led off in handcuffs refused to leave her brain. Had Amilah Alireza been right? Was Jaluwi in reality a cruel dictator who was only masquerading as a man who would unite the Arab countries once and for all?

Was he the wolf in her mother's dream? A wolf in sheep's clothing?

Alireza stepped out of the shower and closed the door. No. The UAR president had taken Amilah Alireza for good reason. He had a right to be skeptical of a mercenary who had once been a Mossad agent, and even a few days before been employed by the Americans. Jaluwi was only insuring that she wasn't a spy. He wouldn't hurt her mother.

And as soon as Talia had proved her loyalty beyond doubt, the president would let her mother go, as he'd promised.

Feeling better, Alireza wrapped the towel around her body and pulled another from the rack on the wall. Slowly she began mopping her hair. Then, suddenly, another disturbing thought crossed her mind. Striker.

Damn him. Every time she felt she'd worked things out in her mind, the big American entered it to confuse her again. But the contrast between the two men—the American and Jaluwi—was always there, and the woman couldn't help asking herself one more question—would Striker ever take someone's innocent mother hostage? Under any circumstances?

No. She *had* made the right decision.

As she walked toward the UAR uniform laid out on the bed Alireza glanced through the window. Past the elaborate flower gardens and statues of lions and bulls in the front courtyard of the palace she saw a jeep crowded with UAR troops and Soviet advisers pull up to the gate. A guard walked out of the metal building to meet them. They spoke briefly, then a Soviet major and a UAR soldier followed him back into the building.

Alireza reached for the clean khaki blouse on the bed. She paused to examine the yellow patches on the shoulders. This uniform was part of the recently arrived shipment designed specifically for the UAR. No longer would the United Arab Republic wear the converted fatigues of other countries. That was all in the past. From now on there would be one unified nation to combat the crimes of the Jews and Americans.

She buttoned the blouse, slipped into the matching fatigue pants and wrapped her gun belt around her waist. She was about to turn away from the window when the three men appeared once more and walked back to the jeep.

The female merc felt a twinge of anxiety shoot through her as her eyes followed the big Soviet major. There was something unsettlingly familiar about the way he walked.

The UAR lieutenant opened the gate, then boarded the jeep with the rest of the men. As the vehicle entered the courtyard and started toward the parking lot at the side of the palace, Alireza's eyes suddenly fell on the face in the back seat. She leaned closer to the window, her heart leaping into her throat.

The face was black.

As the jeep neared, she made out the familiar features in the Libyan uniform.

Calvin James.

Alireza's eyes shot to the man driving the vehicle. Dark, grizzled hair shot out from the sides of his UAR cap. Rafael Encizo.

She didn't need to see more, but her eyes turned to the big Soviet major as if drawn by some invisible force. She studied the hard set of the jaw, the firm determination so deeply etched into the face.

Pivoting away from the window, Alireza raced to the door. She sprinted down the hall, her chest bursting with a combination of excitement and trepidation. If she could reach Jaluwi and deliver the news first, it would prove her loyalty beyond all shadow of a doubt. Her mother would be freed.

But if the news came from someone else, the UAR president might well think she'd been part of the Americans' infiltration plan.

Taking the stairs down three at a time, Alireza emerged on the ground floor in the palace's main entryway. A pair of steel-reinforced elevator shafts faced each other on both sides of the hall and were the only entrances to the underground bunker. She pushed the down button and glanced across the hall as she waited.

The captain at the desk in front of the other elevator eyed her breasts, then looked back down at his paperwork. Like the other palace guards, he knew of her mother's imprisonment and saw no need to question why she was going below in such a hurry.

The elevator door swung open. A soldier toting a Skorpion machine pistol aimed it at Alireza's stomach. Then, recognizing her, he lowered the weapon and stepped back.

Slowly, as if mocking her eagerness, the elevator cranked down to the office level three floors below the ground. The guards stationed outside the door barely look up as Alireza stepped off and hurried down the hall. She smiled, relaxing. Striker and his crew might have planned their infiltration well, but they'd have several more security checks to pass before getting to Jaluwi. She had plenty of time.

Both Jaluwi and Kaganovich's voices drifted toward her as she turned a corner and neared the president's office. Then, suddenly, another voice sounded—not from within the office, but from within Talia Alireza's brain. The woman's hands flew to her ears, trying to block out the sound.

Stop, Talia. Before you go farther, stop and listen to what these monsters are saying.

Her back against the wall, Alireza crept down the hall until she stood just outside the open door.

"Who knows?" Hamoud Jaluwi's voice said from within the room. "In the long run, nuclear devastation may work to our advantage."

Kaganovich's voice answered. "Some of your people will die," he said, "but Eldridge has limited strike potential. And he'll be the excuse you need to retaliate. The world can't fault you then."

Alireza felt as if a thousand tiny spiders were crawling over her skin as she heard the president of the United Arab Republic chuckle. "Yes. You're right."

The chuckle rose to a laugh. "And, after all, what are a few million Arabs, anyway?"

As the men continued to laugh, Alireza suddenly felt as if she'd eaten something very old and rotten. Her hand pressed against her throat, trying to hold back the vomit that threatened to rise from her belly.

The laughter inside the room stopped, and as it did, Alireza's loyalties finally crystallized once and for all. Turning away from the president's office, she hurried back down the hall toward the elevator.

LYONS SWUNG UP the Python in a two-handed grip, his sweating fingers wrapped around the oversized Pachmayer grips. He dropped the front ramp sight on Ali Mahmoud's back as the man ground to a halt next to the zeppelin pilot and bent over the control panel. The Colt's trigger inched back toward the guard.

A sudden gust of wind shook the zeppelin. Dianne Catlin stumbled, falling between the ex-cop's weapon and the UAR terrorist.

Lyons's finger flew back from the trigger. He stepped to the side, trying to avoid the reporter, but she crashed into him and spun him toward the window. The Able Team leader heard the sharp, cracking reports of Schwarz's and Blancanales's Berettas as both they and the UAR terrorists opened fire.

Shoving Catlin out of the way, Lyons reaimed the Colt and squeezed. Another gust of wind jiggled the airship as the big .357 boomed like a cannon in the confined quarters. The shot flew wide, a spiderweb pattern appearing above the pilot in the windshield.

The ex-cop caught his balance and fired again. Ali Mahmoud dropped to the floor, blood erupting from the back of his suit like an angry volcano.

To Lyons's sides, two of the terrorists fell as Schwarz and Blancanales sniped away with their Berettas. The Able Team leader's eyes circled the cabin as a pregnant female against the wall screamed in terror. She and the other hostages weren't bound.

They didn't need to be—there was no place to run even if they'd dared.

Lyons twisted, double-actioning another Magnum round into a terrorist with a black eye patch. The pregnant woman screamed again. A balding man in a plaid sport coat covered his open mouth with the back of his hand, his petrified eyes opening wide in disbelief as the top of the terrorist's head blew off, taking the eye patch with it.

A silver-haired man of at least eighty sat gripping the arms of his chair with bony fingers as Lyons turned the Colt on the pilot. A fourth .357 round drilled through the back of the man's head as Schwarz and Blancanales took out another duo of UAR men. The pilot slumped over the controls.

"Gadgets!" Lyons shouted as he fired yet another blazing hollowpoint through a man with an Uzi. "Grab the wheel!"

Schwarz threw the pilot unceremoniously from his seat as Lyons sent the Python's final slug into the chest of the last standing terrorist, then rushed forward to Schwarz's side.

Suddenly the zeppelin began to rise through the air.

Lyons bent over the controls next to Schwarz. "What's going on?"

Schwarz squinted down at the screen of the computerized control panel and shook his head. "I don't know." Then, suddenly, his face contorted into a mask of horror. "Unless..." The electronics expert pressed several buttons in the console.

The screen explained.

Dump to begin at 10,000 feet.

Gadgets looked up into Lyons's eyes, and the ex-cop saw the raw fear on his partner's face. "The gas, Ironman. Mahmoud... The son of a bitch must have gotten it set in motion just before you dropped him. We're rising so the fumes can spread out, cover more area."

Blancanales hurried forward, his face a duplicate of Schwarz's. He glanced through the broken window as the wind whipped in. "In this wind..." he said.

Lyons grabbed Schwarz by the shoulder and stared at the controls. "Is the zep set to self-destruct?"

Schwarz shrugged. "I can't tell. Maybe."

"Can you stop it?"

"Yeah...sure I could," Gadgets came back. "If I had time to figure it out. But I don't." He looked up again. "Plan B?"

Lyons felt a sudden gust of wind shoot through the bullet hole in the zeppelin's windshield. He stared through the cracked glass. Farther west the black storm clouds that had formed over the ocean were moving their way. The winds had driven the zeppelin back east of the stadium.

Not that it made any difference. Once the gas was released it would shower the residents of Los Angeles indiscriminately.

The Able Team leader nodded. "Put her on auto, Gadgets," he said. Then he turned to Blancanales. "Advise Delta."

Politician grabbed the radio. "Justice to Delta, Justice to Delta..." echoed through the cabin as Lyons sprinted back to where Dianne Catlin still sat sprawled on the floor of the cabin.

A false eyelash had fallen askew over the beautiful media superstar's pale blue eyes. She smiled as Lyons lifted her into his arms. "My hero," she said humorously, regaining her composure. "You saved us."

"Not quite yet."

Catlin's carefully plucked brows fell toward the dislodged lash. She stared in bewilderment as Lyons hurried her toward the window. "What, er, what are you...?" she asked breathlessly as they neared the shattered glass.

"Sorry, I don't have time to explain."

"What—"

"Trust me," Lyons said.

And without further ado he threw Dianne Catlin out of the zeppelin and into the sky over Los Angeles.

THE EXECUTIONER and Phoenix Force followed the frightened lieutenant down the walk through the courtyard to the palace's front entrance. They mounted the steps to a row of elaborately carved cedar doors and stopped.

Katz whispered something to the lieutenant and jammed his .22-caliber finger deeper into the man's back.

A bead of sweat broke out on the lieutenant's forehead. He nodded and knocked.

A small judas hole slid open at eye level. The lieutenant barked something in Arabic to the man who appeared behind it. He got an answer.

Katz leaned toward Bolan, out of eyeshot of the tiny opening. "It's like before," the little Israeli whispered through the clenched teeth beneath his frozen smile. "They're wondering why they didn't receive advance notification."

The lieutenant and the man behind the door continued to converse. A soft click reverberated outside the building, and Bolan knew Katz had just cocked his .22 Magnum.

The lieutenant heard it, too. His arms waved wildly to emphasize whatever argument he was trying.

Bolan looked back to Katz, trying to get a reading on what was being said. The Israeli gave him a slight nod.

A moment later the door swung open and a short, squat corporal wearing the uniform of the UAR Republican Guard ushered them inside. He saluted, then turned on his heels like some Nazi officer and goosestepped them down a long hall toward a pair of elevator shafts.

Katz whispered again as their footsteps echoed down the corridor. "The lieutenant said he knew all about it, and if the corporal knew what was good for him, he'd let us through." The Israeli nodded toward the desk in front of one of the elevators in the distance. "But we'll meet more resistance before we go below. Count on it."

Armed men wearing the new shoulder patches came and went as they headed toward the elevators. The Executioner let his eyes roam over the hall and the rooms that led off it as they passed. With the clock ticking away toward nuclear disaster, there had been no opportunity to work out an escape plan. So far, luck had been with them. If things continued to go well, they'd be ushered into Jaluwi's presence in a matter of minutes. Killing him would be easy.

But after that? He had no idea.

The UAR would eventually crumble without Jaluwi's charismatic leadership. But that wouldn't happen immediately. This wasn't some loose-knit, disorganized tribe that would surrender as soon as its chief fell. The soldiers assigned to the palace would be out for blood.

Escape? Maybe they would, maybe they wouldn't. The important thing was to eliminate Hamoud Jaluwi and the threat he represented to the rest of the world.

The party came to a halt at the elevators. The corporal, lieutenant, and Katz and Encizo posing as Iraqis, all saluted the captain seated at the desk.

The bickering in Arabic began again. This time the ranks on the sleeves of the Executioner and Phoenix Force didn't bring on the intimidation it had earlier. The captain's dark eyes looked hard at the faces of the men who stood before him. He shook his head and picked up the phone.

Bolan glanced at Katz again, trying to key off his reaction. The tiny beginnings of a frown burrowed into the Israeli's face. "Trouble?" the Executioner whispered.

Katz's nod was almost imperceptible as his face returned to deadpan. "He's calling down for verification," he whispered.

The captain pushed several buttons on the phone, then looked up and barked orders to three armed soldiers coming down the hall. The men stopped next to the desk, curling their fingers around the pistol grips of the Skorpions slung over their shoulders. They looked curiously from the visitors to their captain as the man at the desk spoke into the receiver.

Bolan let his hand drift casually toward the hem of his tunic, nearer the big Desert Eagle.

The captain hung up the phone. His eyes flickered nervously from the Executioner to the lieutenant. He spoke again in Arabic as the light came on in the elevator behind him and the car started to rise.

Bolan watched the light above the door as the elevator neared. What was happening was obvious. Someone from downstairs was coming to check them out. In a moment the door would open.

And the firefight would begin.

Around him the Executioner saw the men of Phoenix Force moving their hands closer to their weapons. They all stared ahead at the elevator door.

The door swung open and another lieutenant stepped out. His face wrinkled as he stared first at Bolan, then the other men. His voice was low, gravelly, as he spoke in the foreign tongue.

Bolan's fingers slipped around the big .44. Behind him he heard the bolts of the Skorpions thud closed.

Then a soft bell rang across the hall behind them. The door to the other elevator swung back and a feminine voice shouted angrily in Arabic.

Bolan turned to see Talia Alireza standing in the open car. She waved her arms, and the men with the Skorpions lowered their weapons. Walking directly to the Executioner, Alireza said, "I'm sorry, Major, but I'm sure you can understand how tight security must be right now."

Bolan nodded.

"If you'll please follow me..." She turned and walked back into the elevator.

Bolan, Phoenix Force and the Iraqi lieutenant followed her into the car.

LYONS GRABBED the hostage in the plaid sport coat and hauled him to his feet. "What the—" the man screamed as the big ex-cop tossed him through the window.

As Blancanales and Schwarz hurried away from the zeppelin's controls, Lyons glanced at the chutes on their backs. "Take these two with you and jump," he said, pointing to the old man and the pregnant woman.

Schwarz shook his head. "We'll help you—"

"Go!" Lyons yelled.

Gadgets lifted the gray-haired man as Pol wrapped the pregnant woman in his arms. With a final glance over their shoulders they leaped from the craft.

Lyons went back to the windshield. The wind had blown them back at least two blocks to the east, but they were still rising toward the altitude at which the gas would automatically dump. As he stared through the broken glass, the figure of a Delta Force soldier, diving headfirst through the air, suddenly flashed past the front of the zeppelin.

The Able Team leader looked down to see Schwarz's and Blancanales's chutes open. The falling Delta man reached a speck in the sky Lyons assumed to be Dianne Catlin, then his chute opened, as well.

"Justice to Delta," Lyons said into his face mike. "Get the hook down to me quick." Drawing the Python, he gripped it by the barrel and drove the butt through the bullet hole in the windshield. He swept the shattered glass from the edges, gripped the window frame and hauled himself through the opening and onto the roof of the cabin.

Wind whipped between the cabin and envelope, threatening to hurl Lyons from the roof as he wrapped an elbow around one of the suspension lines. He looked up to see a huge iron hook descending through the sky at the end of a heavy steel cable.

To the west the dark clouds had moved over the land. Lightning cracked suddenly over his head, and Lyons's face twisted in resignation. Just what they needed to complicate things.

As he waited for the descending hook, the ex-cop glanced down again. Two more parachutes opened like suddenly blossoming flowers as the Delta fighters snatched the old man and the hostage in the plaid sport coat from the mouth of death.

Lyons reached forward as the hook fell level with the top of the cabin. Pulling it to his chest with his free hand, he fell onto his stomach before releasing the suspension line. Slowly, the winds of the approaching storm howling in his ears, he hugged the slippery roof as best he could and crawled toward the hole he'd burned earlier. He dropped the hook through the opening, making sure it caught securely in the metal as thunder roared over his head.

The clouds above the zeppelin burst suddenly, sending a torrent of rain down over the ex-cop as he got back on his feet. Lyons tumbled, his arm jerking out for the suspension line as he fell over the side of the roof. Hauling himself back to safety, he shouted into the face mike again. "You're hooked on Delta. Get her out of here." He paused as thunder interrupted him again. "And I'm ready for my ride."

Captain Becker's voice crackled through the electrical static. "Go for it, Justice. See you on the way down."

Lyons looked down once more. They'd moved back over Dodger Stadium. Below, he could barely make out the infield dirt in the pounding rain.

Taking a deep breath, he jumped. The Able Team leader spread his arms and legs to slow the fall as he dropped through the sky. He looked up and saw a tiny dot leap from the Delta helicopter high above the zeppelin. Then the chopper jerked forward, gathered up the slack in the cable and began towing the zeppelin toward the ocean.

Lightning flashed through the sky again as the storm burst open with full fury. Through the wall of water that surrounded him, Lyons saw a figure suddenly appear at the broken windshield of the zeppelin. Then the figure jumped and fell through the sky toward him.

Lyons spread his arms wider, trying to get all the wind resistance he could. As the other man neared, the ex-cop made out the blue suit, flailing arms and terrified face of Ali Mahmoud.

The Able Team leader's jaws clamped shut. His bullet might have stopped the man, but it hadn't killed him. Mahmoud had figured out the rescue plan and decided to pass himself off as a hostage.

The Delta Force paratrooper fell next to Mahmoud, reached out through the throbbing downpour of rain and grabbed the terrorist by the lapels of his suit. Lyons rolled horizontally onto his stomach to get maximum wind resistance, Mahmoud and his rescuer pulling even with him.

The ex-cop saw the name tag on the paratrooper's jumpsuit. Becker looked curiously from Mahmoud to Lyons as the three men continued to fall through the air.

Slowly Lyons shook his head.

Becker grinned and released his grip on the terrorist. As Mahmoud fell away screaming, the Delta leader reached out and caught Lyons by the arm.

The terrorist's screams grew faint, then disappeared completely as Becker slipped the safety harness over Lyons's shoulders and cinched it at the waist.

Lyons looked westward to where the chopper and zeppelin were mere specks against the dark clouds. In a few moments they'd be far enough out over the ocean that if the gas did release, it would dissipate harmlessly before reaching a populated area.

Becker worked the toggles as Lyons spoke into the face mike again. "Justice to Delta," he said. "All clear." He paused, then remembered the terrorists outside the gates, ready to enter the stadium and massacre the baseball fans. "What's the situation below?" he asked.

A voice from above came back, chuckling. "There are enough cops and National Guard down there now to wipe out those mothers six times over," it said. "There was a little initial resistance, but shortly everyone just dropped their weapons and surrendered."

"Do the fans know what's going on?" he asked.

"That's affirmative," the voice replied. "The President decided they had to be told."

Lyons nodded. The Man had been right. They did deserve to know, as long as it didn't compromise the operation. And it hadn't.

A sudden explosion sounded in the far distance. Lyons and Becker both turned toward the noise.

Flames leaped from the tiny dot now far over the ocean as the zeppelin exploded. Above the blimp the chopper rose safely away from the fire, then turned inland.

Lyons and Becker looked down again just in time to hit the ground. Still bound together by the safety harness, the two men tumbled clumsily through the wet dirt of the infield. Lyons felt something firm strike his ribs as he rolled to a halt. Releasing the clasp on the harness, he stood up and found himself standing on second base.

A man wearing a black sport coat, slacks and a short-billed cap came running forward. His white teeth gleamed in a relieved smile. He threw his hands out wide, palms down.

"Safe!" the umpire bellowed at the top of his lungs.

Fifty thousand Dodger fans roared their approval.

CHAPTER FIFTEEN

"We have to hurry," Alireza urged as the elevator descended into the underground compound. She looked up at the roof of the car. "The captain will be calling down right now to find out what the hell's going on." She turned to face Bolan. "I'll get you as far as my limited influence can." She patted the Bernadelli on her hip. "Then we must fight."

Bolan frowned. He knew that the men of Phoenix Force didn't trust her. And why should they? Throughout the mission Talia Alireza's loyalty had shifted as quickly as the Gulf winds.

The Executioner stared down into the woman's dark brown eyes. Somewhere, deep within the mercenary, he thought he saw something. A new conviction. A new permanence in that conviction.

Bolan nodded and turned back to the door. He'd trust her for two reasons. First, his instincts told him to, and it was those same instincts that had been responsible for his survival when so many other good soldiers had fallen over the years.

And second, he had no other choice. Alireza represented their last chance.

The merc spoke again. "We have another problem."

Bolan listened as she explained about her mother. "We'll have to play it by ear," he told her, "but we'll get her out."

The doors swung open. Alireza stepped out and confronted the men sitting at the card table in the hall. She spoke rapidly in Arabic, taking the initiative, and before the guards could reply she held out her hand and ushered Bolan, the frightened Iraqi lieutenant and Phoenix Force past them.

Their boot heels clicking hollowly along the tile, the Stony Man warriors followed Alireza down the hall. "There's another guard station around the corner," the woman whispered. "They'll—"

Alireza never got the chance to finish. As they turned the corner, four armed UAR Republican Guards looked up from their table. The man holding the phone against his ear let it drop and reached for the Skorpion machine pistol, hanging from the back of a chair. The other men scrambled for their own weapons.

Bolan drew his Beretta and fired a triburst at the soldier who'd been on the phone. The man slumped over the table, a red star-shaped cavity suddenly appearing in his forehead.

The surviving UAR gunners opened fire, but their aims were off, hurried. Many rounds pinged off the concrete walls, ricocheting past the Stony Man warriors. Others sailed harmlessly over their heads.

But one burst drilled into the chest of the Iraqi lieutenant, and the man fell forward onto his face.

Bolan took aim and let loose, taking out a man with a black beard. A nanosecond later, Phoenix Force opened up, followed by Alireza.

Suddenly the hall was silent—the quiet before the storm.

The sounds of running feet echoed down the hall behind them. The Executioner turned as a half-dozen men rounded the corner. He drew the Desert Eagle with his left hand. A gun in each fist, he fired 3-round bursts from the Beretta, the Desert Eagle booming like some massive .44 Magnum cannon in the narrow tunnel.

Manning, Encizo, James and Katz joined in, blazing away with their Berettas. McCarter's Browning Hi-Power and Alireza's Bernadelli joined the orgy of gunfire as the explosions bounced off the concrete and threatened to deafen them.

Barely audible within the thunderstorm of lead the Executioner heard footsteps behind him. He turned in time to see another cadre of compound guardsmen round the corner to sandwich them in the hall. Dropping to one knee, he opened up with the Beretta, the Desert Eagle in his left hand continuing to spit flame. The man on the receiving end of the 9 mm rounds dropped to the tile. The soldier catching the big .44 Magnum slug was punched three feet back to smash into the wall before crumpling to the floor.

The Beretta locked open, empty. Bolan shoved it into his belt and continued to fire with the Desert Eagle as he dived forward, somersaulting across the tile to the table where the four corpses sat. He saw Alireza empty her Bernadelli, drop it and reach into her fatigue pants to produce the derringer. A blast of 410 shot caught another advancing enemy in the face, ruining his features.

Reaching up, Bolan ripped a Skorpion from a pair of dead hands above the table and jerked down, feeling the clip tear through the nylon sling around the corpse's shoulder. The sling flopped below the machine pistol as the Executioner rejoined the battle.

More UAR troops arrived. The Executioner and Alireza systematically mowed them down. The gunfire behind them suddenly halted, and the warrior looked over his shoulder to see the last UAR gunner at that end of the hall drop to the ground.

"All clear at this end!" Katz yelled.

"Not for long," Bolan said. "We've got to get to cover." He pulled back on the Skorpion's trigger, and the weapon rattled again in his hands. Two more gunmen trying to round the corner fell to the tile as the machine pistol ran dry.

Bolan reached up, jerking another pair of Skorpions away from the bodies at the table. Alireza grabbed the remaining weapon. "I'll cover you!" the Executioner shouted. "Lead the way!"

With a Skorpion in each hand the Executioner lay down a steady stream of fire that forced the men at the end of the hall to jump back around the corner.

Alireza rose, turned and sprinted back down the hall toward the clump of bodies at the corner. With a final burst from his machine pistols Bolan raced after her. The men of Phoenix Force fell in behind.

Heads and guns popped back around the corner as the fire slowed. Bolan and his team continued to run, twisting to fire every few steps as they followed Alireza. The mercenary stopped in front of a door just before the corner and twisted the knob. Locked.

As Bolan and the rest of the Stony Man crew continued to blaze away at the men behind them, Alireza stepped back, aimed her machine pistol and fired a short burst through the lock. Raising her foot to the knee, she pivoted at the hip and sent a vicious side kick into the door, which swung open.

Bolan and Phoenix Force hurried in after the woman. The Executioner tossed the Skorpions through the air to McCarter and Manning. The Briton and Canadian didn't have to be told what to do. McCarter leaned out the door and continued the cover fire as Manning knelt below him and did the same.

The Executioner scanned the room. Against one wall he saw a giant industrial water heater. A huge metal door set in another wall obviously led to the electrical breakers throughout the compound. A sudden idea flashed through his brain.

Knocking out the lights all over the compound would work against them; the UAR troops would know the twists and turns of the complex far better than the men from Stony Man. But if they could douse the power selectively, and somehow time the darkness to their advantage . . .

Ripping open the door, Bolan stared at the circuit-breaker directory on the back. Arabic. "Talia!" he yelled.

The woman hurried over and looked up at he handwritten information. Slowly her lips curled into a rigid smile as she read the Executioner's mind. "Five and six will knock out the lights in the hall in front of his office," she said. "Eleven and twelve will take care of the office itself."

"How long will it take us to get there?"

Alireza shrugged. "If we run, and meet no resistance, thirty, maybe forty seconds."

"Gary!" Bolan yelled above the ongoing gunfire in the hall. "How's it look out there?"

The Canadian broke fire long enough to turn into the room and shrug. "Fewer than there were, I'd guess. But they're hunkered down around the corner. More could be arriving every second for all we can see."

Bolan hesitated. If there weren't more men there by now, there would be soon. Which meant that if they had to bull their way past the corner, there was no time as good as the present. "Rafael!" he shouted.

The Cuban hurried over.

Bolan pointed to the breakers. "Give it forty seconds from the time we leave, then pull five and six. Wait another twenty and hit eleven and twelve. Another half minute, then switch them all back on again. Got it?"

Encizo nodded.

Bolan, Alireza, James and Katz joined McCarter and Manning at the door. "I'll go first," Alireza said, handing one of her Skorpions to Bolan.

The Executioner nodded. "You're the one who knows the way."

Manning and McCarter lay down bursts of covering fire as Alireza leaped back into the hall. Bolan, Katz and James followed, their weapons spurting a fiery death at two gunners who dared to edge around the corner. Manning fell in behind them, with McCarter staying behind to cover Encizo's back.

More 9 mm and 7.62 mm explosions echoed against the concrete walls as they reached the corner. Pressing his back against the wall, the Executioner risked a glance. He couldn't tell how many men were behind the wall, but a burst of automatic fire sailed past him.

Bolan ducked back around the corner, glancing at his watch. Fifteen seconds had already elapsed. There was no time to play games.

Dropping to one knee, the warrior rolled out into the adjoining hallway, the Skorpion blazing up into the knees, genitals and chests of three surprised UAR men.

The halls fell silent once more.

Vaulting back onto his feet, Bolan headed after Alireza and Phoenix Force, who'd hurdled the clump of dead bodies that had piled up under the onslaught and raced down the hall.

A squad of guards stood shoulder to shoulder across the corridor as the team rounded another corner. With both Skorpions and AK-74s, the guardsmen grinned as they prepared to mow down their outnumbered opponents.

Then suddenly the hallway went black.

The Stony Man crew didn't hesitate. Red and yellow muzzle-flashes lit up the darkened hallway like fireflies buzzing through the night. They peppered the hallway, canvassing the narrow passageway wall-to-wall in the darkness. Seconds later it was all over. The UAR president's last line of defense had been breached.

As the gunfire died down, Bolan felt a hand grasp his arm. "Follow me," Alireza whispered. She placed the Executioner's hand on the back of her shoulder, Bolan following suit for whoever was behind him.

The parade of warriors moved silently down the hall, stepping over the wet, limp obstacles they encountered on the way. A soft light shone through the opaque glass in the closed door. It went out suddenly, and two voices whispered nervously on the other side.

Bolan raised a foot, kicked the frame around the glass and jumped back. Four quick pistol shots sailed through the opening as the door swung inward, opening into the room like the dark mouth of a mausoleum.

The Executioner led the group silently into the president's office. Somewhere across the room he heard breathing.

Bolan's leg brushed against a desk. He turned, gently pushing Alireza and the men filing inside the office away from the desk, then pulled a small penlight from under his tunic. Setting it on the desk, he aimed the beam toward the sounds, switched it on and stepped away.

More pistol fire blasted in the darkness. A round hit the penlight and sent it flying through the air to the floor. Two frightened faces appeared above the flashes. The gunfire continued until Bolan heard two automatics lock open empty.

The Executioner waited. The breathing grew louder, and the stench of nervous sweat filled the office. Then a trembling voice with a Russian accent whispered, "We have gotten them, I think."

The overhead lights suddenly came back on.

"Wrong," the Executioner said. Across the room, huddled together on a couch, he saw Hamoud Jaluwi and Gennady Kaganovich, their empty weapons still gripped in their hands. In a desperate move the Soviet general stood and clawed for what was obviously a gun in an ankle holster.

Bolan tapped the trigger of the Skorpion. Kaganovich's fat mouth opened wide as the top of his head blew off in a flurry of blood, brains and bone.

The Executioner turned toward Jaluwi as the man stood, shocked. The empty Soviet Makarov in the UAR president's hands toppled from his grip, and the slack skin beneath his chin began to tremble as tears formed in the corners of his eyes. "Please," he began.

Bolan dropped the sights on his forehead and pressed the Skorpion's stock against his shoulder. He squinted down the barrel and said, "Give me one good reason why I shouldn't do the world a favor...."

Alireza grasped the Executioner's arm. "My mother," she said softly.

"Yes!" Jaluwi said hurriedly, his voice trembling in time with his chin. "I'll trade her! I'll trade your mother's life for mine."

"Okay," Alireza said simply.

The Executioner walked forward, lifting the phone. He tapped in the number of the Special Forces base and waited. When the ring was answered, he said, "Radio Grimaldi. Get him east of Babylon in something big enough to carry eight passengers. We'll be there in thirty minutes." He disconnected the line and handed the receiver to Jaluwi. "Now you make your call," he said. He nodded toward Alireza. "Get her mother down here."

Jaluwi's eyes brightened as he took the phone. "Yes!" he said in relief. "I'll free her mother. And I'll go with you to ensure your safety." He paused, and a tremor of fear returned to his voice. "But then... you'll free me, as well."

Alireza nodded. "You have my word."

Jaluwi looked down at the phone. After three attempts, his shaking fingers finally pushed the correct buttons. "This is the president," he announced with a quaver. "No...no! Listen to me! Bring the old woman to my office and arrange for transportation at the front gate. Do not attack." He hung up.

Bolan grabbed the collar of Jaluwi's coat and dragged him to the door like a rag doll. He shoved the barrel of the Desert Eagle into the quivering man's ear and waited. A few moments later a cadre of guards led Amilah Alireza down the hall. The bolts on the men's weapons fell forward when they saw the gun at their leader's head.

Bolan leaned down and whispered into his ear. "You just remember. All of us will empty our weapons into you with our last breaths if we have to."

"Lower your weapons, you fools!" Jaluwi yelled at his men. "I'll personally escort you out of Babylon," he said, turning back to the Executioner. Then, hesitation returned to his voice and he looked back at Alireza for reassurance. "And then...you'll free me?"

"How many times do I have to tell you?" Alireza said. The Executioner kept the Desert Eagle in Jaluwi's ear as a guard unlocked Amilah's handcuffs. The old woman rubbed her wrists, then embraced her daughter.

"Let's go," Bolan said.

McCarter and Encizo met them in the hall. "We need to make a little stop before we go," the Executioner said. "Let's go take a look at your nukes, Jaluwi."

The president nodded. Bolan studied his eyes. The man seemed resigned to failure—at least temporarily. But the Executioner didn't kid himself. Jaluwi was no madman with religious delusions like Eldridge. He was in this for himself, and if he survived, he'd regroup and start over as soon as the Stony Man warriors were in the air.

The procession followed Jaluwi down a winding series of halls to a steel door. A Republican Guard colonel hesitated, looked at the President, then shrugged and unlocked the door.

Manning disappeared through the door. The rest waited outside.

Electrical crackles popped inside the room. Fifteen minutes later the Canadian reappeared. "The bad news," he said, "is that they can repair what I've just done in about six months." A grin suddenly covered his brawny face. "But the good news is, it's safe now to launch a direct air strike that will take this place out, and all that's down here. Out for good."

Bolan nodded, keeping the .44 pressed against Jaluwi's skull as they returned to the elevator. When they reached the first floor of the palace, they stepped out of the car and Jaluwi held up his hands as dozens of rifles took aim.

The Stony Man warriors, Talia and Amilah Alireza and the president of the United Arab Republic walked through a tunnel of rifles to a pair of chauffeured limousines waiting at the front gate. Bolan, Katz and Alireza slid into the lead vehicle with Jaluwi as the rest of Phoenix Force helped the old woman into the other.

The Executioner shifted the .44 to Jaluwi's ribs. "Tell your troops to stay behind," he ordered. "If they follow, the first round fired has your name on it."

Jaluwi turned and barked orders in Arabic through the window. The Executioner glanced at Alireza for a translation, and the woman nodded.

The UAR leader's insolent confidence began to return as they neared the edge of the ancient city and his safety began to look more certain. "You'll never stop the Arabs from getting what they deserve," he said suddenly, looking at Bolan.

"No one wants to," the Executioner answered. "But we'll continue to stop dictators regardless of race."

Jack Grimaldi sat behind the controls of the idling helicopter when the limos reached the edge of the city. Bolan grabbed Jaluwi by the collar and herded him toward the chopper. "You'll let me go now?" the UAR man asked.

Alireza laughed. She indicated the two armed chauffeurs who'd stepped out of the cars. "So you can have your men shoot us as we take off? I think not." She shoved the UAR president toward the chopper. "Get on board. I'll let you out when I'm good and ready."

The party boarded, and Grimaldi revved the engine. The blades began to twirl, and a moment later the helicopter rose into the air.

They were five hundred feet above the limousines when Alireza slid the chopper door back open. She turned to Jaluwi. "I'm ready."

A mask of confusion covered the UAR leader's face. "What?" Then the confusion became horror as he realized what she had in mind. "No..." he said slowly. "You promised...."

"I changed my mind." Alireza's foot flashed out in a vicious side-thrust kick, which caught Jaluwi in the abdomen. The president of the United Arab Republic screamed as he toppled backward and fell through the door.

As the screams faded in the wind, Alireza turned to Bolan. A shy, almost girlishly embarrassed grin covered her face. "You know how I am about changing my mind. But I promise you, that was the very last time."

Laughter rose from the men of Stony Man Farm as Grimaldi turned the chopper south toward Kuwait.

A twenty-first century commando meets his match on a high-tech battlefield.

NOMAD

DEATH RACE

DAVID ALEXANDER

He's called Nomad—a new breed of commando battling the grim forces of techno-terrorism that threaten the newfound peace of the twenty-first century.

In DEATH RACE, the second title in the NOMAD series, the KGB is conspiring to bring America to her knees. A supersoldier clone—Nomad's double—has been programmed with a devastating termination directive. Nomad becomes a hunted man in a cross-country death race that leads to the prime target—the White House.

**The Hatchet force is out to splinter
the enemy's defenses in Book 2 of
the HATCHET miniseries...**

HATCHET

SPECTRE

Knox Gordon

**When a highly sensitive experimental aircraft is
shot down in enemy territory, the Hatchet
team is called in to recover the missing
hardware any way they can—even if it means
court-martial.**

**In the air and on the ground, behind the desks
and in the jungles...the action-packed series of
the Vietnam War.**

Available in June at your favorite retail outlet.

A storm is brewing in the Middle East and
Mack Bolan is there in . . .

THE STORM TRILOGY

Along with PHOENIX FORCE and ABLE TEAM, THE
EXECUTIONER is waging war against terrorism at home
and abroad.

Be sure to catch all the action of this hard-hitting trilogy
starting in April and continuing through to June.

Available at your favorite retail outlet, or order your copy now:

Book I:	STORM WARNING (THE EXECUTIONER #160)	$3.50	☐
Book II:	EYE OF THE STORM (THE EXECUTIONER #161)	$3.50	☐
Book III:	STORM BURST (352-page MACK BOLAN)	$4.99	☐

Total Amount	$ _____
Plus 75¢ Postage ($1.00 in Canada)	_____
Canadian residents add applicable federal and provincial taxes.	
Total Payable	$ _____

Please send a check or money order payable to Gold Eagle Books to:

In the U.S.
3010 Walden Avenue
P.O. Box 1325
Buffalo, NY 14269-1325

In Canada
P.O. Box 609
Fort Erie, Ontario
L2A 5X3

Please Print:

Name: _____

Address: _____

City: _____

State/Province: _____

Zip/Postal Code: _____

GOLD
EAGLE ®

ST92-1